# PUCK HAPPENS

HAILEY SHORE

# 1

*Dillon*

Wendy: Hey, you were already gone when I got up this morning. I need you tonight at the Gull. Dave's still sick and it's Friday.

Dillon: I am not working at the bar on a Friday night. That was our deal. Remember?

Wendy: I remember I'm your only sister and you love me.

Dillon: I'll pay someone to work that shift.

Wendy: There's no one to pay.

Dillon: Then I'll pay you to close the bar down. Whatever you'd make tonight – I'll double it.

Wendy: Oh...you know what you sound like?

Dillon: Stop.

Wendy: Nope. I'm serious. You sound like…

Dillon: Don't say it.

Wendy: An elitist dick. Remember when you told me to always keep you honest no matter how big you got…? This is that time. Right now. Don't be an elitist dick and help your sister when she asks.

Dillon: I'm not being a dick. Or elitist. You know how handsy the tourists get when I work behind the bar. Like I'm some kind of genie lamp. Remember that bachelorette party two weeks ago?

Wendy: Indeed I do. They spent a lot of money.

Dillon: They tore the shirt OFF my body.

Wendy: Suck it up. I need the help and it's too late to find someone.

S uck it up was our family motto. So, I didn't text back, I knew when I was beat. I tossed my phone in the cup holder of my Bronco.

I was in the parking lot of the ice rink ten miles north of Calico Cove. It was barely seven in the morning, which made me worry about how much sleep Wendy was getting since she didn't get home last night until two in the morning.

She'd be pissed knowing I'd had half an ear open, waiting for her to come home. Yes, I knew crime was virtually non-existent in Calico Cove, and yes, I knew my sister could more than take care of herself, but I worried. Sue me.

Dad taught us how to handle ourselves in a fight and we both went pro with that knowledge. I was a NHL center forward and my sister spent two years as an MMA fighter before retiring to take over Dad's bar – The One-Eyed Gull.

But for the three weeks I spent in Calico Cove before preseason training, I went hard at being Wendy's protective big brother. And she went hard being my annoying little sister and getting me to work behind the bar at the Gull. All while I slept in my childhood bedroom in the three-bedroom, one bath ranch we both grew up in with our parents.

Try being an elitist dick in a house with your prom picture on the wall.

Could I buy a bigger, fancier house for Wendy? Yes.

Would she let me? No.

Mom let me buy that condo for her in Boston. Dad and our stepmom, Linda, had no problem hightailing their asses down to Naples, Florida when I'd offered to buy them a house.

It was a perk of my job, buying houses.

Per Dad, he'd earned every cent of that house driving me back and forth to this very ice rink as he'd pushed me toward my success. It was true. He had.

There were just times I wish he hadn't been such a dick about it.

No one in my life had a problem taking my money. Except Wendy. She just wanted me to work the damn bar.

I pulled my duffel out of the backseat of my truck and made my way inside.

Hank was behind the front desk. Hank was always behind the front desk. Maybe someone else sat there at night, but every dawn since I was ten years old – it was Hank. I gave him a chin nod greeting and he did the same.

"No fan club today," he said.

"Yeah? The peewees aren't on the ice?"

"Private coaching."

"Nice. Thanks Hank."

The fan club wasn't the peewee team that I usually shared the ice with, it was their parents. Dads who wanted to tell me how my shots on net percentage tanked during the playoffs. Moms who wanted a picture, and if they managed to cop a little feel of my biceps while they did it, so it goes.

Occasionally, there'd be a pretty young thing waiting for me in the parking lot, a puck bunny up from Portland who'd heard I worked out here most mornings, looking to add my number to her list. There was a time I would have been interested, but every NHL player learned a hard lesson about puck bunnies.

Almost always more trouble than they were worth.

Hank had been managing this rink since it was built and he never asked me for anything. Not a signed picture he could hang up in the lobby, or a day to meet and greet fans to promote the rink. Nothing.

He just did his thing and let me do mine. Hank didn't give a shit about how many goals I scored last season, or Hart Trophies I'd earned (two). The Stanley Cup? What? It's just a big silver cup.

Hank and people like him were a huge reason I liked coming back to Calico Cove. Most of the people were real, and everyone who knew me treated me just like they'd treated me before I'd become *The Heart*.

In the tiny locker room I changed into my workout gear. Black compression tights, basketball shorts, nylon runner's top to absorb the sweat and a loose tank over that. The same thing I'd been wearing since high school.

Today was just a skating day. No weights. After yesterday's heavy leg day, I needed the break. We were still a few weeks out from the start of preseason, but I'd learned the hard way over the last ten years of my career that the best way to get into hockey season shape was never to get out of shape.

Ten years? Has it really been that long?

Fuck me.

One of the dads the other day said the *R* word and it hit me like a puck off McDavid's stick.

Retirement.

Not yet. Not for a long time. We had the Cup we needed to win back and I had at least one more shot at the Hart Trophy.

*Retirement. Fuck that guy.*

I pushed through the beat-up door that led to the ice and took a deep breath.

The ice smelled like minerals and chlorine, mud, old popcorn with a touch of dirty gear. I filled my lungs with the cool air and let out a deep sigh.

*Home.* The place I'd been the most comfortable for almost twenty years. Since Dad had driven me to this very rink when I was ten years old and I told him I wanted to play on the junior league team.

On the ice, there were two kids doing side by side drills with hockey sticks in their hands, passing a puck between them, while my old coach, Dan Phillips, stood behind them with a whistle around his neck.

I would stay out of the kids' way, but if they recognized me, that was fine. It had always been my rule, day one after putting on an NHL jersey: Kids first. They got their pictures, autographs and any gear I could give them. Always.

There was nothing I hated more than watching some douchebag player brushing off a group of kids who looked up to him. As captain of my team, I made sure no one on the New England Bruisers ever pulled that shit.

Kids weren't just the fans. They were the future too.

I removed my blade guards and stepped onto the ice. My skates were extensions of my feet at this point. This pair was only a month old, and finally, finally they were starting to feel broken in. I hated getting new skates and limited changes to only five or six pairs throughout the season.

I started with long strides but kept the perimeter of my laps short and away from the kids and Coach Phillips, who gave me a grateful nod and tapped his wrist. I nodded. Yeah, he could bring the kids by when they were done with drills.

I kept my speed steady, letting my body wake up a little.

Not fifteen minutes into it, another person stepped onto the ice.

A woman in a black leotard that clung to every inch of her. She was lean, but with the thick curvy legs and ass that years of skating gave a person.

Her honey blonde hair was in a ponytail and she wore a pair of gloves and bright white figure skating skates. She stepped onto the ice and quickly built up speed along the boards, leaning into the curves.

The girl knew how to skate.

"Uh, sorry, Mr. Le Coeur?"

I stopped short in my tracks and some ice sprayed up at the two kids smiling at me.

"Whoa, that was cool," the one kid said, wiping his face.

"Sorry if we're bothering you, Dillon." Coach Phillips said as he came up behind them.

I shook my head. "No bother. You guys a bunch of peewees?"

"Squirts!" they both said, which made them about nine or ten. I remembered with a pang being that age, and what it would have been like to see an actual pro at my hometown rink. My mind would have been blown.

"Any advice for these two players?" Phillips asked.

"Keep your head up," I said, repeating what Phillips had told me at that age. "And your eyes on that puck. Never lose sight of it. And...ah...do good in school."

In case that hockey dream didn't work out.

"Wow. Thanks Mr. Heart. I mean Mr. Le Coeur," one boy said, his face turning red.

I didn't have a pen or paper on me, but Phillips had a phone in his back pocket. He held it up in a silent request. I crouched down next to the kids and he got a picture of the three of us.

"Thanks. This is a thrill for them," he told me, patting me on the shoulder.

"Not a problem. Okay guys, I've got to get back to work. You want the Bruisers to win this season, right?"

"Yeah!" they shouted in unison.

I took off down the ice and got back into my steady laps around the rink. The woman in the leotard was doing the same, but in the opposite direction. She passed me the first time and her eyes flicked over me and then away.

She was older than I'd first thought. Definitely in her mid-twenties.

So not some junior figure skater. And she wasn't attempting any jumps. Just skating.

Really fast.

Like, really fast.

Her foot work in the corners was top speed.

She had to be showing off.

When she passed me the second time, she passed so close the end of her ponytail brushed my face.

*Great.*

I would sigh heavily if my heart rate wasn't picking up speed. This wasn't my first rodeo. But I needed to focus today on my cardio and I didn't have time for some puck bunny trying to get my attention.

Though that leotard was hard to ignore.

With a hard stop that sent more ice spraying, I changed course and caught up to her pretty ass, although I had to admit, I had to work a little too hard to keep pace.

When I was just behind her, I shouted. "Hey, lady, I get it. You're very fast, but I'm here to work out."

She looked over her shoulder at me and removed an earbud from her ear.

"Sorry?" She shot me a polite smile and slowed down.

Okay, she was doing the whole blasé thing pretty well, but I wasn't buying it.

"No need to show off. I'm not interested."

She made a face. "Excuse me?"

"Look, I'm here to work."

She came to an abrupt stop.

Fucking toe picks.

I slid to a stop and glided back to where she was standing with her arms folded over her heaving chest.

"What's your problem?" she asked.

"No problem, lady. You're pretty enough, I just don't have it in my schedule today to play."

Her jaw dropped. "Pretty *enough*?"

Her voice went real high, and for a second doubt crept in. "Are you saying you don't know who I am?"

"I have no clue who you are. Why would I?"

Okay. She was seriously offended. Did she really not know who I was?

Was that possible in Calico Cove?

Her gray eyes narrowed, and her full lips pursed.

"Wait a minute," she said. "Is this a bit?"

"A bit?"

"Yeah. Do you know who *I* am?"

"No. Why would I know who *you* are?"

She rolled her eyes. At me. "Look buddy, if this is your whole *let me pretend I don't know her to her get her attention* routine, it's not working."

"That's what *you're* doing to *me.*" I accused her. "Aren't you?"

"Hard to pretend not to know who you are, when I don't know who you are. And I'm also here to work out." She took off, skating backwards like a goddamn pro. "Oh, and BTW, you're not pretty. At all."

She turned on a dime and was off like a slap shot.

Of course, I wasn't pretty. I've had three broken noses, a cracked eye socket, and four years ago a blade sliced across my forehead and left a nasty scar.

This was the face of a champion.

I was proud of this face.

But I was left standing there like an asshole. I mean, if she wasn't some puck bunny trying to flirt with me, then I came off sounding like the elitist dick Wendy accused me of being.

I might have apologized, but she'd been pretty mean there at the end.

*BTW, who says BTW?*

Fine. We were both here to work. Nothing more, nothing less.

I started skating again and couldn't help but admire her

transitions. I kept waiting for her to make her way onto center ice so she could start working on jumps and spins before her legs got too tired.

But she just kept building speed along the boards.

To say that I was a competitor was an understatement. They called me *The Heart,* surely because of my last name and its French translation, but I'd earned that nickname too.

I didn't quit. Ever.

There was no game out of reach. No score deficit I wouldn't lead my team to overcome. I played with every ounce of my soul from the start of the game until the final buzzer, and I never let up.

Apparently, today was no exception.

I skated harder in her direction until I caught up to her, sped past her and then turned and skated backwards so I was facing her.

"You're fast, but not that fast," I said with a smile.

Her eyes narrowed again, and her cheeks, already flushed and covered in a smattering of freckles, went beet red. From anger or effort, I wasn't sure.

"You hockey players are all alike."

"What makes you think I play hockey?" I asked, though my size and my skates gave it away.

"Years of observation at the zoo," she said.

Oh! As far as hockey player insults went, that wasn't bad. "Yeah, well, you ice skaters are all the same."

"In what way?"

"You all think you're better than hockey players at skating."

"We are," she said, all smug and competitive. I kind of dug it.

"And you're obsessed with that toe pick move."

"The Cutting Edge is a modern classic, and I won't hear a word otherwise."

"I rest my case," I said.

"You think you're hot shit because you can sprint for what... a few seconds?"

"I think I can go a little longer than that," I assured her. I could hear my sister in my head screaming Elitist Dick, but I shut her out. The same way we shut out Tampa last season.

She came even with me and the smile on her face was nothing but sheer ruthlessness.

I felt a similar smile cross my face.

*Game. On.*

"Okay, you want to go, big boy?" she taunted me.

For the record. I *always* wanted to go.

But I was a professionally trained hockey player with years of experience and about a hundred pounds of muscle on her. It was not a fair match up. At all.

"You scared?" she asked when I hesitated.

Fuck it. Little Miss Toe Pick was going to learn an important lesson today.

"Yeah, I'll go. I'll spot you two laps? To ten?"

"How about four laps to twenty?" she countered.

As one of the best forwards in the league, my line shifts were about sixty seconds. The rink was two hundred feet end to end, around six hundred feet per lap. I did the quick math in my head, because I was a hockey player, but not an idiot. That was a little more than two miles at about ten miles per hour.

Fast, but not crazy fast. And there was no way she would be able to keep up, so I wouldn't have to go all out for the full twenty laps.

Not to mention, it would be a solid cardio workout, which is what I was looking for.

"Deal."

We skated to the home team penalty box. "What do I get if I win?" I asked her.

"Bragging rights."

"I'm not sure I'm going to want to brag about beating a girl."

Her eyebrows went sky high. "No?" She laughed. "Afraid of what the other cavemen will say about you?"

I smiled. Wendy would like this woman. I liked this woman. It was in me to ask for a kiss, but I wasn't *that* kind of caveman.

"Ready?" she asked, getting into her crouch. That leotard made the most of every muscle in her body.

"Always," I shot back. "Set," I said, and she went still. Her eyes focused. Why was that so hot? "Go!"

She took off like a speed skater and I hung back.

One lap, two laps, three laps.

Shit, she wasn't slowing down even a little. No, she was getting *faster*.

When she passed me on the fourth lap I took off. I was three laps in when I realized I had a problem. I was skating all out, and of course I was catching up to her, but not at the pace I needed to overcome her head start.

Five laps in, I passed her, making up one lap.

Ten laps and I passed her again, but I was breathing heavily from the effort. My heart rate was way up. My mouth dry and my vision narrowed.

Didn't matter. I'd let my heart explode in my chest before I stopped.

The good news was, I didn't have to get to that point. I was just hitting my eighteenth lap when she finished.

The bad news was, I'd lost.

To a girl.

She let herself glide along the ice after her victory. Fists on her hips, head tilted back. Chest heaving up and down. And that smile. The smile of victory was absolutely glorious on her face. It almost, *almost* took away the sting of defeat.

"So…" she said as she skated by me where I was doubled over, my hands on my thighs. "The question is…what do I… win?"

"Whatever…you want." I meant it. This woman had me intrigued.

"Tempting," she said, as we both got our breath back.

"Tell me… your… name," I shouted to her.

She shook her head and skated toward the exit that led to the women's locker room.

"That's it? You beat me and leave?" I asked.

She smiled and waved at me. Although, I could hear it in her voice - the pure smugness – when she said:

"Toe pick!"

Fucking figure skaters.

## 2

---

*Later That Night*
*One-Eyed Gull*
*Dillon*

F riday night at the Gull during the summer was pure
insanity. Every tourist looking for some local flavor
came to take advantage of Wendy's drink specials –
especially the women. There'd been a line two deep at the
bar for hours.

Luckily it was too busy to have to do more than pour
beer, take some pictures and sign some bar napkins.

"You owe me!" I shouted to Wendy over a group of
women singing a Taylor Swift song at the top of their collec-
tive, drunk lungs. All of them had my autograph scrawled
on some part of their body.

A PG part of their body. I wasn't that kind of caveman
either.

Wendy shot me her evil grin and rang the bell behind

the bar. "My brother is buying a round!" she shouted, and the place went apeshit.

During a lull in the action, I went into the back to bring out some more cases of Allagash and Bud, and, thanks to Wendy's drink specials, Margarita mix and tequila.

When Dad ran this place, that was after Mom left and his career as a professional wrestler had collapsed under the weight of injuries and poor management, the Gull had been a sleepy dive bar. A locals only hang out.

Lately, my sister was turning it into more of a kitschy destination. She'd leaned in on Dad's cheesy old nautical decorations and the scary mermaid painted on the far wall. She'd even started to serve better food, even though all drunk people wanted at midnight was french fries.

The other really smart thing she'd done was put in the sound system upgrade.

At some point every weekend, the place turned into either a karaoke song fest or a dance party.

That was usually when I left.

By the time I got the booze organized and put away, the tourists had mostly cleared out.

"Hey," Neil Hayes, a fisherman who'd been holding down the end of the bar all night, slid a napkin across the scarred oak bar towards me. "That group of women?"

I knew exactly who he meant, and I was slightly terrified. "Yeah?"

"The tall one left her number."

"Thanks, Neil," I said. I took the napkin and subtly tossed it in the trash. "Another Bud?"

"A'yup."

Matt Sullivan, another local and the town's ferry boat captain, came in and sat down next to Neil. They exchanged silent hellos.

"Sullivan," I said with a smile. We went to high school together back in the day. He'd been a track and field star and had always been joined at the lips with Carrie Piedmont, who'd gone on to be a giant movie star.

Coincidentally, the gorgeous redhead was in town filming a Christmas movie. The cast and crew came in sometimes to sing karaoke and blow off steam.

"What can I get you?"

"Bud," he said. He did a double take when I handed it to him.

"Dillon?" he said, cracking a rare Sullivan smile. "What the hell are you doing behind the bar?"

"NHL doesn't pay him enough," Neil said. That had been his joke all night and it was old the first time he said it. "He needs a better agent."

"Just helping out my sister," I said.

"Team's looking good this year," Sullivan said.

"I like that new kid you got," Neil said. "Novice?"

"Novek?" Sullivan shook his head. "He's a prima donna."

Sullivan wasn't wrong, but I had yet to meet our new European hot shot, so I was keeping my mouth shut.

"How are you doing?" I asked Matt. "I hear Carrie's back in town. It must be great to see..."

Neil was making some shut the hell up gestures over Sullivan's shoulder.

"Her," I finished lamely.

"She's a menace," Matt said, and walked away from the bar. Neil shrugged and took a big swig of his beer. I wasn't a believer in true love, really. But in high school Matt and Carrie had seemed like a fairy tale. It was sad to see it fall apart.

"How you doing?" Wendy asked, coming up beside me. "It's after eleven."

Shit. That late. As a professional athlete, I was serious about a lot of boring stuff that made a huge difference in my career. Getting enough sleep was at the top of the list.

"Past your bedtime, Dillon?" Neil joked. I ignored him. Wendy didn't.

"How's that professional hockey career working out for you, Neil?" Wendy asked. "You drink beer out of any big trophies lately? Break any league records? No?" She cocked her head and Neil had the good grace to look abashed.

"My defender," I said, slinging my arm around her shoulder. "I wish I could take you out on the ice with me."

"Me too," she said. "I'd have given Kadri a little payback after that cheap shot he gave you in the playoffs last year."

I gave her a squeeze and she rested her head on my shoulder for just a second before whirling back into action, pulling a rack of clean glasses from the dishwasher.

"Good night, huh?" I asked her.

"You, my dear sweet older brother, are very good for business," she said.

Wendy had long black hair that she wore up on her head while she worked, and bright blue eyes that men kept falling for. She was a dead ringer for our mom who'd been Miss Maine when she was twenty years old.

But Mom didn't have 10-inch biceps, a championship judo belt and a wicked arm bar.

"Happy to help," I said. "I don't like you closing up on your own."

She rolled her eyes at me. We'd been down this road before. A million times. "I've got Sheriff Bobby on speed dial and Neil here is almost always the last one to leave and he walks me out."

So if someone jumped Wendy she'd have to defend herself and Neil. Awesome.

"I need a keg switched out," she said.

"Fine. But then I'm going home. I'm tired."

"Aww, is my poor bitty bwother twired?"

"Some respect, Wend. That's all I ask."

She beamed at me. "I'll respect you after you change out the keg."

Yeah, yeah. I turned back towards storage when the door to the Gull opened and the last person I ever expected to see stepped inside.

It was *her*. From the ice rink this morning. Little Miss Toe Pick.

Oh shit. Did she figure out who I was? Ask around? Was she here to tell everyone in this bar, maybe this entire town, that she beat me in a race?

I cringed at the thought of what Neil would do with that.

Much less my sister.

Forget the embarrassment factor, it was no secret I was getting up there for an NHL player. The minute you got to the other side of thirty, you started counting down your days and strangers started saying the *R* word in front of you.

I didn't need my team, or any other team, or anyone in this town, thinking I was losing a step.

She was looking around the place curiously, not like she was looking for anyone in particular, and I started to relax.

I was also struck again by how cute she was. Thin, compact little body that she had no problem showing off in tight jeans and a plain black t-shirt. Her hair was still tied up into a ponytail. Even from here I could make out the freckles over her nose and cheeks.

Cute. Her face was really cute.

And her ass was really hot.

A classic combination I was very into.

I grabbed Wendy who was shelving clean glasses.

"Hey, what?" she said. "I'm working here."

"I'm not a hockey player," I said in her ear.

"Okay, is this like some existential crisis you're having right now?"

"What? No. See that woman?" I nodded in the skater's direction. "I don't think she knows me and I want to keep it that way. Okay?"

Wendy smiled. "Someone who doesn't know you? Hmmm, me likey."

"Whatever. Just play it cool," I said.

"Please, Dillon. Remember who you're speaking to."

My mystery lady crossed the room toward the bar. She still didn't seem to see me, but then there was a lot of distraction in the Gull.

"Does she look familiar to you?" I asked my sister.

Wendy watched as Little Miss Toe Pick took a stool at the end of the bar.

"No. Definitely not from around here."

"No, I mean... is she someone famous?"

"Like someone working on the movie in town? No, I know the whole cast. You gonna get her order or just stand here being weird?"

I swatted at my sister with my bar towel and made my way toward the beauty at the end of the bar. There was no point in hiding, and now I wanted to know what she was up to. Showing up at my family bar? That was too much of a coincidence. Wasn't it?

"Here to rub your victory in my face?" I asked her.

It took her a second to recognize me and her eyes went wide. Then her pink lips settled into a smug little smile.

I liked her cocky attitude so much.

"Oh, hey, it's you. Funny meeting you here."

"Hilarious." If she was lying, she was a really good actress.

"You work here?"

I lifted my arms as if to state the obvious. "Yeah."

"Huh. For a second I wondered...yeah, I don't know what I was thinking. I think we got off on the wrong skate. I'm Liv."

She held her hand out and I looked at it for a second wondering if she could really be trusted. Was this all a game? What was pretending not to know me going to get her in the end?

"Come on," she prompted me. "We're obviously going to see each other at the rink again, might as well be civil."

Fine. I shook her hand. "Dillon."

"Nice to meet you, Dillon. So you like to skate, huh?"

Geez, was she for real?

"You could say that."

She leaned back on the bar stool as if assessing me. "Couple of broken noses, a killer scar. Really good on skates. Let me guess, you're in some local beer league?"

"League champions," I said, without missing a beat.

"Well, I'm sorry if I tweaked your pride a little bit. I sort of have... an advantage when it comes to skating."

"Let me guess," I said, leaning my elbows down on the bar. "Former junior figure skating competitor?"

"Junior?"

"You didn't jump. If you were any good at it you would have been doing those twirling things," I said, and made a spinning motion with my finger.

She smiled. "Yeah, something like that. So why would you think I knew you?"

"You know how it is. Former high school hockey stud in

a small town. Most folks recognize me when I skate. Why would you think I knew you?"

"Ah well, I wasn't just a competitor. I actually won a few times. You know, back when I used to do the twirls." She made the same motion I had with her finger and I had a deep rooted suspicion I was getting played. But I was also being entertained so I didn't care.

"You in Calico Cove on vacation?" I asked her, and yeah, I went there in my head. She was cute. She was feisty. She made me smile, and a little vacation fling, no strings attached, right before the season started, was just what the doctor ordered.

Me, being the doctor.

"Yes, just for a few weeks. I start a new job in September in Portland. So I thought I would come, check out Maine early. I heard about Calico Cove and your beaches."

"Well, my beaches are amazing."

She rolled her eyes at my bad, mostly nonsense innuendo.

"Hey, brother," Wendy called across from the bar. "I thought it was past your bedtime?"

"Bite me," I barked back, and turned back to Liv who was smiling. "Can I get you something to drink?"

"Gin and tonic with lots of lime please."

"Coming up," I said and got to work on her drink.

"You're probably tired after me pushing you for twenty laps... oh wait, you only finished like eighteen, right?"

"Get this woman a microphone. She's a comedian," I said, and slid the drink in front of her. She reached for the small purse she had strung over her shoulder and I touched her hand, stopping her. Her skin was soft. "On the house."

"Well, thank you. You sure know how to welcome someone to Calico Cove."

"We're a friendly group up here," I said. "You enjoying our little town?"

"It's really something special. Good people. Good food. Super competitive beer league hockey players."

A couple walked behind Liv and I held my breath. Pretending to just be a local has-been hockey player couldn't last forever. If anyone was going to ruin it, it would be Sheriff Bobby Tanner, who was a bigger gossip than hockey analysts.

"Hey, Heart," Bobby said.

"Bobby, Mari," I said.

"Good luck this season," Bobby said and then Mari pulled him forward. She waved at me over her shoulder and I waved back.

"People take their local hockey around here pretty seriously," Liv chuckled, as she sipped her drink.

"Something like that."

"Heart? Is that your last name?"

"Yep." It wasn't exactly lying. I just didn't mention the French translation. Because the truth was, I liked her not knowing me. Right now, I was just a guy, flirting with a girl, wondering if he might get laid.

Trust me, I wasn't usually that guy. Even remotely. I wasn't a monk, but I didn't like random hook ups because you never really knew how that shit was going to go down. You only had to wake up once in a strange house with a girl taking pictures of you sleeping to know you never wanted to do that again.

And relationships, right now, were a no-go for me.

I was taking the Derek Jeter approach to life. Play my sport to the best of my ability for as long as I could, and when I was done, I would settle down and do the family thing.

Basically the opposite of my father's approach to life when he married my mom. And that had blown up in four people's faces.

So, I had to work in careful, short term, no strings affairs, when I could. Which was never easy when the woman knew who I was. They wanted all the strings.

But this. Maybe?

If she liked me.

"You going to be at the rink again tomorrow morning?" I asked her.

"I am. Why? You want to get your ass beat? Again?"

Yeah, she liked me.

The way she leaned forward on the bar. How that smile played on her lips and her lashes fluttered over her eyes. They were gray, not blue, gray. Like the sky at dawn.

*Damn, they are beautiful.*

"That sounds kinky," I said, leaning on my elbows, just a little into her space. She didn't back up. "I was just thinking we might race again, but if you want to go there..."

"Someone get this man a microphone," she quipped, parroting me.

I was smiling. She was smiling.

Yeah, this was on.

Her eyes caught on something over my shoulder and widened. "Holy shit, is that...*Mon Ami*?"

Inwardly, I groaned and cursed my sister for keeping Dad's old publicity picture up.

"Sure is," I said, looking over my shoulder only to be confronted by the most ridiculous version of my father. Wearing his pro wrestling get up, standard trunks in the colors of the French Flag, a scarf tied around his neck and yes...dear God, yes...a beret.

That beret had been ruining my sex life since I had a sex life to ruin.

It was no wonder my sister and I had to become professional athletes just to live it down.

"You're a professional wrestling fan?" I asked.

"My brother was as a kid. Huge. Why do you have Mon Ami's picture?" she asked. "He was kind of a B level guy, wasn't he?"

Oh God. Dad would die if he heard that out of a beautiful woman's mouth. I couldn't wait to tell Wendy about it later.

"When his career was over he bought this bar," I said and left it at that. "So, where are you-"

Before I could even get the subject changed, Liv pushed her now empty glass forward on the bar.

"Another gin and tonic?" I asked, hopefully. For someone who'd claimed exhaustion not an hour ago, I suddenly felt alive.

"I'm a one and done girl."

"I hope that doesn't apply to...everything."

She blinked and I waited to see if she thought I was charming or creepy.

But she laughed, shook her head and pushed herself off the stool. "See you around, Dillon."

"You need me to walk you home, Liv?"

"No thank you, but nice try."

I shrugged. "Can't blame a guy. Hey, bring your A-game tomorrow. I'm coming for retribution."

She gave me a jaunty finger salute and I returned the gesture.

Wendy came up behind me as I watched Liv make her way through the dwindling crowd. She stopped to look at the mermaid painting with the creepy crossed eyes.

"We have to get rid of that picture of Dad, Wendy. It's ruining my sex life."

"No way," Wendy said. "If that picture ruins your sex life, you have a terrible sex life. Locals love it."

"I hate it," I said, as Liv's excellent ass walked out the door.

"She's cute," Wendy noted.

"Yeah. She is."

"And she really doesn't know who you are?"

She could have been lying. But nothing about her felt like a lie.

"I don't think so."

Either way, I was showing up tomorrow at the rink to find out.

*Liv*

Hockey guy is bartender guy?

With the broken nose, the ice blue eyes, the buzz cut... and dimples? Both sides.

They changed him from hot in a very menacing kind of way, to hot in a holyshitwhoisthisguy kind of way.

Dimples that filled up both sides of his whole face. They were more than dimples. They were Dimples Grande.

And his mouth... that mouth was completely unfair. A perfect cupid's bow. Soft full lips.

He stood behind that bar, built like a brick wall, flirting like a rock star and flashing those dimples at me. It was amazing I wasn't a puddle on that bar stool.

It was amazing I had the strength to leave.

It had been years since my body responded to a guy like this.

Did he really not know who I was?

My car – a beat up old Honda I called Tonya – was a champion. She'd gotten me from Seattle to Maine and, sure, her air conditioner didn't work so well anymore. And the passenger side door didn't open, and, it seemed she was getting a little tired of starting. Just a little.

She just needed some convincing.

I turned the key three times. I patted the dashboard. Turned the radio off so she wouldn't be distracted. Said a quick prayer to her patron saint Kristi Yamaguchi, and finally, with a sputter and then a roar, she started.

*Atta Girl, Tonya.*

I ran back over the conversation I'd just had with the very handsome and charming bartender...what was his name? Dylan Hart? Something like that.

I guess it was pretty arrogant to think I was still a household name. It was just that for a time there, after the last Olympics, I was everywhere. Or at least that's how it felt.

One thing for certain, he was totally flirting with me.

As I drove through town, to the little Airbnb I'd rented, I tried to unpack how I felt about that. Which was a testament to how long it had been since a guy had flirted with me. It was nice to be flirted with. Fun, even. It had been years since I'd thought about fun. Since I'd thought about anything more than putting one foot in front of the other.

Getting back on the ice.

Even with the dimples and those lips, he was not my type, that was for sure. I wasn't into the big and brawny muscle guys. Too many years spent fighting with hockey players for ice time and respect.

He was also naturally competitive, which given my

competitive nature, could be an explosive combination. But maybe also fun? I mean, who wanted a guy who didn't want to compete? Fight? Try hard and win?

That was my whole life.

I should be thinking about my new job. Not distracting myself with men and flirtations. That job was going to be an uphill battle and I knew it. If I even made it past the first few weeks.

So yes, all of those things were true.

However, I was still going to the rink tomorrow morning.

## 3

---

*The Next Morning*
*Dillon*

I'd forced myself out of bed early just to make sure I was the first one at the rink. Last night while I set my alarm, I decided that if I'd been properly warmed up, I wouldn't have lost.

Much to my dismay, when I stepped onto the ice Liv was already there. Not going particularly fast. Just gliding effortlessly. She was wearing a one-piece creamy beige leotard that for a second gave the impression she was entirely naked and my dick took notice.

She was fit and trim, but the leotard made the most of her round ass and perky apple shaped breasts.

Wait. Could I race with a hard on?

Fortunately, my loose shorts hid the evidence of my interest. I stepped onto the ice and quickly fell in time with her easy stride.

"Good morning," I said with a cheeky grin. It felt good just seeing her.

"Good morning," she said with her own cheeky grin.

We had the ice to ourselves today and the building was empty, beyond Hank who was presently and permanently located at the front desk. He told me the high school would be in to practice at seven am so we had an hour.

"So I was thinking," I began. "I'll give you one lap to five."

She shook her head. "No way. You know you'll beat me at that pace."

"Isn't that the point?"

She came to a quick stop on the ice and I had to slide into my stop.

"Look, Dillon, you're a mildly charming guy-"

"*Mildly*?"

She laughed and shook her head. "And I have a sense of where this is going. But I'm really not looking for..."

"A race?" I supplied, when her voice trailed off.

"Yeah. *Races* can be distracting. I've got this new really challenging job coming up. I need to be focused."

"How long until this job starts?"

"Beginning of September." That was my countdown, too. Maybe she was a teacher?

"Perfect, you have a few more days of vacation," I argued. "You don't have to be focused while you're on vacation do you?"

"I'm not looking for trouble, that's for sure. And you reek of it."

"Okay," I said, taking my defeat like a man. "Can I still skate with you to warm up or do you want to listen to whatever's on your phone?"

That seemed to take her by surprise. Like maybe she

didn't think I would give up that easily. But I didn't pursue women who said straight up they weren't interested.

Don't get me wrong, Liv was interested, but something was holding her back and that was enough for me. Guys who pressured women after they held up the no sign always seemed a little pathetic to me. Like, have some self-respect.

"We can skate. Sometimes I like...I like to just listen to the sound of the blades on the ice. You know?"

She took off on her right foot and I joined her, the *snick, snick* of our blades across the freshly Zambonied ice the most familiar, comforting and exciting sound in my life.

"So, if we're not going to race, and now I know you are in fact a figure skater, why don't you show off with the twirls and such?"

She looked at me with a gleam of suspicion in her eyes again.

"What? You forgot how or something?"

"No," she sighed. "Jumps and spins are the words you're looking for. Not twirls. But I can't do them anymore. I had a bad accident a while back and the spins mess with my brain."

"Sorry," I said, regretting being so flip. "I've been pretty lucky in the concussion department, but I've had plenty of friends who have had their careers ended by a brain injury. Their local league career, that is."

"Yeah, it was a little worse than a concussion, but it's all good now. I'm fine. But the doctor says no more jumping and if I spin too fast sometimes it triggers my vertigo."

"That sucks," I said, genuinely. But then I added everything up, and it occurred to me how bad that accident must have been. "Should you even be on the ice?"

"Take me off the ice and what's the point of anything?"

I stopped and she stopped too.

"That sounds dramatic," she said, obviously embarrassed by having admitted something so personal. And to any other person might sound weird.

"No. I know exactly what you mean. If I couldn't skate I'd feel...trapped."

She nodded. "Yeah, it's like those motorcycle gangs. Instead of Ride or Die, I'm more Glide or Die."

I groaned at her terrible pun and she took off again, grinning over her shoulder.

"You loved it," she shot at me.

I was a big lumbering body next to her, but it felt good to have company who was able to keep up. Sometimes I made Wendy come out to the rink with me, but she was an average skater at best. Some of the high school teams liked to give it a go, but they didn't have the stamina or the attention spans.

I knew without asking that Liv could do this all day.

"Shouldn't you be wearing a helmet on the ice?"

"What are you, my doctor?"

"No. But I bet he'd be pissed if he saw you out here without one."

She held a finger up to her lips. Nice plump lips. Especially her bottom lip. "Don't tell my mother."

"My mom can never watch any of my games," I said, and then immediately corrected myself. "Back in high school that is. She was always afraid of watching me get hurt. Said it was too stressful for her. Which is hysterical considering what her daughter used to do for a living."

"Wait, last night, didn't the bartender call you her brother?"

"Wendy runs the bar now but she used to be an MMA fighter."

"What? Like she used to kick people's asses? In a cage? That's so badass."

"Yeah, she was pretty tough. But for the record, my mother couldn't watch her fight either."

We took the corner, each of us on our right skate. Her shoulder bumped mine and my hand reached out to steady her, but she didn't need my help. Our hands brushed and I felt like a teenager.

"My dad would come to every event but he would keep his eyes closed the whole time," she said. "When I asked him what was the point of coming, he said he wanted to let me know that he supported me, but if he kept his eyes closed he could just pretend I landed every jump."

I chuckled. "Did you skate solo?"

She shook her head and her expression changed. Became a little sadder. "Pairs."

We stopped talking for a while, just skating. Not racing.

Except after ten minutes, I could feel her getting a little faster. So I went a little faster too. She crouched, getting lower, changing her center of gravity. So, of course I had to do the same. She took the corners with footwork so fast and pristine there was no way I could match her. So, I just turned up the gas and passed her on the straightaway. She came for me on the next curve, going full out.

Naturally, I had to go full out.

We were both laughing and breathing hard, when she finally cried, "I give!"

I've scored a lot of goals in my time. Won a lot of fucking games, including a game 7 Stanley Cup overtime, tie breaker.

But this win was so flipping sweet, I fist pumped through my entire victory lap.

"Goodbye, Dillon!" she called out as she left the ice and left me to my victory.

"See you tomorrow, Liv."

Because she would be back. In my gut, I knew it.

*Two Days Later*
*Liv*

THIS WAS SO STUPID.

If I kept showing up day after day, I was only going to encourage Dillon. I'd basically told him in no uncertain terms I wasn't up for...racing.

Which, let's face it, we were both adults. We knew that meant sex.

Because he knew I was on vacation, it's not like he was looking for anything beyond that. A bartender, who looked like him, in a summer tourist town? Short term affairs were probably his bread and butter.

Which was why he backed off so easily when I put up the stop sign.

On to the next tourist.

Some sunburned blonde, with highlights in her hair, would be all over a guy like Dillon.

*Ooooh, show me your big muscles? Are you big everywhere? So you used to play hockey? That's sooooo cool.*

Shit. This woman was a made-up fictional character and I was already really annoyed with her. Even worse, I was pissed at him for finding someone like that attractive.

"This is your problem, Liv," I said out loud in my car so my ears would hear it. "You can't get out of your own fucking head. He's just a guy you've been spending time with. No. Big. Deal."

Except getting in my head was my favorite thing to do. And skating next to Dillon these past few days had been nice. I'd forgotten what it felt like to be in sync like that with someone. He certainly wasn't my former partner Brian.

Brian was all lean muscle and graceful movements. Skating next to Dillon was like skating next to the Hulk. Only he wasn't green and he was pretty funny and actually sort of good looking in his own way.

He was also fast and he didn't pull back because I was a girl. He liked to compete and that was my second favorite thing after skating.

Not to mention the allure of him not realizing who I was. The anonymity of just being me, and not a story, was addictive. If he went home and Googled me, would Olivia Tyler-Branch even pop up?

All he knew was Liv and figure skater.

Except now he knew Liv, figure skater and accident.

Figure skater and accident would definitely put me on top of the search. Or maybe not. It was three years ago, but who knew if Dillon was a snooper.

I had some well-meaning friends do some snooping for a blind date I had seven months ago, and they immediately shot him down with a detailed Power Point presentation on every red flag his social media account alluded to.

Needless to say I hadn't tried that again. The dating thing.

So what was I doing back here at six fifteen am, hoping the bartender/local hockey league guy would show up too?

I got out of my car and headed to the rink determined to just enjoy my morning workout whether anyone joined me or not. Except when I came out of the locker room, Dillon was already on the ice and skating.

It made me happy to see him.

Damn it.

I stepped onto the ice and started warming up my legs, pretending he wasn't even there when he glided through my peripheral vision.

"Morning, Liv. Bit of a late start today?"

We'd been trying to one up each other on the ice these past few days. Today was a win for him.

"Geesh, it's just after six," I grumbled. "Plus, you're a bartender. You should hate the morning."

I always liked to be the first one on the ice and I suspected he was the same. He slid in beside me and again I thought of The Hulk on skates and laughed.

"What?"

"You make me feel like I'm skating next to The Hulk," I told him.

He pumped up his chest and beat it with his fists.

"Okay, that's King Kong, not The Hulk. Get it right."

"Guess you're used to being around *figure* skaters," he said with a smirk.

"Don't disparage. I know male figure skaters who can lift and hold their weight above their heads while skating close to twenty five miles per hour."

"Twenty-five miles per hour?" he asked, grudgingly impressed.

"That's how fast the fast ones go," I told him.

He grunted in exchange. "Hey, I know you don't want to...race."

I gave him a side eye, because he dropped his voice several octaves on the word race.

"But it's wing night at the Gull tonight," he continued. "All you can eat for twenty bucks and there is a contest-"

"A contest?" I perked up.

"Yeah, who can eat the hottest wings."

I snorted. "No contest then."

"You can't handle hot wings?"

"No, the opposite. My grandmother on my dad's side was Mexican. I grew up with her cooking and jalapenos were her love language. There is no level of heat I can't handle."

"Wow. Those are some big words."

I shrugged. "Just a fact."

"Good. Then I'll see you tonight?"

Stupid, Liv. So stupid. I'd basically walked right into that.

"Maybe," I said, even though I already knew I was lying to myself. "Now are we going to chit chat or are we going to skate?"

"Me, Hulk. Me skate," Dillon grunted. "You, Jane. You follow."

I rolled my eyes. "That's Tarzan, doofus."

His dimples flashed like the joke was on me and he sped off, all but daring me to chase him.

"So I'll see you tonight?" Dillon pressed as we left the rink. The sun was out and humidity had jumped a couple dozen degrees since I'd gone in. We both slid sunglasses down over our eyes. I had changed into a pair of shorts and a tank top and took a little satisfaction in the way he kept checking out my bare legs.

"I said maybe," I insisted.

"You said yes with your eyes."

Did I? Probably. "No, I didn't."

He laughed. "Alright, maybe you didn't but it will be a good time. All the studs in Calico Cove come out to prove how tough they are, eating the hottest wings imaginable, only to cry like a baby when they're slamming gallons of milk. It's hysterical."

That did sound fun.

A minivan pulled up to the building and four young boys of varying ages piled out of it.

"Wait for me! Stand there and wait for me!" shouted the mom from inside the van, but the boys were having none of it and raced toward the building.

One of them spotted Dillon and stopped dead in his tracks.

"Whoa. The Heart. Guys, guys! It's The Heart!"

"Sorry," Dillon said to me as he was rushed by the four kids all talking at once so I couldn't understand a thing they were saying.

He was some local hero. I shook my head and crossed the parking lot towards my own car.

"Later!" I called over my shoulder. Then, because there was a part of me that liked to be difficult, I said, "Maybe."

**4**

_____

*One Eyed Gull*
*Later that Night*
*Dillon*

"Dillon! Earth to Dillon." My sister yelled in my ear over the general roar of wing night.

"What?" I snapped.

"You going to keep watching that door or are you going to pour drinks?"

"Maybe," I grunted, but started drawing a few pints. Not easy with one eye on the door.

Liv had said she *might* see me later, which we both knew when she said it, was a crock of shit.

We were vibing. There was no getting around it. These past few days had been...something. Whether she wanted to do anything about it or not was her choice. But I knew, sex or no sex, we were always going to have fun together.

We could shoot the shit and make two hours of skating go by in a blink. Or we could do laps in silence, listening to the sound of our blades cutting through the ice, and that was cool, too.

I was going to have to come clean to her about who I was, though. Those kids that rushed us as we were coming out of the rink could have given it all away. Fortunately, they used my nickname, which she just thought was my last name. But I don't care how small a town was, or how blasé some people in town were about me, no one who played in a local hockey league demanded the kind of attention I got from people.

And at this point, I knew her well enough to know she was not the type to be impressed by a professional hockey player.

She thought I looked like The Hulk. Which...not an ego boost. But the way she said it as her eyes drank in the width of my shoulders and the size of my legs more than made up for it.

I also doubted my piles of money would make her care one way or the other.

Liv was too real for that shit. It's what I liked about her.

And I was as real as I could be with her, beyond lying to her face about my job.

Which was why I was surprised she still hadn't shown. It was getting close to nine and the kitchen would close at ten. I could always make up the wings myself, I'd spent formative high school years working that fryer.

I had a five-alarm habanero sauce that even Jolie Bettencourt couldn't handle, and everyone knew Jolie was the queen of the hot wings.

I was going to watch little Miss *I can handle any heat* light up like a fire truck and laugh my face off while she did it.

Unless she changed her mind. Unless she was starting to sense, like I was, that our eventual hook up was becoming inevitable and she needed to take active steps to avoid me. Like not showing up here tonight and not showing up at the rink tomorrow.

Fuck that. She wasn't going to ditch me entirely, was she?

Oh hell. Maybe she was. I didn't know her last name or where she was staying.

Nothing.

This was a beach town in August. There could be a hundred places she might have rented, including a room at The Dumont Hotel. Although she didn't strike me as the fancy hotel type.

How the hell was I going to find her if she didn't show up?

More importantly, why was I freaking out about it? If she didn't show, she didn't show. I was Mr. No Relationship Until My Career Was Over.

There was nothing more going on here, just two people hitting it off. I liked her. She liked me. Our chemistry was off the chart. She was here for a temporary amount of time. It was simple.

Wasn't it?

The door opened. Liv walked in through pink and blue neon lights and I thought...

*Shit. Not simple.*

I was too damn relieved to see her. Too damn happy.

I turned away and saw that stupid picture of my dad hanging on the wall. More than stupid, it was a reminder that you couldn't have everything. You couldn't do the thing you loved – even if it was in a stupid beret - and have relationships. Family.

You got one or the other, try for both and you lost it all.

*Get your shit together Le Coeur. You don't do relationships. You don't do feelings.*

*You do fucking. And you do hockey. That's it.*

Right. This wasn't about feelings. This was about me getting my hands on her hot little body. That was it.

Phew. For a second there I thought I might have been in trouble.

"Oh good, your girlfriend's here. Now maybe you can focus on the job," Wendy said, sliding behind me with two espresso martinis. Another one of her upgrades to the Gull – cocktails.

"You know you don't pay me, and I can leave whenever I want," I reminded her.

She smiled and tossed her hair behind her shoulder. "Yeah, but you won't or I would have to kick your ass."

"Oh, like I'm so scared of you," I snorted.

I was totally scared of her, for the record.

"Also, she's not my girlfriend. This isn't a thing," I insisted. "We just like spending time together."

"Hookay," Wendy drawled. "Look, I'm only busting your chops. Bar's cooled down enough you can go have your fun. You know, with the woman you just like to spend time with."

Wendy was right. The tables were filled with people eating all the chicken wings they could stuff in their face, but there was only a handful of regulars sitting at the bar.

Liv sat in the same seat she had that first night she showed up. This time she was in jeans, a flowy blue top and her hair was down.

Wavy and bright, it fell around her shoulders. Long enough that I could get a grip of it in my fist, but not so long it would get in the way.

I groaned just thinking about it, knowing it was getting harder to shut those thoughts down.

"Hey," she said, hanging her purse on one of the hooks under the bar.

"Hey," I said. I gave her a cool smile. Like I was happy she was here, but it wouldn't have bugged me if she'd never shown up.

*Like I am in fucking high school.* "You bring your appetite?"

She nodded enthusiastically. "Wing me, Heart."

I blinked at her use of my nickname, but then remembered that's what she thought my last name was. Guilt exploded in my chest.

"Hey, about that..."

"Hi, I'm Wendy." Wendy held out her hand over the bar and Liv shook it.

"He said you're an MMA fighter," Liv said, her eyes alight with curiosity. "Is that true?"

"Formerly. My fighting days are over. So if you break his heart you don't have to worry about me kicking your ass."

"Geez, Wendy. Lighten up," I admonished her.

But Liv was laughing.

"I'll keep that in mind."

"Drink?"

"I'll go with your best beer on tap. Something I can gulp down with wings. My understanding is that there is some sort of contest." She steepled her fingers like a cartoon villain.

Wendy shook her head in warning. "You don't want anything to do with the habanero sauce. Trust me."

"Hey," I said. "No inside information for the newbie."

"I'll get you a beer," Wendy said, walking away. "But I'll bring you a glass of milk too. You're going to need it."

"How does this contest work?" Liv asked, clearly not deterred.

"We call it the Five Levels of Hell. Five wings, each wing

gets hotter, if you can eat all five, then all-you-can-eat wings are on the house."

"Sweet," Liv said, wiggling her butt on the stool like a kindergartner on the first day of school. "Free food. I'll take it."

"No one tonight has made it past level four," I warned her.

Liv shrugged. "I guess the good people of Calico Cove have weak palettes."

I chuckled, impressed by her trash talk. "Your funeral. Wait here and I'll bring them out."

In the kitchen each freshly made and sauced wing was put in its own container by our cook, William, who wore gloves. The fifth wing, the habanero sauce, looked radioactive. Poor William's eyes were watering.

Maybe I would wait until she was crying and her mouth was on fire and then I'd tell her who I was. She'd be in too much pain to get mad about how I'd lied to her these past few days.

*Yeah. Class act, Heart.*

I set the wing baskets down in front of her and crossed my arms over my chest. I gave her the very serious instructions about not rubbing her eyes with her hands or a dirty napkin.

"Please. This isn't my first rodeo."

"Oh, this is going to be fun," I announced.

"Watching a person eat entertains you?"

"No, watching you try not to freak out, when I know your whole mouth is on fire, is going to be fun."

She shook her head, her hair bouncing around her shoulders, like she was shaking me off. "I can do this all night, buddy."

"Do you want to give me your next of kin's number before you go down this path?"

"Hardy har. Let's go."

She ate the first wing like a pro. Pinched both ends and twisted it so that the meat fell apart. Popped the whole thing in her mouth.

"Delicious," she said.

The next wing went down the same way. Again, she didn't flinch.

On the third wing she breathed through her nose, but other than that she was showing no signs of slowing down.

The fourth wing made her blink. That was it. A single slow blink. She took a sip of beer and looked down at the fifth wing. The five-alarm habanero sauce.

Not only was it hot, but it also didn't taste great. Neil had rushed to the bathroom after trying it. And he hadn't looked right since. Suddenly, I didn't want Liv to get sick. This wasn't fun if she had to go home. I found myself doing something I never did – flinching in the face of a competitor.

"You don't have to do it," I said, tugging the edge of the basket away from her. "I'll give you all the wings you want. Don't punish yourself just to prove something to me."

Her lips twisted into a smirk. "Uh, that's the whole point of competition. Hand it over, Heart."

She'd drawn some attention from a few of the locals hanging out at the bar.

"Yeah, let her try it, Heart. She's already finished four and she's not flinching," shouted Frank, a gruff old lobsterman, whose beard and ear hair had grown into one magnificent pelt.

"Stuff it, Frank," I barked back. "She doesn't have to if she doesn't want to."

Too late.

She picked up the wing, twisted the ends to break it up, and cleaned the meat off each side of the wing with her teeth. She dropped the bones in the basket and then licked the sauce off her fingers.

Holy shit.

"Man, she did it!" Frank shouted, gathering everyone's attention to Liv at the bar. "She beat the Five Levels of Hell. Hey everyone, we have a new Queen of Heat in the house!"

The bar erupted in applause, but I said nothing. I just watched her face, like waiting for a volcano to blow. Her cheeks turned red and her eyes teared up. There was absolutely no mistaking the signs that the heat was getting to her.

But she only smiled at me.

"You okay?" I asked, breaking first.

"Do you have one of those wet wipes?" she asked, with a wiggle of her fingers, like she was ordering another beer.

Maybe she really was impervious? Was it possible the heat didn't impact her even a little bit?

"You're a beast," I acknowledged, conceding the win. "A hot wing beast."

I ducked down toward the other end of the bar to grab some packets of wet wipes, but as soon as I turned back around I could see Liv chugging the glass of milk Wendy had given her. She emptied it, slammed the glass on the bar and a laughing Wendy already had another glass in front of her.

"Ha!" I shouted. "I knew it!"

"Knew what?" Liv gasped, and then chased the milk she'd been given with some water. Tears streamed down her face.

"Impervious to heat, my ass," I laughed.

"There was a contest. I won. That's all that matters."

"You're insane, you know that?"

"I'm a winner. I know that."

She hiccupped and grimaced, but after another glass of water and another glass of milk she was back to normal.

People came up to congratulate her on her victory and it was obvious she was in her element. After half a beer, and some chit chat with the locals, she wiggled her eyebrows at me.

"Feed me, Heart. I'm a girl on a budget."

I brought her a basket of ten wings, nothing crazy hot and a few hot and honey for sweetness and set them down in front of her. She was not a woman who got weird eating around a guy, which I secretly loved.

I couldn't remember the last time I went on a date with a woman who didn't order a salad as their main course. "What's this budget you're talking about? I thought you were starting a job in a few weeks."

She squirmed on the stool again and I had a sudden image of her doing that while sitting on my lap.

"Yeah, it's only a few weeks and I'm not sure what's going to happen after. It's sort of an...experimental position."

"Are you like a scientist or something?"

She laughed. "A little bit. What I do is essentially a study in physics."

"Well, I'm just an old hockey player, I don't know anything about physics," I said.

"Please, skating is all about physics. It's force and motion. Acceleration and angle. It's the purest form of math on ice."

"You make it sound kind of beautiful."

"Because it is."

I leaned over the bar until I was close enough to feel the

heat off her shoulders. The smell of hot sauce and shampoo wafted off of her. She had a little wing sauce in the corner of her mouth and I wanted to lick it off. I was going to kiss her tonight and it was going to be hotter than the five-alarm habanero sauce.

"You going to let me walk you home tonight, Liv?"

She smiled, even as she was shaking her head. Like she was losing her own internal battle.

"You know you want to," I sang in high falsetto.

"Maybe, I'll let you walk me home because you've got all those big muscles so no one will mess with me."

I closed my eyes and groaned. "That's right, Liv. Use me for my muscles."

She pushed against my shoulder. "You're such a dork. And I'm not done eating. You said all-you-can-eat. I need another basket."

"Your wish is my command."

IT WAS LATE. After midnight. Way past my bedtime, but Liv and I were walking together like the destination didn't matter. The moon was high over the ocean and it felt like every star was out to guide our way.

We crossed Harbor Road towards the center of town where the Christmas movie was being filmed, and the sets with all the fake snow were still up.

"Wow, your town really loves Christmas."

I explained the movie as our shoulders brushed and my hand kept touching hers. It was the most pleasurable torture I'd ever experienced. Most of the set was behind fences, but we stopped in a section of fake trees covered in fake snow.

"What's it called? The movie?"

"Something stupid," I said. "I can't remember it."

"This is a little weird," she said, spinning around slowly, taking it all in. "Christmas in August."

"Usually, there's a bunch of street vendors and food trucks," I told her. "You haven't lived until you've tried Birdie's falafels. Oh, and you can get your fortune told by Madame Za."

"A fortune teller? Seriously?" Liv asked with a raised eyebrow.

"People swear by her and she makes a living doing it."

"I like to have control of my future rather than leaving it up to the whims of fortune."

I snorted.

"You think that's crazy?"

"Not at all, it's just a little crazy how much you sound like me sometimes."

"Not a believer in fate?"

"I'll tell you what a buddy of mine told me. You can control how you get to your future, but you can't control your future. You never know what's coming."

I hadn't seen her coming, that was for sure.

"Fair enough. Although you're so big, I'm going to assume most people see you coming."

"Hey, stop making *big* jokes. You're hurting my feelings."

She stopped walking and turned to face me. Her expression lit up with mischief. "I'm sorry, is that the moon out there over the water? I can't see it over your big head."

"Fine. Go ahead then," I said, twirling my finger. "Get it out of your system."

"Your head's so big I bet you have to step into your hockey jersey."

"That's it. Now you've done it." I made a motion to grab her around the waist, but she danced back. She was quick, but I was a professional athlete. Another two steps and I had my arm around her waist.

She didn't struggle even a little bit.

"Is this the part where you kiss me, big guy?"

"Yeah," I pulled her closer. "This is the part where I kiss you."

I was not a man who over-thought my kissing technique. I didn't get in my head about the angle of my head, or how much tongue I should use. Kissing was something you just went for and let the drive and the heat take over.

But as soon as my lips touched hers, something hit me. Like a puck to the solar plexus. I felt nervous and winded and excited all at the same time. My lips grazed hers and then pulled back. I wanted to breathe her in first. All that heat, all that feistiness. I wanted to ingest her, absorb her into my skin.

I wanted *her*. Her body and her quick wit and her non-stop trash talk. I wanted her last name and the whole story about what happened to her. I wanted to see what she would look like in my bed tomorrow morning.

Her lips fit mine. Her tiny frame tucked against my chest like she was this missing limb I never knew I was supposed to have. Under mine, her lips opened with a quiet gasp.

That's right, I wanted to say. This isn't going to be simple. Or just a kiss. This is going to be all night. And maybe a good chunk of tomorrow. And every day before she left to start her new job.

When that punch hit, you know the one deep down in your gut, the one that grabs you by the balls and says, *Yes. Let's fuck...*when that hit, it made my knees go weak.

I wanted more. I wanted all of her. I hadn't even realized it, but she'd lifted herself up into my arms, wrapping her legs around my waist, so I could have better access to her mouth. Like a move we'd choreographed and practiced over a thousand times.

"Liv," I breathed, and she pulled away, her wide eyes meeting mine, like she couldn't believe this either. This heat. This connection.

*I know, right?*

She dove back into me and sank her teeth into that spot where my neck met my shoulder. It sent chills down my fucking spine.

"You smell good," she whimpered, and ran her tongue over my skin. "Hmm. You taste good too."

"Mouth, babe. I want your mouth."

I wrapped a hand around the back of her head, my fingers sinking into her blonde silky hair. I tugged on it until she was forced to crane her neck back and then her mouth was offered up, so I took it.

It could have been minutes, or hours, or days for all I knew. I only knew I didn't want it to end. I wanted to kiss her all night. Taste her all night. She did a full body squirm in my arms and shit got real.

I was hard and primed and we needed to get serious about a location or I was going to lose my shit and fuck Liv in the middle of the park in downtown Calico Cove.

"Uh, hello. 'Scuse me. Yeah, uh Dillon, I hate to break up what you're doing there, buddy, but I sort of have to remind you about public decency laws."

Liv broke away from our kiss and we realized a police car had pulled up next to where we were making out on the sidewalk.

"Go away, Bobby," I growled.

"Yeah, I can't do that. But maybe you two could... I don't know...go somewhere a little more private."

"Wow, the police in this town are so strict," Liv said with

a smile, and she dropped her legs from around my waist. I had no choice but to let her go.

"I think I hate you right now, Bobby." I glared at him with my fiercest scowl. The asshole had the nerve to smile.

"Sorry, Dillon. I get it. But you'll thank me."

"I don't think so."

"Well, when tomorrow's headlines don't say New England Bruisers captain and star center forward Dillon Le Coeur caught having sex in the middle of Calico Cove– you'll know it's because of me. Have a nice night and go Bruisers!"

Oh shit.

Bobby hit the gas and pulled away from us and I was left frustrated, rock hard, and standing in the lie I'd been telling.

"What did he mean?" Liv asked, taking a step away from me. Her lips were swollen but her eyes were narrowed. "He called you Dillon Le Coeur."

"Hey, I was going to tell you tonight. I just forgot with... everything."

She took another step back. "Tell me what?"

"My last name isn't Heart. Well it is, but you know, in French. Heart's my hockey nickname."

"Your hockey nickname."

I rubbed my hand over my face, felt the scruff of hair on my cheeks and wondered if it had bothered her soft skin.

"Listen, don't freak out. But I don't play in a local hockey league. Unless you consider the New England Bruisers a local hockey league."

"The New England..."

"Bruisers."

"No. No, no, no, no." Horrified, she put her hand up over her mouth, like she wanted to wipe the kiss off her mouth.

Not an awesome reaction.

"I know. You're mad I didn't tell you, and I get it. But I have a lot of women who come on to me just because of what I am, instead of who I am. You didn't have a clue I was a professional hockey player and I...I liked that."

"I need to go. Right now." She was still backing away from me.

"Liv, come on. You know we have something. Let's talk this out." I reached for her and she flinched away.

Flinched.

"A kiss. One kiss. That's all we had. Past tense," she said.

"Liv..."

"No, Dillon," she held up her hand. "I'm dead serious. This isn't happening. You and I are going to pretend we never met. Do you understand? Never met."

I reached for her again, feeling like I was sinking. "Don't do this. This can be so good."

She looked at me like I was a worm. A worm she wanted to step on. "You lied to me. You tricked me. None of this is good. Don't follow me or so help me God I'll scream so loud I wake up the entire town."

"Liv! Come on. Let's talk this out..."

She shook her head and jogged away from me. Then ran. Then she was full out sprinting.

I could have caught her. If I started running after her, I could have caught her. Except what the hell would that accomplish?

Instead, I pulled my phone out of my pocket and called Bobby's cell.

"Uh, didn't I just leave you two?" he answered after a single ring.

"I pissed her off," I told him. "And she took off. I don't want her running at night alone. Double back and head east on Beach Street. Then give her a ride home, yeah?"

I didn't have to say anymore. "A'yup."

The call disconnected and I stood there in the street for a minute. Not ready to walk away. Not willing to accept that was the last time I was going to see Liv. Talk to Liv.

Kiss Liv.

No. No way. This wasn't the end. I wouldn't let it be. I just had to figure out how to win her back.

Then I remembered I didn't even know her last name.

"Fuck!" I shouted into a Christmas movie set in August.

# 5

---

*Three Weeks Later*
*Bruisers Training Facility*
*Portland, Maine*
*Dillon*

T he atmosphere in the team conference room was
electric. Charged. Legs were bouncing. Shit was
talking. There were handshakes and hugs. There
were pencils and notebooks set out in front of each of our
chairs, like it was the first day of school.

The first day of school with a bunch of driven, competitive, sometimes asshole, grown men. Everyone was excited.
Everyone was five pounds overweight.

Everyone was ready to get the season started.

Except our brand-new, star forward, Balak Novek, was
nowhere to be found.

"Fucking phenoms," Ron Morgan muttered next to me.

Ron was a senior player, in his late thirties, plagued by

an ankle injury. Bounced around from team to team for the past few years, he was a specialized defensive player. But it was clear from the moment he stepped onto the ice with us at the end of last year, that he wasn't looking to make friends or bond with the team.

He was here to collect his paycheck and that was it.

I didn't like it. You didn't build a team that made it to the finals with role players.

Or guys with bad attitudes.

"Listen, if Novek gets sixty goals this season, he can be late all he likes," said Derek Smith, our gigantic, red-headed, Canadian goalie. He sat with our other new rookie. Some corn fed kid out of the prairies who'd won the NCAA Championship with the University of Michigan. He had come with a laptop like he was going to take notes. The rookie seemed nice enough, but it was doubtful he was going to be sticking around. Collegiate champs got chewed up by the NHL all the time.

No point in even learning the kid's name.

"This is bullshit," Skalsberg muttered. Skalsberg was our big Swedish defenseman, a man of extremely few words and the best blocked shot average in the league. "It's disrespectful."

There was a murmur of agreement in the room.

"Calm down," I said. "Coach isn't here, yet."

You weren't officially late until coach showed up. But as the captain and a guy who liked to be the first one in every room, I would be having a little talk with Novek about time management and team dynamics.

Novek was a big part of our plan to get our hands back on the cup this year.

This was what I lived for. Had lived for, for the past ten years.

I was amped up, the whole room was. But it wasn't just hockey that had made me restless and on edge. For the last few weeks I'd felt like a tiger pacing in its cage. I couldn't train or run or skate this feeling away.

I checked my phone again.

Nothing from my sister. Before leaving, I'd asked her to keep an eye out for Liv, but Miss Toe Pick hadn't been back at the bar and Wendy said she hadn't seen her around town either.

She'd packed up and left Calico Cove all together.

Which seemed a little extreme to me.

Okay, I lied about who I was, but it wasn't like I was a serial killer. I was just a pro hockey player for Pete's sake.

The door to the conference room opened and Novek strolled in with his mullet, wearing some Balenciaga bull-shit like he didn't have a care in the world.

"Wait." The rookie asked. "Aren't we supposed to be in team workout gear?"

"Yes," I muttered. Everyone in the room was wearing team kit. Except superstar over there with the fanny pack.

"Hello," Novek said with his thick eastern European accent. He smiled, revealing his extremely white teeth. That he had all of them was a miracle. "I am here."

"You're late," I said.

"I am never late," Novek said, slipping into a seat at the front of the room. "Nothing starts without me." Beside him, Beroski reached forward to shake his hand. Novek ignored him.

"Fucking phenoms," Ron muttered again. "You going to do something about that, Captain?"

Before I could, Coach opened the door and walked in exactly at the top of the hour. He wore the same warm-up gear he always wore, circa 1990. The guys joked that he wore that warm-up gear under his game day suit. That he went to bed with that whistle in his mouth.

He was trailed by our offensive and defensive assistant coaches and our conditioning coach.

"Men," he said and we immediately quieted down.

Coach Lawrence McKay had been with the team for four seasons. There were rumors this might be his last year and he wanted to go out with one more championship attached to his name. The coaching staff and team had built up trust over the last several seasons, which is why I felt like we were all primed for a deep run into the playoffs. There would be no real surprises going into this year, other than Novek and the rookie. But new players, and incorporating them into the team, was expected.

No team stayed exactly the same year to year.

Father Time and Mother Injury always saw to that.

"Welcome to preseason. I've called you all here for this meeting to talk about one topic," Coach said. He picked up a magic marker from the tray of the white board and wrote a single word:

SPEED.

"Our transitions are slow. Our footwork is slow-"

"Speak for them," Novek said, pointing at the rest of our team. "My footwork is perfect." The tension in the room hit the ceiling. Skalsberg growled, like a Viking.

"Hello Novek," Coach said, deadpan. "Everyone in this room can improve. Guys like Oshie make us look like we're standing still."

No one could argue that T.J. Oshie made everyone look like they were standing still. But that was an excellent red flag to wave in front of a room of elite competitors.

"We've hired a preseason skating coach who is going to help us get our speed up."

"What happened to Anton?" Ron asked.

Anton was our old skating coach. A former NHL forward who'd had his career cut short by an eye injury during practice.

"Anton didn't agree with our change in direction," Coach McKay said.

Oh. Shit. Everyone in the room sat forward. Whatever this was, it was going to be...different.

Coach held up his hands to get us all to calm down. "Olivia Tyler-Branch is a pro. You'll listen to her."

"A girl?" Novek sneered. I could feel a few other guys in the room echoing that sentiment.

"A professional," Coach corrected him, his gaze sweeping all thirty of us sitting there. "I don't think I have to tell you respect is expected for any member of the team. From me to the towel kid. Understood?"

"I've never heard of her," Ron said. "Why are you bringing in some unknown?"

"Girl," Novek sneered again.

"I know her," the rookie said. "I mean of her. She was a world class figure skater a few years back. Pairs."

"Oh shit. Her!" Someone said from the back of the room. I wasn't really paying attention because I had this weird buzzing going on inside my head. "She wiped out at the last Olympics. Like splat."

"It was bad," rookie said, with palpable sympathy. "Ended her career."

"To answer your question, she is not unknown," Coach said. "She comes highly recommended by legendary skating coach Don Bruno. And she's been revolutionary for the US Junior National team."

"You mean *boys*," Novek said.

"You guys need to get in this century. Lots of teams are hiring figure skaters as skating coaches," rookie said.

"No. Hockey is *not* figure skating," Novek snorted. "If she steps on the ice with us, she will get hurt."

Was that a threat? It sounded like a threat but I couldn't do anything about it right now because my brain was still short-circuiting.

I thought of Liv. Daring me to go faster. Liv, beating me over the course of time.

Liv.

*"I wasn't just a figure skating competitor. I actually won a few times."*

*"It messes with my brain. I had a bad accident a while back."*

*"You and I are going to pretend we never met. Do you understand?"*

Now I was listening. To everything she ever said to me. Because it felt like one of those movie reveals, where all the clues are shown together at the same time so the audience could come up with the answer just a few seconds before it was all revealed for the idiot main character.

I was the idiot main character.

"Come on in, Coach," McKay called out.

"Gentlemen," Liv said, as she stepped in the room and up to the white board. She smiled at everyone. Except me. "Good morning."

*I am so fucked.*

"This is a mistake," Ron muttered in a voice low enough only I could hear.

That caged tiger living in my chest roared.

I wanted to tear the room apart. I wanted to flip over the desk and chair. I wanted to haul her up over my shoulder and start running as fast as I could back to our cave.

Because that's how this felt. Primitive.

She looked different. Her honey-blonde hair was in a tight bun on the back of her head. She wore a navy blue pantsuit with a white blouse. Way too formal for this bunch, but it was her first day and she no doubt wanted to make an impression.

The pantsuit said she was all business.

She had mascara on her eyelashes, making her gray eyes luminous.

I wondered if she was standing in that hallway listening to every word these idiots were saying. Except rookie, he'd been the only reasonable one. While I'd been wrestling with the realization that the only woman I wanted to fuck was now the one woman completely off limits to me.

*This* was why she took off that night. It wasn't because I lied to her about who I was, it was because she knew today was coming.

The pencil I'd been rolling between my fingers snapped.

That smile on her face faltered and she shot a nervous glance in my direction.

"Okay, let's begin," she said. "I don't need to tell you that the best hockey players in the league are the best skaters. I'm going to throw a lot of numbers at you which will probably make your eyes glaze over, but it's important we start with the basics. How fast do you skate?"

"Slow, baby. I can go as slow as you like," Novek said.

There were a couple of nervous laughs, and before Coach could say anything I remembered I was the fucking captain of this team.

I stood and everyone immediately shut up, as they should.

"You know what, Novek? You were a big deal in the European Leagues, but you're in the NHL now and everyone in this room is a big deal."

Novek sneered and reclined even further in his chair like a petulant baby.

"Skalsberg?" I said. "How many championships have you won?"

"One," The Viking said. "With you, Captain."

"Smith?"

"Two, baby!"

"Coach?" I said, my eyes still on Novek. "How many rings do you have?"

"Three."

"How many do you want?"

"Four."

"Funny," I said. "Me too."

The room cheered.

"If Coach says this is how we get there, this is how we get there," I said. "Cut the shit. We're going to listen to what Miss...I'm sorry I didn't catch the full name?"

Yeah, I was a dick, but I felt justified in this case. She could have just told me what was happening instead of bolting that night.

"Olivia Tyler-Branch."

"Right. Coach Tyler-Branch is going to make us better, Novek. And if we get better we might win more often. Show of hands, who likes winning?"

The room put their hands up.

I moved to return the stage to Liv and saw she also had her hand raised high above her head. I lifted my eyebrow at her and fought my smile.

"Oh, you meant them," she said, then slowly lowered her hand.

"Sorry for the interruption," I said.

"Thank you. Now back to those numbers..."

She turned back to the white board, took a marker off

the tray and started writing equations I didn't give a shit about.

Liv was here. She was in this room. I knew her full name, and she wasn't going anywhere.

It was time to get some answers.

*Liv*

"Excuse me, Coach Tyler-Branch, can I have a word? I want to get clarification on that force vs. angle equation you put up on the board."

It was Dillon. Of course, it was Dillon. Did I think he'd just file out with the rest of the guys?

No. But I'd been hoping he would.

I set the marker back down on the tray, unwilling to turn around and face him just yet.

Earlier, standing out in the hallway, I'd only been half listening to the guys talk shit about me, because I'd been preparing myself to face *him*.

Which made me want to scream. Biggest professional moment of my life after the accident and I was distracted by the cute boy I'd met this summer? The cute boy who'd lied to me?

Shame on me. I was tougher than that.

But when I finally saw him, sitting in the bottom corner of the room, all intense and shocked and handsome and big and familiar... my palms got sweaty and my heart pounded.

I was worse than a teenager.

Obviously, he waited until most everyone had cleared the room. There was no option but to turn around and face the music. Was he going to yell? Probably. Say something reasonable like that kiss meant nothing, and we had to be professionals now?

That's what I'd been saying to myself the last three weeks.

"Cap, you coming?"

It was Cody O'Rourke. I'd already studied the entire team's roster. He was a rookie on the team, fresh out of college, and the only one who looked like he understood the math I spent the last hour talking about.

"In a second," Dillon said, without looking at the younger man waiting by the door. His eyes were on me and me only. "I need a math refresher."

The door swung shut behind O'Rourke and it was just the two of us.

Staring at each other.

"Look, I know what you're going to say," I said, beating him to the point.

"I'm pretty sure you don't," he said, crossing his big beefy arms over his wide chest.

I kept telling myself I didn't like muscles, but my eyes kept lingering on his bulging biceps.

*Focus, Liv!*

"You're going to apologize," I said. "For lying to me."

"I'm not. Because I already did that. But that's okay, because *you* are going to apologize for lying to *me*."

"Please," I scoffed. "It was hardly the same caliber lie. I didn't tell you my last name. You let me believe you played in a beer league."

Even saying it out loud I felt stupid. Of course he didn't play in a beer league. Sitting in this room full of professional athletes, he'd been the biggest, most intense, among them.

"Once I told you the truth-"

"Told me the truth?" I screeched, and then lowered my voice, my face getting hot. "You were outed by the town sheriff!"

He had the good grace to look guilty.

I took a deep breath and got control of myself. This had been exactly the scene I wanted to avoid.

"If you remember, I said this job was temporary. I am mostly an unknown and Coach McKay is taking a risk with me. You can see what I'm dealing with. The guys don't respect me because I'm a woman telling them this information."

"Not true," Dillon said. "They don't respect you, because you're a figure skater, not a hockey player, and you haven't earned their respect."

"Fine," I conceded, I could respect that. "But they're certainly not going to respect me if they think I'm messing around with the team captain, so anything that may or may not have happened between us..."

"May *not*?" Dillon snorted. "Babe, you climbed me like a tree and swallowed my tongue."

"Shhh!" I hushed him, looking to the door. "My point is, nothing can happen now. I work for the team. And now you understand why I had to put a stop to things."

"You mean ran away. You could have just explained it all then, but instead you bolted."

I hated that he characterized it that way. I wasn't a coward and I didn't run from difficult things. But the realization of who he was and the mistake I'd been about to make had sucker punched me.

He'd worn me down with that grin and nuclear grade sexual chemistry. I'd made the decision to have sex with him. Sex wasn't something I took lightly. It required a level of trust I didn't just hand out to people. That he'd earned my trust over a handful of days felt a bit scary, but I knew I would be safe with him.

However, as soon as I'd made that decision, the sheriff was telling me who he really was and I was instantly pissed.

No, I wasn't a coward, but I wasn't a fool either and he made me feel like one.

But I was also...sad.

Sad because it felt like I was losing something I didn't get a chance to have.

Like treating yourself to an ice cream cone only to drop it on the ground after only one lick.

I gathered myself to every inch of my five foot four height and lifted my chin.

"You lied to me," I said. "Tricked me. I felt like a fool, Dillon."

His cheeks flushed. "I am sorry. I just...I really liked you. Things were normal between us. I was afraid if I told you the truth it might change things between us. I didn't want that."

"Would you have slept with me without telling me the truth?"

"No," he said. "I would have told you before we got that far. I swear."

"Okay. I believe you," I said, grudgingly.

"How did you not recognize me by the way?" He asked. "Your new job is with the team. My face is all over the place."

I winced, feeling foolish again. Yes, I'd studied their names and their careers. But I hadn't paid much attention to their team pictures.

"Well, mostly you wear a helmet. And with that hair cut..."

He ran his hand over his head, the close buzz cut.

"Also, it honestly never occurred to me that the guy at that small town rink and behind the bar in Calico Cove was freaking Dillon Le Coeur. But it doesn't change anything between us. I'm not going to ask you to lie and say you don't know me. But if anyone asks, maybe you could classify our acquaintance as a casual friendship that happened while I was on vacation in Calico Cove."

He sighed while nodding and a sense of relief poured through me. I'd been dreading this day for weeks, not knowing how he was going to react when I showed up. Now I knew. He was going to be reasonable.

Damn it.

Because, not going to lie, part of me wanted him to smile at me and crowd me against this white board until I couldn't think straight.

*No, I did not. Get it together, Olivia.*

"Yeah, that makes sense," he said. "You're going to have an uphill battle with some of the guys. If we're fucking around, they will sniff that out and make your life hell. And if word gets out that you sleep with players-"

"I will never get hired again. With any team."

He nodded. "So...I guess...I'll see you on the ice?"

"On the ice," I said, smiling as he walked out.

This was the best possible outcome.

So why did it feel so shitty?

# 6

—————

I took a deep breath and prepared myself to step out on the ice and lead my first practice. I had my cones. I had my stop watch. I had my whistle.

For four days I'd been watching their dynamic on the ice, looking for areas of improvement, planning my drills and individualizing them for every player.

This was going to be fine. Great, even. I was knowledgeable. Charming. I was going to earn their respect and they were going to love me.

I felt like I was going to vomit.

McKay blew the whistle and the team gathered at center ice, Novek taking his sweet time. While McKay was talking to them, I looked over my edge work drill notes.

I wasn't going to push anyone too hard or too fast. This was just a little get to know you drill. Should be fine.

*Please be fine.*

"Hey, it's time for figure skating lessons," Novek said. I was gratified no one laughed with him, but when I turned around I realized it was because Dillon was giving them a death stare.

It was strange that two groups of athletes with so much in common, struggled to find mutual respect. Yes, it was true. The NHL was using more figure skaters, female figure skaters too, as skating coaches, but the mountain we had to climb was steep.

Hockey players thought figure skaters were frivolous, and my former partner, Brian, thought hockey players were all dumb thugs who did nothing but fight. It was slightly shameful, but I may have thought that too at one time.

My brother, an up and coming star hockey player, had obviously changed my mind.

But so did Dillon.

By every definition he was a leader. He never went easy in practice. He always executed his coach's vision.

Helped the guys who needed help.

Checked the guys who needed to be checked.

Inspired all of them to work harder.

And he looked really hot doing it.

That was not something I was thinking about. At all.

After our conversation the other day, he hadn't done or said anything to me. We passed each other in the hall and he gave me the same chin nod he gave everyone. Like I was no one special.

Which of course was the plan, but I didn't love it.

Whatever. I was here to do a job. Whatever the guys thought of me, I had knowledge that could help.

"Remember. Respect." McKay said to his guys, and then turned to face me. "Coach Branch, they're all yours."

The sensation was like breathing to me. That first glide out onto the ice. With the dimensions of a standard US hockey rink, I could feel the size of the guys on center ice. If one of them barely bumped into me I was going to go flying, but I wasn't going to let that bother me.

Overcoming fear was something I'd been doing since my crash and burn.

Recovery had been a slow and steady journey. I had to relearn how to walk, then run, then bicycle. Until finally, a year after it happened, I was able to step back on the ice.

That day I'd cried the entire time I skated. Scared out of my mind, but so happy to be flying again, even if tentatively. It was like no emotion I'd ever felt before. Not even winning Olympic Gold had felt like it.

So this was another fear I just had to conquer. Facing down a large group of men and telling them what they were getting wrong.

I set out my cones, bending to shift one over a few inches. Someone whistled as I bent over, and I had a good idea who. I knew I couldn't respond to the sexism. The second I did, I would be called difficult and I'd lose even more of them.

But honestly, you'd expect more from a group of professionals.

"Excuse Novek," O'Rourke said. "He was raised on the back of a mule."

"Fuck you," Novek said, good naturedly. "I was raised on the front of the mule."

A few of the guys laughed.

Yeah, that guy could be an ass and I had to just keep working.

There was a strategy to earning respect. Always.

Take down the big dog first.

I turned and faced the team, all leaning on their sticks, looking like they'd been born on skates.

"Right leg, inside out drills."

"Come on," Skalsberg groaned. "Give us a challenge."

"Show me you can meet this one and I will," I shot back.

The boys oohed and Skalsberg scowled. Dillon's eyes met mine and something about his gaze was intense. I tried to have no reaction, so I blamed my suddenly hard nipples under my team training gear on the cold air.

"Novek," I said. "Why don't you go first?"

"My pleasure," he said, with a little more smarm than was necessary. His dark mullet streamed out from underneath his helmet. Hockey hair, honestly, were these guys fourteen? He skated up to me, and I was reminded of our size differential. If he wanted to, Novek could knock me halfway across the ice.

"Right leg only, stay between the cones, stay low. Head up. Speed and control."

"You think I don't know this?" he said to me, the smarm gone under an edge of defensive superiority.

"Let's go, then," I said, lifting my watch. Novek got positioned and I blew my whistle. "Captain," I said. "You're next."

I got them all moving. Each of them five loops. Then I moved the cones closer to each other.

Smith, the goalie, groaned.

Another five laps. I moved them closer.

Now half of them groaned. I smiled. The tiny muscles used to stabilize their legs would be screaming at them.

Across the ice, Dillon smiled at me. I had to look away.

This round I started to give some corrections. O'Rourke soaked up my coaching like a sponge.

Ron grumbled but gave it his best shot. I made a note to give him some of my ankle mobility exercises.

Then I went after my big dog.

"Novek, when you dig you're making two mistakes."

"Mistakes?" his voice practically cracked on the word. "I don't make *mistakes* on *skates*. See what I did there...with my rhyming?"

"Very clever," I snorted, and rolled my eyes even as the guys were laughing around me. Pretty sure at my expense.

"You're cutting down your momentum in the c-cut. You have all this bulk that you're not using to your advantage."

"Novek, I think she just called you fat," one of the players commented.

Again more laughter from the group.

Just power through this, I thought. If I show them techniques that actually work, and I can prove it's going to increase their speed, they will listen to me.

At least I hoped so.

"In the middle of the c-cut you shift your weight back, when you need to be pushing even more of your weight forward, out over the skate-"

"No," Novek said, cutting me off.

I blinked. "What do you mean no? You didn't even let me finish."

"Hear her out, Novek." Dillon's voice cracked across the ice.

Oh God. I did not want Dillon getting involved. I needed to fight my own battles.

"We are the best skaters in the world," Novek said, facing the team. "What does this... *woman* know about what it takes to do our job."

I gritted my teeth. "If you would just trust me-"

Dillon talked over me. "Novek, shut your mouth for once and let Coach Tyler-Branch talk."

Yeah, did I mention he only ever called me *Coach Tyler-Branch* in front of the other guys? That was fun.

"Novek," I said. "Your time on that drill was three seconds slower than O'Rourke's."

The guys all oohed and aahed. A couple of them high-fived O'Rourke. "See what happens when you run your mouth off, Novek?" Dillon said.

"Captain?" I said, trying not to smile. "You were three seconds behind Novek."

Dillon stopped laughing. "Well...it's practice. I'm conserving energy."

"You know what we call that in figure skating?" I asked. "Slacking off."

The team whooped and I smiled.

"Let's go," I said, and put my whistle back in my mouth. "No more...slacking off."

Dillon grimaced. "Conserving energy."

"Right, conserving energy," I repeated.

Still smiling, I blew my whistle.

The men came huffing to a stop in front of me when they were done. "So?" O'Rourke asked. "Who was fastest?"

"We all know who was fastest!" Novek said, his chest heaving from the exertion.

"Do we?" I asked him, smiling a little. And whew, he did not like that. "Because it was Dillon."

Everyone applauded but Novek... and Ron. But Ron did not give the impression of a guy who clapped.

"Good work today guys," I said. "See you back here tomorrow."

"See you Coach," a few of them said back, and I took it as a win.

*Later That Afternoon*
*Dillon*

Practice ended at two.

PT ended at three.

Some of the guys ate a late lunch in the cafeteria. They didn't leave until four.

I waited all of them out until it was just my Bronco, coach's BMW and Olivia Tylor-Branch's POS in the parking lot.

If she was trying to prove she was a hard worker, mission accomplished. I'd also say she proved herself to be a surprising asset to the team.

But she'd also made a few enemies today.

Novek had run his mouth about the new skating coach to the other guys all fucking day.

I wasn't his number one fan, but she needed to back off a little or she was going to fuck with the chemistry of the team. The last thing I needed in the locker room was a pissed off and resentful star forward.

The Bruisers needed Novek.

I leaned against the door of her car and it groaned. Half the thing was rust, the other half was made of reflector tape. Whatever the Bruisers were paying her, it clearly wasn't enough.

It would take nothing to send an email to Joyce in the

front office asking for Liv's contact information. As players we had full access to our coaches. But I didn't want to raise any eyebrows asking for the temporary skating coach's address and cell phone number.

Seemed...extra ballsy.

And I was being plenty ballsy already.

After I found out her full name I did a social media deep dive. Every news article, every Instagram photo I could find.

The basics were easy. She was twenty-six and grew up in Seattle. Started competing by age eleven. She and her partner, Brian Sampson, also her ex-boyfriend – *put a pin in that* – had won gold at World's four years ago and were the favorites for gold in the last Olympics when she had her *accident.*

There were hundreds of videos that would show me what happened, but I had no interest in watching her get hurt. I didn't need to see it when the headlines were bad enough.

*Brian Sampson Drops Partner During Complicated Lift.*
*Olivia Tyler-Branch Hospitalized After Gruesome Fall On Ice.*
*Olivia Tyler-Branch's Career Ending Crash.*

Yeah, I didn't need to watch it happen. But it made me want to know more about her partner. This Brian asshole. It also made me wonder how safe it was for her to be skating around hockey players.

It didn't come from a place of misogyny, rather real concern. If one of the guys ran into her at top speed, it could be trouble.

From her Instagram feed I knew she was a Swiftie. Her cat, Max, of fifteen years, had passed away last summer. Her parents were alive and they seemed pretty tight. And she clearly adored her younger brother, who was a stud on the Junior National hockey team. I went back further and there was a real long break, and then it was nothing but her life as a world class athlete.

I mean world class.

I ate every stupid joke I ever made about figure skaters.

I remembered our first encounter at the rink in Calico Cove and how she thought *I* should have recognized *her*. The only figure skating I'd ever watched was waiting for them to clear off the ice at various rinks I'd gone to when I was younger, but if she'd said her name was Olivia Tyler-Branch, something would have clicked.

Her crash had kicked off another round of debate about the impact of serious head trauma for all teenage athletes. Restrictions on lifts, speed and jumps had all been considered.

Then rejected.

All athletes understood the risks. At least that's what we told ourselves.

Myself included.

Until we all got together at award ceremonies with former NHL players. Then you were confronted with what really happened to a hockey player's body ten, twenty, thirty years after they stopped playing.

Some guys maintained a good shape. However, some were on walkers or used canes. Their hands shaking with early onset Parkinson's disease. Some of them were way worse. Hockey wasn't as bad as football, but head trauma was real. And it was serious.

As serious as Liv's career had been shaping up to be.

The side door opened up and she stepped out, the wind picking up her hair and blowing it across her face. She'd ditched the business suits and the Bruisers' training gear for jeans and a plain white t-shirt, that skimmed her breasts and her thin waist. She had her gear bag over her shoulder and was digging through that familiar little purse for keys.

God. She knocked me out.

She was practically in front of me when she finally looked up, saw me and screeched.

"What the hell, Dillon? You scared the crap out of me!"

I frowned. "I shouldn't have. You're a woman alone in an empty parking lot, you should pay better attention."

"Thanks, Dad. Is there something you need?"

*Yeah. You up against this car. In my arms. Licking my skin like you did that night. I need that full body shimmy and I need it right fucking now.*

"I can tell you, you need a new car."

"Don't speak ill of Tonya."

"Tonya? You named your car after…"

"The first woman to land a triple axel? Yes. Yes, I did."

No. Nope. I wasn't going to get distracted.

"You did a good job today," I said.

She couldn't quite contain her smile. "Thanks."

I pushed off her garbage car, stepping up into her space. "But you need to ease up on Novek."

"What?" She snapped, that smile gone like it never was. Her gray eyes were immediately thunderstorm dark.

"Yeah. I'm trying to get this team to gel, and I can't do that if you keep poking Novek with a stick."

"I'm not poking anyone with a stick. I'm pointing out places he can improve, and he just doesn't like it because he has an overinflated ego. You wouldn't be saying any of this to me if I was a coach who had a dick!"

That made me smile. "Baby, trust me. I am so glad you don't have a dick."

"Ugh! Men. Focus, Dillon. I'm doing my job. I'm doing it well. You just said that."

"Yeah, and now I'm telling you if it comes down to you or Novek, I know who will get fired. It won't be our star forward."

"That's...wrong."

"That's the NHL, babe."

"Don't...you can't call me that."

I knew that. She wasn't allowed to be my babe. I didn't like it, but I knew it.

"That reminds me," she said. "You can't keep jumping to my defense. You said I had to earn their respect and I can't do that when you're fighting all my battles for me. The guys are going to start to wonder."

Again. She wasn't wrong.

"Fine. We need some ground rules," I said.

"Good idea. Stop fighting my battles for me and stop calling me babe. Stop waiting by my car to talk to me in the parking lot."

"Okay. Stop making trouble with the guys."

"I'm not trying to."

The wind kicked up again and her hair blew across her face. I didn't even think about it, I just reached forward and pulled her hair from her lips where it got stuck. My fingertips brushing the satin smoothness of her cheek. The delicate strands of her hair and every instinct in me wanted more. Demanded more.

She took a deep breath, her eyes dilating. If I picked her up in my arms, right now, what would she do? Where would she wrap her legs? Her arms? How would she kiss me?

"Dillon," she breathed. "Please stop looking at me like that."

Fuck.

"Just be careful," I said. I thumped the top of her car and walked away.

*The Next Day*
*Liv*


Yeah. So I was going with the opposite of careful. Like... the polar opposite. I showed up even earlier this morning and I still wasn't the first one in the parking lot. Jeez there were a lot of overachievers on this team.

I walked by Dillon's Bronco and felt myself flush.

Ridiculous. That just knowing he was in the building was enough to rattle me.

My office was at the end of a long hallway and down a flight of steps. It had, quite obviously, been a windowless storage room hastily made into an office with a too big desk and an office chair with a squeaky wheel.

Joyce, who worked the front office, had been very apologetic when she walked me down this long hallway my first day. Apparently, another assistant coach had claimed the skating coach's old office and since I was only temporary, she was really hoping this was okay.

I assured Joyce it was all right, while secretly delighted I had an office at all.

Today's workout was going to be a risk, but if I played my cards right, the payoff would be extraordinary. These long shot odds were like candy to me. I couldn't get enough. Taking the easy way was not my style.

I found the things that were hard, and I made them my bitch.

Wondering if I should have brought a few tutus, I opened my door and got smacked in the face with an overpowering stench.

Corn chips.

Not the good kind.

The sweaty, disgusting hockey gear kind.

My desk and my chair were covered in thirty pairs of used professional hockey gloves.

Lovely.

Solid prank. But I wouldn't give it more than a B- for creativity.

The guys must have told the equipment manager to dump yesterday's gloves in my office instead of taking them to the drying room where they were cleaned and left on racks to dry.

"Having a problem with your office there, Coach?"

I turned to find Novek, wearing a pair of bright red Jordans and again with the fanny pack. His mullet was in top form..

Yesterday he'd come out of the PT room and run right into me. I'd nearly bounced back three feet. He didn't apologize, he just smiled that gold tooth smile and walked away.

Jennifer, one of the trainers, just rolled her eyes and mouthed *baby* behind his back.

The assessment was spot on.

"Nope." I said, not giving him the satisfaction. "Perfectly fine. Why would I think there was a problem?"

I had to breathe through my mouth and not my nose.

He leaned forward, looking at my desk and all the gloves. "Oh," he feigned innocence. "How did those get there?"

"No idea," I said.

"You're not auctioning those off are you? Because that would get you in trouble."

Yeah, suddenly this prank didn't seem so innocent.

"Nope. No plans for that," I said.

"It isn't some kinky sex thing, is it?" He asked, leaning forward. I stepped back. "Because there are easier ways to get into my gear..."

I leaned forward too, baring my teeth. "Not. On. Your. Life."

"Novek!" It was Dillon at the end of the hall, looking like an angry Hulk. "You're late for the team meeting."

"Coming Cap," Novek said, and strolled away.

Yeah, we really were going to be doing things the hard way today.

AFTER STRETCHING, which...have you seen hockey players stretch? That shit was pornographic. I love a good hip flexor stretch as much as the next gal, but that was some straight up humping happening on the ice. Though that might have just been Dillon, who looked up at me at one point and winked.

*Stop winking was going to be added to the list of rules.*

How was it possible that the guy could turn me on, make me laugh and cringe all at the same time? It was a real gift.

They circled around at center ice and it was impossible not to notice a few of the guys smirking at me as they stood side by side with Novek. Just a few of them, and fewer than I expected, really. However, they were making it real clear who my enemies were.

"Today," I said, "is footwork day. You can put the sticks down."

"We don't skate without our sticks," Dillon said. Not exactly helpful.

"Okay. Keep them. We're doing a basic sequence. Right leg lead and then left leg. Easy enough, right?"

They looked at me dubiously, which made me smile.

I laid out the moves. Back inside edge, mohawk, back outside edge three turn, mohawk. Outside bracket and a cross sequence that was actually a grapevine (but I wasn't telling them that.) Tap toe jump. Forward inside edge, three turn. Tap toe jump. Repeat.

These guys were some of the best skaters in the world, and while they picked the sequence up pretty quickly - it wasn't pretty. Smith skated with his tongue between his teeth. Skalsberg mouthed the steps as he did them.

There was zero elegance, but the footwork was tight.

"Nice," I said. "Faster."

"Again," I said when they were done. "Faster."

"This feels like choreography," O'Rourke finally said, and I had to hand it to the kid. He was often the smartest guy in the room.

Dillon kept skating. "Because it is, rookie," he said, proving he was always the smartest guy in the room.

Most of the guys skated to a stop, looking at me suspiciously.

"Everyone in a line along the boards," I said pointing in the direction I wanted them. They went begrudgingly.

"Top speed guys," I said, bringing my whistle to my mouth. "You go until the music stops."

"Music?" They groaned.

I lifted my finger and Donny, one of the assistant coaches up in the booth, hit play on a track I'd asked him to cue up.

Taylor Swift's Love Story blasted through the rink.

There was some good-natured groaning, but they all started to skate.

"Faster!" I yelled over Tay-Tay and the sounds of their blades on the ice. "Keep the pace." I started clapping my hands to the beat and felt like Coach Judy, my first figure skating coach.

O'Rourke put down his stick so he could really get into it.

But then Novek yelled, "This is bullshit," and stormed off the ice.

Some of the guys paused, looking after him like they might follow, but I skated through them, smiling and clapping, encouraging them to just keep going. I could feel Dillon behind me ready to bark at them if they moved a muscle towards the locker rooms, and I willed him to keep his mouth shut.

It was like he said: I had to earn this respect for myself.

Those guys stayed on the ice but half-assed the routine.

However, the rest of the guys did what I expected them to do, they turned it into a competition. They all ditched the sticks, and by the time Romeo pulled out a ring they were going top speed.

The song ended and they came skating up, a little winded, but almost all of them were smiling.

"Grab your sticks, we're doing it one more time," I said. I pulled the puck out of my pocket and dropped it on the ice. "This time it's a passing drill."

The guys lined up. Dillon took the puck. I gave the signal and Donny hit play again. They looked freaking amazing out on the ice.

I sat back, reveled in my victory and sang along with Taylor.

*Dillon*

"Cap, a second?"

Coach was on the edge of the rink, his hands tucked into the pockets of his joggers. Next to him, Gary, our offensive coach, looked like he'd eaten something sour.

Fucking Novek. He must have skated off the ice and gone right to their office like a tattletale.

I skated over. "What's up?"

Coach nodded with his chin toward the ice. "What do you think of her?"

Now, that was not an easy answer. I had many thoughts about Liv.

In fact, I jerked off in the shower this morning to thoughts of Liv.

That was not something to be shared with the coach.

"I mean, seriously, Taylor Swift dance routines?" Gary said. "Anton didn't do this shit."

Anton was a bitter old man who wouldn't know fun unless it came at the bottom of a bottle of booze.

"It's unorthodox, but the guys are having fun," I said, leaning against the boards.

"Not all of them," Coach said. "Novek is not happy, and I don't need to tell you that we need Novek to be happy."

What we needed was for Novek to grow up, but I wasn't going to say that. Not in front of Gary.

"I told you, you couldn't bring all that equality bullshit onto an NHL team," Gary said.

"Equality isn't bullshit. It's something to strive for. She's not asking to make the team, Gary," I said. "She's making us better skaters."

Even I could admit as silly as that routine was, it had been hard. Once she threw the puck on the ice, it was obvious how improved footwork would help.

On the ice, Liv was skating in front of the rookie, facing him as she easily glided backwards on the ice. Doing that thing that figure skaters did, like they could rotate their heads one hundred and eighty degrees to make sure the ice was clear behind them.

He was holding up fingers and she was shaking him off, until finally, she tilted back her head in laughter.

That wasn't jealousy, making me grind my teeth. No way. Did she have to smile at him like that? Like with her whole mouth?

Together they skated over to me. Liv looked like her gray eyes were lit from the inside.

"We're going to race," she said.

"Race?" Gary snorted.

"Yeah, I heard she beat you, Cap," the rookie said. "So I thought I'd teach her a lesson about respecting her elders."

Me? I was the elder in this situation?

"Go get Novek," Coach told Gary, who trotted off to do what he was asked. It was crazy to me that the coach was letting Novek get away with such prima donna behavior, but when a kid was getting millions and millions of dollars to play a game, you knew the balance of power was going to be lopsided.

When Novek got back on the ice, Coach put the whistle to his mouth and blew hard, getting everyone's attention.

"Take it away," he said to Liv.

"Cody and I are going to race," she said to the team. "You all know damn well I shouldn't have any hope of coming within a sniff of him. So I'm going to show you what technique can do for your speed. Not just muscle. Technique."

"This should be good," Novek muttered.

"I'm going to give her a head start," The rookie piped in. "Five lap advantage to ten."

Fifty percent? It was going to be tight.

"Yeah, but no tricks," she told the kid. "No bumping me or anything when you pass me. Give me a minute to warm up."

She skated out onto the ice while everyone else took a seat on the bench to watch the show. Rookie was shaking his head like he couldn't believe he was about to race a girl.

I hated to break it to him, but he was going to get beaten by a girl and that was going to make me feel better about having been beaten by a girl.

He pushed off the boards, but I grabbed him by the back of the jersey and pulled him back towards me.

"Check her and I end you, rookie," I growled, as visions of her flying across the ice flashed in front of my eyes. "You skate. That's all."

"Of course, Captain," he said with a huge smile on his face. "I'm not going to hit a girl."

I joined the team while the coach served as the official race starter.

Ron was giving me the side eye. I could feel it.

"What's wrong, Ron? Too much Taylor Swift to start your day?"

He shrugged. "You seem a little invested in the figure skater."

"Invested? What the hell does that mean?"

"Don't know. Just feels like you're watching her all the time."

Was I? Probably.

She fascinated me in so many ways. The way she laughed, the way she moved. The way she was surprising everyone around her. The woman was out to prove something all the time, and it felt like I understood her on a deeper level despite not knowing her very long.

This was a problem.

Ron was a problem.

Novek was a problem.

Which meant Liv was a problem.

The coach blew the whistle and Liv took off while O'Rourke, yes, I knew his real name, just kept skating in tight circles until she'd gotten in her lead. Then he took off.

The boys cheered as O'Rourke sailed past her in the straightaways, but Liv lowered her body weight like a speed skater and crushed him in the corners with the precision of her crossovers.

It was close. Like super close. One more lap and he would have had her. But she - and her technique - pulled it out in the end.

Coach blew his whistle and in victory she started doing alternating fist bumps, with alternating leg kicks. The boys went quiet in horror. It was like watching someone dancing really badly at a wedding. You felt awful for them because they didn't seem to know how stupid they looked, but at the same time you couldn't look away.

"I'm sorry, Coach, but that's the worst victory dance I ever saw," O'Rourke teased her. "You seriously need to work on your moves."

"What? The fist pump is classic. Alternating fist pumps. Yeah. Yeah." She did another demonstration of her alternating fist pumps. "And the kicks."

She did some kicks and looked utterly ridiculous.

Ron skated past me, his eyebrows raised, and I wiped the smile off my face.

"Come on, boys," I said, pushing myself into motion. "Back to work.

**8**

———

*Later That Afternoon*
*Liv*

The short term lease the team got me was about as welcoming as my office. One bedroom, fully furnished with extremely uncomfortable furniture in an apartment complex on the edge of town. I had one window that wouldn't open and one window that wouldn't shut all the way.

It also came complete with a creepy downstairs neighbor guy.

All of this I omitted from my daily phone call with my parents, who weren't exactly thrilled with my decision to move cross country for a short-term contract and a job they didn't think I should take.

My mother:

*"Honey, I know how hard this must be for you, but your*

*skating career is over. Finding ways to get around that is only going to cause you more heartbreak."*

My father:

*"Kiddo, you were the best. You achieved at such a high level, but now it's over. It's time to hang up your skates and focus all that intensity you have on the next part of your life."*

*This* was me trying to figure out the next part of my life. They just didn't understand that.

I didn't have a college degree and I wasn't interested in going back to school.

And no one was going to hire a figure skating coach who couldn't demonstrate sit spin technique.

Which left me speed and footwork. And the New England Bruisers.

Today, I crushed it.

I watered Harry, my spider plant, and Styles, my cactus, and took a second to do what I hadn't done almost all day. Go pee. My days were long. It wasn't just the ice time, it was the endless meetings too. Staff meetings. Team meetings. Today I had a meeting with Jennifer, the trainer, to talk about Ron's ankle mobility.

It was like I had time for one coffee on my way to work and then I didn't stop all day long.

There was a hard knock on my door and I jumped so hard I bashed my hand on the cheap countertop of my bathroom.

"Shit," I hissed, pulling up my pants and washing my sore hand.

I knew no one in Portland outside of the Bruisers. Which left my creepy downstairs neighbor. Maybe he wasn't creepy? Maybe I was just judging him harshly because I was alone in a new town. It wasn't like he'd done anything; he just gave me a weird vibe.

Another knock as I made my way toward the door.

I checked the peep hole.

*Dillon.*

I opened the door with a scowl on my face because his stopping by my apartment was a really bad idea, and I also wanted to hide the fact that I was happy to see him.

"How did you get my address?" I asked him, as soon as it occurred to me he wasn't supposed to know where I lived.

"I have all the coachs' personal information," he said, walking past me into my apartment and making it even smaller. "Including phone numbers, so be prepared for me to call you."

"I don't answer unknown numbers," I told him.

"Then get me known. Jeez, they really moved you out to Siberia, didn't they?"

"I don't mind it."

"Who's the creepy guy downstairs?"

"He *is* creepy, right?"

"Pretending to wash his car so he could stare at your door." Dillon shook his head in disapproval.

There was some comfort in that the creepy downstairs guy now knew I was friends with a big hulking guy.

A big hulking guy making his way into my apartment like he owned the place.

"Nice plants," he said, testing his finger against Style's spikes.

"What are you doing here?" I asked.

"We need to talk. For real," he said, and then just made himself comfortable on my couch that his size turned into a love seat. Or tried to anyway. "Jesus," he muttered, shifting his butt around. "What is this stuffed with, rocks?"

"Let me guess, you want to talk about how awesome I was today?" I asked him. I didn't join him on the couch.

He looked me up and down and smiled. "You look nice."

"Yeah?" I said. "This look works for you?"

I was in what I wore to work: leggings and a Bruisers' jersey. My feet were bare and that seemed more than a little intimate. Mostly because I did not have pretty feet. Nearly every toe, down to my pinky toe, had been broken and reset at some point. I didn't wear toe polish because that felt like trying to shine up a turd.

But he didn't look twice at my gnarly feet.

"Whose jersey is that?"

I peeked over my shoulder but couldn't see the name on my back. "I don't know. I asked the equipment guy for a spare jersey, and he gave me this."

I turned and showed him my back.

"Carver," he grunted. "He got traded at the end of the year."

"So, am I breaking some unknown rule by wearing a traded guy's jersey?"

"No, I just don't like you wearing some other dude's name on your back. I'm the captain, you can wear my jersey."

"Your jersey," I snorted. "What are we, in high school?"

"Nah," he stretched out his legs looking every bit the professional athlete he was. "I wasn't as good at sex back then. You know, just starting out, learning the ropes. You want fully mature me. But you should be wearing the captain's jersey."

"That's not going to happen."

"You gotta be careful with the sensitive male ego, Coach. You're going to hurt my feelings."

"Or you could grow a pair."

He laughed and the Dimples Grande came out. Funny thing I realized just then. The beer league bartender smiled a lot. The professional hockey player not so much. I liked his dimples. So much.

Too much.

"I'm pretty sure you being here is against our rules," I said, as my entire body pulsed and tingled with full awareness of him.

"No, the rule was we couldn't talk in the parking lot. Since your apartment is in Siberia, no one will ever see us."

"Fair point," I conceded, mostly because I liked him in my apartment. I liked how he filled it up. Made it warmer. "Only, I still don't actually know why you're here."

"What was going on with you and Novek in the hallway before practice?" he asked.

I shook my head. Not going to go there with him. "Just a little prank."

"In your office? Hmm. It was either gloves or jockstraps and I need to know it wasn't jockstraps."

God, jockstraps would have been so much worse. So glad they didn't think of that.

"Okay, I'm not admitting to anything, but what difference would it have made if it was gloves or jockstraps?"

"Because their penises touch those jockstraps," he said, deadly serious. "And no one else is getting their penis anywhere around you. Except me."

"Except you? Uh, we have rules about meeting in the parking lot. I'm pretty sure those rules extend to your penis. You have to stop talking like we're going to be a thing, Dillon."

"Did I mention I don't give a fuck about rules?"

This time I crossed my much smaller, less beefy arms over my chest and glared at him.

"Okay fine," he said, backing off. For now. "No more talking about my penis. Unless you want to. But the reality is, Liv, if the guys are messing with you like they're third graders, that's one thing. If they're messing with you like they're high school boys, that's something else entirely."

"They didn't tell you about the prank," I concluded. That's why he was here. They were operating behind his back, which, like rules, was probably something else he didn't care for.

"Because they knew I'd shut it down. We're professionals. Not kids."

If I told him what Novek did, or worse, what he implied in that hallway, Dillon would most likely go ballistic on the guy. I'd lose all the ground I'd gained today.

"Well, I'm not telling on anyone," I told him, sitting down on the other side of the tiny couch. "But if I said I can handle third grade shit, would you be satisfied?"

"Sure," he said.

He was so big and the couch was so small he made it feel like a love seat. Our thighs touched, our shoulders touched, our arms brushed. I would have shifted away if there was anywhere to go.

Then he did the craziest thing and lifted my thigh and draped it over his, which made us fit better. I jerked, but he settled his hand on my knee as if he was holding my leg in place.

He wasn't. I could have moved, but I was frozen by the contact. I hated that we fit like this. I hated that it felt so perfectly right. Because it only made the knowledge that we weren't allowed to have this, that much harder to swallow.

"Dillon," I sighed, but I wasn't really protesting. I wasn't even moving.

"I know," he said, his voice rough. "Probably against the rules. But we're just talking."

It was hard to focus with his rock-hard thigh under mine, but I gave it my best shot.

"Tell me what's really bothering you," I nudged him. "That the guys left you out?"

He shook his head. "I'm worried Novek is going to make trouble for you," he said with a deep sigh.

"It was just a prank, Dillon."

"No. I mean today, when he left the ice, he went right to the coaches and gave them an earful."

Uh oh. That made my stomach twist with sudden nerves.

"Yes, but then they made him come back to watch the race to show him what I could do. Honestly, I think the other coaches are on my side," I said. "Maybe not Gary."

"Hmm. Until they're not. What's your contract? A couple thousand bucks for a few weeks?"

Basically, but I wasn't telling him that because I knew where he was going. Novek's contract was twenty-eight million dollars for three years. So mine was...less.

"This sucks," I said. "I'm doing good work and he's being a baby."

And a bully. But again, I wasn't going there with Dillon.

"Yep."

"So? What do I do?"

"You could quit," he suggested.

"Are you shitting me?" I tried to get up off the couch and his thigh, but he held me down.

"Stop. Hear me out. The team wouldn't announce it until you got another job. A better one," he said. "Me and Coach could put in a few words for you with other coaches around the league. Minor league teams with less drama."

"This is because you want to sleep with me?" I snapped, absolutely vibrating with rage.

"No. Well, I mean, yes, it would certainly be helpful in that regard, but I'm trying to think of you and your future."

"The future of your dick, maybe."

"Liv-"

"Do you think I'm a quitter?" I said, my jaw tight, my eyes spitting fire. I'd never been so offended in my life.

He looked at me for a long moment and then sighed. "No," he said. "I know you're not. I've known you for a handful of days and I can see you're a force of nature. You won't stop. You're going to run face first into any challenge."

"Damn right I am," I snapped.

He frowned. "I'm just worried you'll push him too hard and he'll hurt you without even trying."

"He won't get me fired," I said, and I believed that. Mostly. Maybe.

"You know how bullies are. Push them and they push back. I'm also scared of what he might do on the ice."

"Is this about my head injury? I can't spend my life hoping I don't get hit in the head again, Dillon. It took a lot of time, but I've let that fear go. I had to or it was going to take over my life."

I relaxed back on the couch, my leg over his. He reached over and pinched my chin between his two fingers. I should have stopped him, but his touch felt so good.

"It was that bad?"

"No one likes the nitty gritty, dark part of the story," I told him as a way to warn him off. "Everyone wants the over-coming all obstacles music montage."

"I hate music montages," he said and I laughed.

Only he didn't laugh, and maybe that more than anything, convinced me he was taking me seriously. Let me know it was safe to open up to him.

"I almost didn't make it. They put me in a coma and had

to drain fluid from my brain three times. No one knew if I would wake up, and if I did, if I would be...functional or even...me."

He cupped my face, running his thumb along my cheek. I should remind him about the rules, but we were in Siberia, and I'd been so cold for so long.

His touch felt like summer. It felt like stepping out onto the ice after a long recovery.

"I didn't watch the video," he said. "I didn't want to see you get hurt like that."

I shook my head. "Please don't. I'm sure it's not pleasant. My family wouldn't let me see it either."

Ignorance was bliss.

"Where was your partner in all of this?"

I blinked at the unexpected question. "Brian? It wasn't his fault if that's what you're asking. It was my mistake that caused him to drop me."

Maybe there was a tiny window where he could have gone down with me, taken part of the impact of the fall... instead he'd done exactly what he'd been taught to do every day of pairs training. He'd let me go.

"Wasn't he more than just your skating partner, weren't you a couple?"

That made me uncomfortable. Uncomfortable enough I swung my leg away from his tree trunk of a thigh and stood up.

"Why does it matter? It's in the past."

He put his hands on his knees and stood up as well. I kept misjudging how big he was. I felt his gaze on the top of my head and refused to meet his eyes. No good would come of it.

No good would come of any of this.

"Because if you were mine, I would never drop you."

For a moment something so bright and hot spread through me I could barely breathe.

That's how Dillon would love a woman, I thought. All the way.

*Rules! You made them for a reason. Come on, Olivia!*

I stepped back, pushed my hair behind my ears, did everything but look at him.

"Brian and I were pros. We knew the risks. There was no blame game on either side. It was a lot of stress to put on a relationship, that, if I was honest, had a few cracks in it already."

Dillon nodded as if that made sense and I was glad he didn't push for more. I was rattled and shaken. A lot of old ghosts out of the closet where I normally kept them shoved deep inside.

"Hey, I'm starving, how about we go grab dinner?" he suggested.

I nodded, before I thought about it. "Sure, that sounds... wait, no. Dillon, I'm not having dinner with you."

He chuckled. "We could order in?"

"We can't do that here," I said.

"Well, your couch is pretty shit, but-"

"Here. In this town. You know that."

For a heartbeat we just looked at each other. It was like a fork in the road. If I gave him the slightest nod, he'd have me back in his arms. I knew that. I also knew it would be amazing, I had no doubt about it.

But it would also put everything I'd worked for, to get back here, with a job on the ice, in jeopardy.

In the end, he was the one who nodded and headed to the door. It was on the tip of my tongue to add *stop coming to my apartment* to our list of rules.

"See you tomorrow," he said, at the door.

*Do it. Tell him. Say; you can't come over like this.*
But instead, I said, "See you tomorrow."

*Dillon*

I DIDN'T KISS HER. That was the win.

I left her apartment knowing full well I should never have gone over there, but the way I saw it, the rules didn't give me a whole lot of choice. We needed to talk about Novek, and maybe I should have brought up what Morgan said, but I didn't want her to know that one of the guys was on to us. Or me, anyway.

I could handle Morgan.

What I couldn't handle was the idea of her getting hurt. I didn't want her to get checked on the ice, or offended by a bunch of athletes. I didn't want her to get fired.

I wanted to protect her from all of it.

It felt like every second we spent together we got closer, and we weren't even trying. It just happened. Like breathing.

She was right, we shouldn't go out for dinner. I was enough of a name in town that people would want pictures and then we'd be in real trouble.

Well, she would, and the injustice of that made me want to smash something.

Novek, maybe.

I paused at the bottom step and looked over my shoulder to the apartment directly below hers.

There, real quick, the curtain drifted back over the window as if it had just been moved. Creepy neighbor guy was seeing if I was leaving or staying overnight. I considered the trouble I could get into, especially if he had a phone and was already recording, but I couldn't leave without saying something.

I could see the headlines now:

*NHL MVP Threatens Innocent Civilian.*

Coach would be furious, and if I had to guess, Liv wouldn't be all that thrilled either.

But whatever, I had a little aggression that needed to be dealt with.

I walked over to the door and pounded on it. He opened the door far enough that I could see the chain was still in place. One heavy push and it would snap, but I was just here to offer a warning.

"What?" he snapped, his nose just under the chain. His beady eyes told me he was shitting a brick.

"Lose interest in the lady upstairs," I told him. "She's not for you."

"I'm not-"

"This is a warning," I said, not bothering to hear his explanations. "Next time won't be. We understand each other?"

He nodded and shut the door.

I made my way to my Bronco and got inside. I still didn't like it. Leaving her here in this shitty apartment complex didn't feel right. I owned a penthouse condo in downtown Portland. Maybe I would check out the building and see if there was anything open, where she could stay.

Maybe, as in I definitely would.

That decision made, I drove home feeling a little lighter.

## 9

*The Next Day*
*Liv*

There were no stinky gloves on my desk the next day. There was something worse.

A pair of hockey skates in my size.

With a note from our equipment manager.

*Shooting practice today. You need skates that protect your feet better.*

It was stupid. This was stupid. I was a professional ice-skater.

*You were a professional ice-skater.*

Shut up. Inner voices sucked sometimes.

They were skates. Nothing scary about them.

Except they didn't have a toe pick.

Toe pick wasn't just a line from the greatest movie of all time. It was about that instant stop.

It was about control. I didn't realize until just this moment that I had a thing about control. In that I really, really liked it. Needed it.

If I got hit in the ankle by a puck slapped by one of the Bruisers, I'd be in a cast. So, hockey skates made total sense. Perfect sense. Nothing to be scared about.

I changed into my gear and headed down to the ice where some of the guys were already doing their porn stretches.

The skates felt weird on my feet, but so would any skates that I hadn't broken in yet. I held onto the boards and let my feet glide back and forth, trying to get the feel of them. Ankle mobility was shit, but that was the sacrifice for protection.

"Hey, you good?"

I lifted my head and saw Coach McKay making his way toward me. Instantly, I let go of the boards and pushed myself forward to meet him.

Yes, this was fine. I could do this, even on strange skates. There was nothing to be worried about.

Smiling, McKay pointed at the guys. "Look what you've done."

Out there in front of the home net, half the guys were doing the foot work routine from yesterday, passing the puck. Smith was singing the song off-key and at the top of his lungs.

It was awful.

It was amazing.

Novek sprinted across center ice to steal a puck from O'Rourke. They scrambled for a second and Dillon swooped in and peeled it off Novek.

"Come on, I want you to work on some speed drills," McKay said.

"With you?" I asked. I hadn't been incorporated into the main practice. This was new.

"That's how it works," McKay said, and blew his whistle,

gathering the team.

"What's next," Novek said. "More dancing?"

McKay ignored him and split the team. He took the forwards. I took defense.

Which meant I had Ron and Skalsberg.

I was fine on these skates. I had no problem with them. They were already starting to feel like extensions of my feet.

*What if I can't stop?*

Stupid. Of course I could stop. I knew how to use an edge. This was old nervous shit bubbling up to the surface. Like after the accident, when I started walking again for the first time and I would wonder if my legs would hold me up.

Of course, they would.

"Hey, Coach!"

I glanced up and saw Cody skating towards me. I blew out a breath and slid to a stop.

"Hey, Cody," I offered. "What can I help you with?"

"I think I'm losing momentum in my backward c-cut."

He was asking me a question. A legitimate question.

"Let's take a look," I said triumphantly.

*Dillon*

I TOOK myself to the bench for a new stick and to adjust my laces. I'd finally caved and gotten new skates today. I didn't need them. Didn't want them, but it was an excuse to go down and talk to Leroy about how Liv was still wearing figure skates during practice.

As expected, he was outraged.

Liv on the ice in the proper gear only made me happy.

Though if she had my jersey on over that fleece, I'd be happier.

"What a suck up," Ron muttered next to me.

"What'd you say to me?" I growled.

"Not you," Ron said with a slight scowl, jerking his thumb towards the opposite end of the ice. "The rookie. He's sucking up to the girl. Probably thinks he has a chance of getting in her panties."

I let the panty remark go by, but just barely. Ron was looking for a fight and I was trying to fix this team chemistry, not pull it apart. But who was to say? Sometimes a good brawl was just what the doctor ordered.

Me, being the doctor.

I shook my head. "He's a rookie, he should be eager."

"He keeps flirting with the skater and the guys are going to give him a raft of shit," Ron said, selecting his own stick, testing the balance. "Unless of course he manages to nail her. Skater does have a sweet ass. Then they might just applaud him."

I crowded him back towards the boards. "Morgan, you talking shit about a member of the coaching staff, whether she can hear it or not, is disrespectful and that's not cool with me. The kid is working hard, that's what we're getting paid to do."

Ron smirked, leaning on his stick. "Settle down, man. I was just trying to get under your skin."

"Why the fuck are you trying to cause trouble?"

Ron shrugged. "I'm not an idiot like these other boys. I see how you look at her. Figured I would talk some smack and see if you blew. Congratulations, you did."

"You're full of shit, Morgan. I would have said the same thing about any member of the staff."

"Nah, you've got a thing for the figure skater, and I'm

telling you now, man, shut it down."

"The fuck?"

I was annoyed he'd been able to spot it. Annoyed he was telling me to do something about it. Annoyed in general.

Ron skated closer until I could see the silver in his mustache. Those crow's feet around his eyes. Someone should say the *R* word to him.

"Look, I know everyone around here thinks I'm a bitter old hanger on. And maybe that's true. You get traded four times in the last three years of your career and we'll see how you feel. But I'm telling you, this team has a chance to do something this year. *You* are the captain. That means you need to be focused. Totally and utterly fixated on one thing and one thing only. Winning. You can't do that if your eyes keep sliding away to the figure skater."

"She's got a fucking name," I growled.

"No," Ron said. "She doesn't. Not to you. Not if you want a clear vision for the season."

I was about to tell him that I could walk and chew gum at the same time, except I heard a slap shot heading the wrong way, then a scream.

Olivia's scream.

*Liv*

I DIDN'T SEE it coming. One second I was skating beside Cody, correcting the alignment between his foot, ankle and knee, and the next second it felt like I was getting shot in the ass. Like for real shot. I barely had a chance to realize I'd been hit by a puck when I felt something else hit my skate.

It caught me off guard and my left skate shot forward, throwing all my weight off balance.

Instinctively, I tried to apply my non-existent toe pick, but that only made it worse. Now I was falling face first. I twisted, caught myself with my shoulder and slid into the boards.

I'd fallen on the ice since my accident. Hit a wet patch once and was skating too fast. My blades got gluey and I fell on my ass. It had been scary, but I'd been fine.

*I'm fine. Fine.*

It was my mantra. The thing that helped me to breathe through the panic. It wasn't about the pain, although my ass and elbow did hurt. I got up on my knees but couldn't seem to get to my feet. All I felt was my feet slipping out from under me.

"You hurt?"

I looked up. Dillon was like a freaking giant blocking out all of the light from the rafters above.

I turned away from him towards the boards because I didn't want him to see my panic attack. This wasn't pretty or cute or even remotely cool. It was terror and panic and tears leaking out of my eyes. I couldn't catch my breath or get my heart rate to slow down. I settled my hand on my chest, felt my heartbeat fluttering beneath it, and focused on my breathing again.

In and out. In and out.

"Don't you turn your back on me, I need to know if you're hurt."

He sounded mad. Why did he sound mad?

*I'm fine. Fine.*

Another second and my heart rate was out of my ears and my eyes weren't leaking. One more deep breath and I looked up to see all the guys who had been on the ice, in a half circle around me.

Great. Just great. Not only was I embarrassed, I was publicly embarrassed.

Dillon crouched down in front of me, moving me so I was facing him, his face a stormy cloud of fury.

"What happened?" he barked at me.

A puck hit me in the ass, then in my skate. That had finally registered. As did the insistent throbbing in my right butt cheek.

"Stop yelling at me," I mumbled, finally feeling in control of my body again. I reached out a hand to have someone, Dillon presumably, since he was the closest, pull me back on to my skates, but my gesture was ignored.

"Novek!" Dillon yelled.

"Wasn't me," Novek said, all innocent. "I think we all know I have better control of my pucks."

"It was my fault, Captain," Anderson said, a third line defensive player, standing next to Novek. "I was shooting a few at the net and a couple of pucks got away from me."

Novek's smile would suggest otherwise.

"Really? Seems kind of crazy...you know, for professional fucking hockey players. Rookie, help her up," Dillon said and then he skated away.

Skated the fuck away.

Wow.

Unreasonably, it hurt worse than the puck to the ass.

It made sense though. He had to keep his distance. Hadn't I been the one to tell him that he couldn't keep charging to my rescue because of how it would look? I just hated that he'd actually listened to me so well.

Emotions and logic battled inside my head for a bit. On the one hand, I was butt hurt. Literally and figuratively. On the other, if the guys suspected we had feelings for each other, it most likely would cost me my job here, as well as future job prospects.

The worst it would do to Dillon was...nothing.

Absolutely nothing. He was a big time hockey star, after all.

In the immortal words of Taylor Swift: Fuck the patriarchy.

I'd been getting up off the ice on my own since I was five years old. I shrugged off Cody's offer and climbed back onto my blades.

"You sure you're okay, Coach?" Cody asked me.

"Fine," I said, and resisted the urge to put my hand on my ass to feel for a welt.

Coach McKay blew his whistle. "Let's take ten and come back and work some battle drills. Coach Branch, we won't need you on the ice when we get back."

Thank God, I thought.

I made my way toward the edge of the rink, my ass seriously throbbing, when I felt a giant looming behind me. I didn't have to look over my shoulder to know it was Dillon.

"You sure you're good?" he muttered it under his breath as he skated by me.

"You sure you care?" I snapped back, then immediately regretted it.

In the grand sum of things, we'd only spent a few days total together. That's it. Which meant none of this should matter so much.

I didn't matter to him and he didn't matter to me. That's how it had to be.

Also, I was reminded of the most important lesson I'd already learned once.

When I fell, it was a solo effort.

# 10

*Liv*

"Honey, can I just say again you don't need to do this?"

I was driving back to my shitty apartment, in my shitty car after a shitty day, and for some reason had thought it would be a great idea to call my parents. My mom of course heard the defeat in my voice and pounced.

At the red light I rested my head on my steering wheel.

"Mom-"

"No, hear me out," Mom cut me off, which only proved how frustrated and worried she was. "You come home, you live with me and Dad, you can go to college. We're only talking four years. Or maybe less if you double up your course work. School and grades were never a problem for you."

She was right. They weren't. I wasn't afraid of going back to college because I couldn't handle the course work or because I would be older than all my peers. I didn't want to go back to college, because I had no idea what I wanted to do that wasn't *this*. Exactly what I was doing.

Also, having to live with my parents again? Hard pass.

I loved my parents, and I had a lot of friends who still lived with theirs because Seattle was so expensive. But being able to live independently again after my accident had been a major milestone in my overall recovery. Moving back now, would feel like taking a step back.

I couldn't do it. I didn't want to do it.

"I agree," my dad said, obviously they were on speaker phone. "You belong home with us. Do you think they intentionally hit you with that puck?"

I know they did. Because there had been more than one. They'd been using me for target practice.

"Because if that's the case, honey, I have a good mind to fly out there and give them a piece of my mind. Using very firm words."

I smiled as I pulled into a parking space closest to the stairs. This was why I loved my father. He was the most peaceful man on the planet, who believed every problem could be solved with thoughtful words over a good cup of tea. But hurt his little girl, and he wouldn't hesitate to confront an entire professional hockey club with a *piece of his mind.*

"Dad, it was an accident. Mom, I'm not going to come home. I think I'm actually helping this team," I continued. "Today one of the players asked me for help. Most of them are good guys."

"Except when they're hitting you in the ass with pucks," Dad said.

"Well, you know we will always support you no matter what," my mom said.

"How is Billy? How is the season going?" I asked after my little brother, trying to distract my parents. Despite the almost nine-year age gap between us, Billy and I were still tight.

"He's fine," Mom relayed. "The season is going well. Except now he insists we refer to him as Bill."

I made a mental note to never refer to my brother as Bill.

"Oh, and he told us he wants nothing but a signed jersey from you for Christmas. What's that one player, Miguel? The one they call The Heart. Billy wants a signed game jersey."

Yeah, that's not happening. I wasn't going to give that guy the satisfaction after that bullshit today.

The big oaf.

"Dillon Le Coeur is the team captain, Mom. And he's not very...approachable. Tell Billy to set his sights a little lower."

"Whatever you say, honey."

"Okay, I'm home. I'll let you both go."

"Ice that sore bum," Dad offered, just as I was hanging up.

Hopping out of my rental car, I started towards the stairs to my apartment but came up short when creepy neighbor guy burst out his front door.

"Can I help you?" I asked, stepping back to keep a couple of feet between us.

He kept nervously checking over my shoulder.

"You know lady, I was just trying to be a nice neighbor. I look after the people in this complex. That's all. You tell that hockey player boyfriend of yours, I don't want any trouble."

"My boyfriend?"

"Yeah, that Le Coeur guy. It took me a minute to recognize him, but I finally did and I don't want any trouble with a Bruiser. I was just minding my business."

Dillon. He must have had words with my neighbor, who now knew who Dillon was and that he'd been at my apartment.

Well, wasn't this all awesome.

I wanted to be mad at Dillon all over again for interfering in something I could handle myself.

"He doesn't want any trouble either. I promise. Everyone's cool."

Creepy neighbor guy nodded quickly and I sighed. Dillon must have really scared him.

"I'm Liv, by the way."

"Stu," he said, but didn't offer his hand and I didn't offer mine.

"Well, see you around, Stu."

"Not much, probably. I got a lot of shit going on."

This from the man who spent most of his time looking out his apartment window.

"Oh, well, then good luck with all that."

I left him and made my way up the stairs to the 2$^{nd}$ floor landing and opened the apartment door. Dropping my stuff by the door, I made a beeline for the bathroom.

With my back to the mirror, I used my phone so I could get a good view of what I was dealing with as I lowered my leggings and took in the bruise that was forming on my right butt cheek.

Man, that was nasty. Swollen, purple and black, with those red spider veins. That was a solid slap shot. Initiated at Novek's suggestion.

Dillon was right – Novek was going to be a problem.

Oh, well, nothing to do but ice it down and call it my first official hockey injury.

My phone beeped with a text. It was from a number, not a contact.

1-888-209-7788: How bad is it?

Maybe if he hadn't told me that he'd already gotten my number, I might have been surprised. Or maybe I could have dismissed the text entirely because it was an unknown number. But I knew who it was and I updated his contact information.

Liv: I told you I'm fine.

Dillon: That's not what I asked.

There was no way I should let him get away with this. No way he could Mister Tough Guy on the ice and blithely skate away and now be all concerned for me.

Feeling a little cheeky, I used the mirror and the camera on my phone to get the perfect angle. Once again bearing my butt cheek, I snapped a picture and sent it to him.

Liv: Kiss this.

Liv: PHOTO.

Dillon: Did you just send me a naked picture of yourself?

Liv: I sent you a pic of a bruise so you'll get off my case and stop asking if I'm okay.

Dillon: I need context. Show me the other cheek.

I bit back my smile. This guy.

Liv: Go away.

I waited for him to reply. But there was nothing.

No sense in getting disappointed. I took a hot shower and used an Ace bandage to wrap an ice pack around my ass.

An hour later, I was trying to get comfortable on my uncomfortable couch with my uncomfortable ass when there was a hard knock on my door. I'm not going to say I knew who it was just by the sound of his knock, but my heart pounded just a little harder.

Dillon.

I opened the door to find him flashing his dimples with hands full of plastic bags.

"Oh my God, Dillon! You can't keep coming here!"

"I know," he said. "But it was like my car was on autopilot. Do you want me to leave?"

No. I didn't want him to leave, which was part of the problem.

"What's in the bags?" I asked instead.

He lifted one hand. "Dinner." He lifted the other hand. "Gifts."

"We agreed dinner was against the rules," I reminded him.

"No, we agreed we couldn't go out to dinner together and we couldn't order dinner in with me here. But me picking up dinner and dropping it off for a coach who is butt hurt... not only is it not against the rules, it's practically part of my contract."

I considered this and caved. "Okay," I said and reached for the dinner bags. "Mostly because I'm starving."

Behind him I saw Stu looking up at us. I caught his eye and he ducked away.

Shit. Even Siberia wasn't safe.

In my kitchen, Dillon was taking to-go containers out of the bag. "I hope you like Thai. I told them they were making food for the Calico Cove Hot Wing Queen so not to skimp on the heat."

The reminder of that sweet night put a little squeeze in my heart. I still remember how it felt to be held in his arms. To absolutely know with such certainty how much he wanted me. "Good," I said, in an attempt to feign casualness.

He found my plates and forks and he split the Pad Thai and spring rolls and we sat down at my tiny little table. I sat gingerly, on just half my butt.

"How is the ass?" he asked, watching me carefully.

"I've had bruises before," I said with a shrug, like it was no big deal, when we both knew it was a huge deal.

"You and I both know it wasn't a stray shot," he said, everything about him focused and intense. I nodded in agreement.

"Hey, you should be proud of Anderson. He hit the bullseye on the first shot."

"It's not cool, Liv."

"Dillon. It's hockey. Puck happens."

I took a bite of a crunchy spring roll and he stared at me blankly.

"You really went there with a puck joke," he asked me. "I don't think you even did it right."

"I'm channeling my inner hockey girl. Also demon- strating how chill I am about the whole thing."

"You're making jokes now, but you looked pretty shook up when it happened."

We were having a nice time and the adrenaline from earlier had long since faded. I didn't want to talk about my minor panic attack. It was something I had to live with just like anyone else who carried irrational fear around inside them.

"I'm fine," I said, and shoveled a forkful of noodles in my mouth.

"Oh," he laughed. "So we're just going to avoid it, is that it?"

Yes, we'd kissed. And we'd flirted. Today, he brought me food that I was grateful for.

However, opening myself up to him wasn't necessary or prudent. It would only complicate our already complicated situation even more. So I said nothing. After a minute, he nodded like he got it.

"Fine. Ready for the gift part of the evening?" he asked, his eyes twinkling.

He reached for the bags on the floor beside him and set them on the table. Then, like he wasn't a multimillion dollar star athlete, he cleared the containers and plates and took them into the kitchen.

It was really, really hard not to be charmed by the guy.

Until I remembered how he left me on the ice today. Everyone saw me put my hand out while he skated away. The message was clear. I wasn't that important to him. I needed to remember that.

I stared at the bags instead of opening them. There was no reason I should say anything. No reason to call him out on his hypocrisy where one minute he was Mr. Concerned and the next, he was Mr. Distant.

Except it felt wrong. Like I needed to know one way or the other who this guy really was. I also didn't want to be disappointed when I found out.

"What's wrong?" he asked.

"You left me hanging on the ice today," I said. "Skated away like I was...nothing."

He braced his hands against the counter and nodded. "I did. I know it was a dick move. This whole situation is messing with my head, Liv. I nearly went ballistic out on that ice today. Fucking Ron..." he stopped and I shifted in my seat to face him.

"Ron what?"

"He just reminded me that I have one goal this year and that's getting back the Stanley Cup. But this...stuff between you and me, it isn't going away. Obviously, because I'm here now."

"Stuff?" I asked. It seemed a little vague. Maybe I shouldn't want clarification, but I couldn't help it.

He pushed off the counter and crossed my tiny apartment like some kind of apex predator. He was so big, he filled the space completely. Took half the air. Filled my brain with cotton. Made my body crackle with electricity.

Leaning down to me, he put one hand on the table and the other on my chair.

His eyes were on my lips like all he could think about was kissing me.

*All I can think about is kissing you too.*

"Yeah, stuff," he breathed. "This *can't stop thinking about you* stuff."

He lifted a hand and touched my face. His thumb on my cheekbone. It took everything in me not to close my eyes. Not to lean forward the three inches necessary and put us both out of this misery with a kiss.

"We can't do anything about it," I whispered. Because the reasons we couldn't do anything were serious. Real. My job. My future, the only one I wanted, hung in the balance.

His thumb pressed against my lower lip and I gasped with the sensation. Heat spilled through my body, pooling between my legs.

I was already wet. One touch and I was wet. Sex with this man, with his control and intensity, with our chemistry, would have changed the game for me. I was forcing myself to be glad it never went that far.

"We can't do anything about it at work," he said, his voice low and dark. "But we're in Siberia now."

"After that little speech you gave my neighbor, he recognized you. Siberia is not exactly safe. He knows you're here now."

He took a deep breath, that massive chest rising and falling.

"Damn, I wish we were back in Calico Cove," he said, and then stepped back and the world around us came back into focus for me. "Open your gift."

I gave my body a little shake to gather myself and he groaned.

"That fucking shimmy," he muttered. "I have dreams about you doing that shimmy on my cock."

Blazing heat filled my cheeks and my resolve weakened even more.

"Gifts," he said, and crossed the room, putting as much distance between us as possible. He leaned against the kitchen counter and crossed those giant arms over his massive chest.

With trembling hands I opened the bags and pulled out a helmet and what looked like an impact shirt. All in my size.

"What..." I whispered.

"If you're on the ice you need to be protected," he said.

"Skills coaches-"

He shook his head. "I *need* you to be protected. Today took ten years off my life."

He looked at me like he'd been hollowed out and it was enough to make me reach for the gear.

"Is any of this a butt pad?" I asked, breaking the tension.

Trying to make him smile. "Because that's what I really need."

*Dillon*

WHAT SHE REALLY NEEDED WAS A SOLID fucking kiss. She needed to be pressed down on the floor and given half a dozen orgasms. I was sure I was the man to do it for her.

Not gonna lie, that had been my plan coming over here. I'd started to convince myself as long as we were away from the team it was okay. This apartment complex was Siberia. Only I had to go and ruin that by running my big mouth to the downstairs neighbor.

Fuck me.

I was still dealing with my reaction to what had happened earlier today. I'd heard her scream, in obvious pain, and it twisted something inside my chest.

Something that felt really big. Like, irrationally big.

Then Ron Morgan was in my head telling me to shut it down. The guy was an asshole, but he wasn't wrong about distractions.

You had some wives and girlfriends who understood the life. When their man was playing during the season, they basically treated them like deployed troops. The women knew their men were going to be gone, they knew communication was going to be infrequent. They also knew they had to take a backseat to the game. Support was its own full time job.

For the most part they were okay with that.

Or at least they told their boyfriends and husbands they were okay with that.

But I'd seen guys fall, and fall hard, for women who didn't understand how the season worked. Who chaffed against the loss of their own identity.

Carver, who had been traded last year, had a wife who had been a chemist when they got together. When he got traded, she gave up her job, her family and friends, to go with him. Of course she did. Only I just heard through the grapevine they were now getting divorced. That kind of shit happened over and over again.

Why risk the heartbreak?

We were a privileged few who got to participate for a limited time in a game we loved and got paid well for doing. No sense in potentially ruining the time we had, dividing our focus.

Those guys who fell for a woman during the season, a woman who didn't understand how to fit into the life, those guys would turn themselves inside out trying to serve two masters and it never worked.

Either the relationship crashed and burned or their play on the ice did.

Morgan was right. Liv was a distraction.

Taking a puck to the ass was something that the coaches, assistants, hell, even the Zamboni driver, accepted as part of the job.

Like she said – puck happens.

The problem was me. Her reaction when she fell nearly undid me. So much I could barely talk, barely look at her. I'd been ready to tear Novek's head off. I was furious and worried all at once.

What the fuck was that?

Where did all that emotion come from?

More importantly, how did I shut it down?

Not coming to her house with dinner and gear and nearly kissing her would probably be a good start.

She tried on the helmet and I adjusted it for her. Tightening the setting, pulling the straps until it fit snugly on her head.

"This is not comfortable," she grumbled.

"Turn around," I said, ignoring her complaints. "You got anything on under that sweatshirt?" I asked.

Without a word she pulled the sweatshirt over her head. It got caught on the helmet and I helped her pull it off. Under the sweatshirt, she had on one of those tank tops she wore all the time. Thin little straps. Thin fabric. I could feel the heat of her skin. Smell the shower she must have taken after practice. If I stepped forward, one tiny step, my chest would be pressed to her back. My aching cock, constantly at half-mast around her, would be pressed against that perfect ass of hers.

Perfect ass with a giant bruise.

*Get a grip!*

"This is a bit much, isn't it?" she asked, as I pulled the five pad shirt with adjustable chest straps over her head and then turned her around to make sure the fit was right.

"You're copping a feel."

"Babe, I'm not." I was shifting the pad on her shoulders, so she was balanced and even. Then I secured the Velcro straps. "If I was copping a feel, I'd do this."

Making sure I didn't get the sore side, I gave her perfect little legging-clad butt cheek a squeeze, eliciting a fake sounding squeal on her part.

*Another thing you shouldn't be doing.*

"That's copping a feel," I said, and quickly removed my hand.

It was meant to be a joke, not an aggressive move. The way she swatted back at my hand told me she took it good-naturedly.

"You're such a guy," she accused me.

"Guilty. How does that feel?"

She wiggled her shoulders. "Fine, I guess."

I stepped back and took a look at her.

"Well?" She put a hand on her hip like an old-school pin up girl.

"You're smoking hot, babe." She'd be smoking hot in a garbage bag.

"I feel like a Pillsbury Dough Girl." She thumped the chest pad in the shirt. "Am I done?" she asked. "Or do you have any more armor in there?"

"You're done," I said, and pulled the straps so she could get herself out of the gear.

My phone buzzed in my pocket, and while Liv was pulling off her helmet and the pads, I read a text from my sister.

> Wendy: Hey, dearest brother. Fall festival next weekend. I can count on you behind the bar. Right?

> Dillon: No

> Wendy: But I signed you up to be in the dunk tank.

> Dillon: Not funny

> Wendy: For you, probably not. For me? Hilarious. It's for a good cause. The local arena needs a new Zamboni.

> Dillon: Low blow, Wendy. Low blow.

No chance I was working the bar at the Fall Festival, and now I would be buying the arena a new Zamboni. I can't believe Hank never said anything when I'd been there.

But she gave me an awesome idea, a solution to this problem Liv and I found ourselves in.

> Dillon: Thanks for the reminder.

I put my phone back in my pocket and watched Liv pull her shirt down where it had ridden up, exposing her taut abs. Her creamy skin. I caught a glimpse of a little birth mark near her ribs and the urge to investigate made me take a step back.

"You got any plans next weekend?" I asked, gathering up the garbage from the gifts.

"Studying tape," she said. "Why?"

"Calico Cove does this start of the Fall season event. I think I'm going to go." I was playing it very cool as I shoved the garbage in the plastic bag.

"You should go then."

"I think you should go too."

She gave me that look. "Dillon…"

"No, hear me out. We're not going to go together. I'm just letting you know that my home town, a town you have visited and loved, is having this Fall festival and given that you'll also have a few days off this weekend, you might want to check it out. Just as a fun Maine thing to do."

She eyed me suspiciously and so I brought out the big guns.

"There will be games."

"Games?" she asked, her eyebrows lifting.

I nodded. "And prizes."

"Prizes?"

"Contests galore, where you can win things."

"Win?"

I laughed. "You're like one of those TikTok dog videos where the owner says all the dog's favorite things and their head keeps tilting back and forth."

She scowled. "Am not. What kind of prizes?"

"Stuffed animals, free baked goods from Bobette and Belle. All kinds of stuff."

All kinds of stuff...away from here. From the job. From Novek. Fucking Morgan. I saw that realization hit her. What I was really suggesting.

Beneath that thin tank top she wore, her nipples beaded up and I groaned low in my chest.

"Say yes," I growled.

"Maybe." She said, because she loved to torture me. "Maybe."

"Good," I said, knowing maybe wasn't maybe, it was instead yes. I played it very cool, but inside I was doing her ridiculous double fist pumps with the over-the-top kicks. "Then maybe I'll see you there."

# 11

_Dillon_

We crashed into the locker room, the guys giving each other some good-natured hell.

"How many was it?" Skalsberg asked Smith, pretending to be confused. "I lost count. I blocked so many shots I should be getting part of your salary."

"Yeah," Smith shot back, taking off his goalie mask, his red hair plastered to his forehead. "If you'd blocked that well during the Calgary Games we might have beaten them."

The boys oohed and I collapsed onto the bench in front of my locker listening to Novek spout off about how many goals he got in the scrimmage.

"O'Rourke got just as many," Coach said, coming in after us. The boys looked over at the rookie, who shrugged but was smiling. "And he beat just about everyone down the ice, every shift."

"What can I say?" He said, standing up to peel off his pads. "I'm listening to Coach Branch."

Novek said something in his native language and a few of the guys who understood laughed.

"If I have to speak English," Skalsberg said, with his thick accent. "So do you."

"I said," Novek spoke, wearing only his cup and jock. "I also like to listen to her." He put his hand over his dick and stuck out his tongue like a fucking deviant.

I stood up to shut that shit down, but I caught Ron's smirk and turned to grab my phone on the shelf behind me, pretending to check my messages.

"Novek," Coach McKay said, sounding good and pissed off, which I liked. "Shower, get dressed and meet me in my office. We're going to have a discussion about how you respect staff on this team." Coach stormed out of the room and all the boys oohed.

"Someone is in trouble," Smith said.

"Fuck you guys," Novek snapped, all petulant baby. He shucked the last of his gear and walked naked, big dick swinging, to the showers. The rest of the guys went in after him and I heard them all laughing.

Novek was a dick, and I hated the way he talked about Liv, but the team was managing it. That was the thing I loved about teams, you could be the hottest shot in the world, and the boys would still bust your balls. On a good team, on a team firing on all cylinders, everyone pulled in the same direction and no one got special treatment.

Egalitarian as fuck.

"Cap," The rookie said. I didn't realize he was still in the room. He sat in his compression shorts looking down at his phone. "Can I ask you a question?"

"Shoot, kid," I said, stripping off my gear.

"Do you think they're going to send me down to Maryland?"

Maryland was where one of our feeder teams was located, and if I was being honest, at the start of preseason it would have been an unequivocal yes from me. I would have said the kid didn't stand a chance at staying in Portland. Most rookies coming directly out of college didn't.

"I'm asking because my wife-"

"You're married?" I cried, dropping my shin guards. "How old are you, ten?"

"Twenty-four."

"Jesus, kid, what did you go and do that for?"

The rookie looked at me like I was the one who was out of my mind. "Childhood sweethearts, Cap. What can I say? When you know, you know. Anyway, she found this house in Portland that she loves and...I don't know. It kind of feels like I have a shot of making the team."

I took a deep breath and looked at this kid. Really looked at him. He was hard-working, respectful, extremely coachable. Smart as all hell. "What does your wife do?" I asked.

O'Rourke blinked. "I mean, she went to school to be a teacher, but you know with my position on the team it's not like she can just get a job if we're going to move."

"She doesn't mind that? Putting her career on hold like that?"

The kid blew out a big breath. "She doesn't love it, but she understands. It's our life. We're in it together."

I tried to imagine Olivia's reaction if I said: *Hey, babe, you need to stop doing that job you love so much and follow me around the country because I just got traded to Tampa.*

There was no fucking way. No way I'd say it, and no way she'd go for it.

"So?" O'Rourke asked. "What do you think?"

*I think you're an idiot and your wife is going to grow to be resentful. In five years you're going to be paying alimony and maybe child support.*

But that wasn't what he was asking me.

"Yeah, kid, you keep working like you're working and I think you have a real shot. But don't buy a house. Not yet."

I don't know if it was the answer he wanted, but he typed something on his phone and a second later he was smiling at whatever came back at him. He threw his phone back in his locker and went to the showers with the rest of the team. I heard another round of laughter but didn't move.

I grabbed my own phone and pulled up the text thread with Liv.

The smart move was to tell her to forget Calico Cove. Meeting there was a mistake. On every level. Why risk her career for something that didn't have a future?

I had no intention of taking this anywhere, except to the bedroom.

Right?

"Cap!" The guys were coming back, led by Novek, whose mullet was slick down his neck. "I have heard the most amazing thing," he said, looking honest to God like a little kid.

"What's that?" I asked.

"Your father was Mon Ami?" he said.

"How the fuck do you know Mon Ami?"

"Wrestling is big in Europe. We know all the wrestlers. So, it is true? Your dad?"

"Yep." I said with a smile, that this kid from half a world away knew his name would make Dad so happy. "Mon Ami was my father."

"I wore a beret when I was ten because of him," Novek said.

"You get the shit kicked out of you?" I asked.

"Yes. Very much. But I loved his swagger," Novek said, twirling a fake mustache the way my dad used to.

"I'll let him know."

"He should have been featured more."

"Yeah, well, life got in the way," I said.

My mom hated him traveling. Hated the fact that he was away from us growing up. If he'd told me once, he'd told me a hundred times, you couldn't have everything in life. You had to pick what was most important.

In the end, I suppose he'd picked mom and us over his career, because he dropped out of wrestling. But the damage had already been done. There was no saving their marriage. That's what both of them had told us as kids.

A conversation kicked off about everyone's favorite wrestler, but I tuned them out.

I needed to call off our detour to Calico Cove. I needed to stop all of this before it spiraled out of my control.

*Hadn't it already?*

I looked down at my phone again. What the hell was I supposed to say to her?

*Scratch next weekend.*

Seemed a little abrupt.

*Let's call it off now.*

Calling *it* off, implied there was something to be called off. It wasn't like we were making plans to fuck at the Festival. I just wanted to be in a space where she was without any team eyes around.

I shoved the phone in my pocket without typing a thing. I didn't know what to say to her. I certainly didn't know how to say it.

So maybe the best play here was to not say anything. Focus on practice, on my job, and pretend – try to fucking pretend – Liv was nothing more than a coach on the team.

## 12

---

*Calico Cove Fall Festival*
*Liv*

W as I fool? I felt like a fool. Down to my toes, I felt like a fool.

Calico Cove's town square, which had been covered in fake snow at the end of August, was now full of carnival games and vendors. The gazebo was home to a biggest pumpkin contest. The winner was a monster grown by a ten-year-old girl and her grandfather.

It was so wholesome it hurt.

Except I was walking through all of it like a dark bitter cloud, sick with my own hope and foolishness.

I shouldn't have come.

This week of practice had been great, to start. The Taylor Swift routine had become part of the team's warm up program. The guys were really embracing the more complicated footwork routines. I'd really started to feel like I was contributing. That this experimental job was becoming something solid under my skates.

The only downside, Dillon had ignored me all week.

He'd worked hard. He'd done everything I'd asked. He called me Coach Tyler-Branch respectfully...and that was it.

No texts. No surprise visits to my apartment. No mention of this weekend at all.

At one point I'd tried to get him isolated on one side of the rink, away from everyone else, so I could confirm one way or the other if our little rendezvous was still happening.

*"Hey, can I talk to you about the Fall Festival?"*

*"What about it?"*

*"There is an apartment above a bookstore, I can rent just for the weekend-"*

*"You should do that if you want. I've got to get back to practice."*

That had been it. He'd cut me off about the apartment, then skated away. The sum total of our exchange for days.

Of course I'd already rented it before I'd even talked to him. I suppose I could have canceled and gotten my deposit back, but I decided it could at least be an overnight vacation from my terrible apartment.

Once I got here, I contemplated just curling up in the lovely bed with the window that overlooked the town and reading all weekend. Or maybe taking a hike. There seemed to be a lot of trails in Calico Cove. But that seemed like too much effort and bug spray.

And after twenty minutes of reading the same page of my book, I cried uncle, threw on my shoes and headed down to the festival.

I could still play the games and contests and win shit.

Winning shit would make me feel better.

The clown game was a classic. Shoot water into the

mouth with a water pistol until the balloon over the clown's head filled with air and eventually popped. You had to have a steady hand and clear vision. You couldn't stand around thinking about a guy who brought you dinner one week and then ignored you the next. You couldn't think about how he made your knees weak and infuriated you at the same time.

You couldn't remember how his kiss had made you wonder if you'd been doing sex wrong your whole damn life.

"Hey, excuse me," A woman said from behind me. "My son would really like to play the clown game, but you've taken up a spot now for almost thirty minutes."

"The sign says I can play until I get beat," I said, pointing out the sign on the side of the booth.

The woman, holding the hand of a boy I imagined to be around ten, gave me that look. That look that I'd seen so many times from skater-moms who all sort of hated me because I was better than their daughters.

I didn't take it personally.

"These games are for the children."

"One of the prizes is an aura reading from a psychic," I gave her a sideways smirk, not taking my eyes off Bozo and the balloon I was filling. "I think these games are for everyone."

A spot opened up two slots down and the woman huffed and pushed her son into it.

I handed over another dollar to the teenage kid working the stand.

"Am I being a jerk?" I asked. The kid had a name tag that read Nick.

Nick smiled. "Yeah, a little bit, but I think it's hysterical. I sort of have a...competitive family, so I understand where you're coming from."

"No mercy, am I right?"

"You stay until you get beat. Those are the rules," he agreed.

"Bet your ass," I said.

"I'll beat you."

My entire body went still at the voice behind me. My heart skipped a beat. My lungs held a breath. And then I felt him.

The kid who'd been sitting beside me vanished, a ten dollar bill in his hand, and Dillon took his place.

"Oh shit," Nick said, his attention fully on the pro hockey player. "You're..."

"Not today," Dillon said. "Today I'm just here to play some games." He slapped a bill down on the counter. "Twenty bucks should cover me until I beat her."

"In your dreams," I muttered.

"Unfortunately, yes," he shot back.

Not fair. Not fair at all. He didn't get to ignore me for a week and then sit down and insinuate he'd been dreaming about me. That was garbage.

He was garbage.

I went back to ignoring him.

"Okay everyone, take your spots and wait for the bell," Nick announced, moving down the line to help the other kids with their water pistols.

"I didn't come here for you," I said, filling the awkward silence as the kids laughed and talked smack around us.

"Oh really?" He asked.

"Yes, really. I'm here because I love this charming town and I really love the water balloon clown game."

"Too bad I'll be kicking your ass at the water balloon clown game."

"You can try, Le Coeur."

He pivoted the squirt gun and sprayed me in the side. Eyes wide, I glared at him.

He flashed his Dimples Grande.

What an asshole.

Nick rang the bell and we were at it. My balloon popped first and I shot him a cheeky smirk.

"Let's go again," he muttered.

"You really don't like losing, do you?"

"My job is not losing."

The bell rang again. I won again. This time he got a double fist pump right in his face.

"If you start kicking your legs people are going to think you're having a seizure," he said, and I laughed.

"Poor baby," I said, forgetting that I was mad at him.

It took him four tries, before he finally won.

"Yes!" Dillon shouted, his head tilted back like he'd just won a playoff game. "I win. You lose! Finally! Victory is mine! Nick, that's your name right? Bring me the finest prizes in all the land."

"Uh, you only won once, so that just gets you another turn," Nick explained. "You have to build points."

I smiled triumphantly. "Yes, Nick. Tell the man how many points I've won."

"She's up to twenty-five. Here's the list of things you can get," he said, and handed me a paper flyer.

"Hmm," I said, perusing the list. "Let's see. So many options to choose from. A pick two of anything from Bobbette and Bell. A lunch special at Pappa's Diner. The aura reading by Madame Za... I have to admit that's kind of what I was playing for."

Dillon scowled at me. "You don't want that one."

"Yeah, he's right," Nick agreed.

"Why not? It sounds fun."

"Well, it's just sometimes, Madame Za...she can be *right*," Nick said cautiously. "If you know what I mean."

"I have no idea what you mean," I said.

"Mostly, she's wrong," Dillon said. "But when she's right, she'll change your whole life."

"Sometimes she knows when you're calling from jail," Nick said.

"Hookay," I said, glancing between the young man and the man I wasn't supposed to be speaking to. "Can I have my tickets, Nick? I think I'm ready to try another game."

Nick handed me a line of red tickets, showcasing my incredible water balloon clown game skill, and I shoved them in my back pocket ready to move on to the next event.

Dillon fell into step beside me. I ignored him.

"Liv."

I didn't stop walking.

"Liv."

Nope. Kept going.

"Liv!"

I turned around to shush him.

"Don't make a scene," I hissed. "Do you want people to think we're here together?"

He caught up to me in three ridiculously easy strides.

"You're mad," he said.

"You're a genius."

He grabbed my arm and pulled me between an apple cider booth and a craft booth where little kids were making corn husk dolls. "I wasn't going to come," he said, and I tried to shake him off, but he held tight. "But I couldn't stay away."

"That's not the compliment you think it is."

"I don't know what to do!" He cried, and he looked so

upset I almost took pity on him. "It is such a bad idea for us to be together, but you are all I can think about."

I swallowed but kept my mouth shut.

"I know I've been an ass the last week, but...I have to choose the team. You get that, right?"

He was a competitor in his prime. Of course, I got it. I just didn't have to like it.

"Of course, I get it," I said, letting him off the hook. Maybe too easily, but it was becoming clear to me I was a sucker when it came to Dillon Le Coeur. "Look, this doesn't have to be a big deal. Let's pretend we're just two people here to play some games, and that's all."

His dimples showed up and then vanished. "Some friendly competition," he said.

I shrugged. "What's wrong with that?"

"Not a damn thing." This time the dimples came out and stayed out. "The three-legged race is about to start."

"Race?" I tilted my head like one of those TikTok dogs he'd accused me of being. I really had to stop that.

"You're unhinged, you know that?"

I was. He was. This whole situation was completely unhinged. Someone was probably going to get hurt.

Unfortunately, I bet it was going to be me.

*Dillon*

THE ONLY WAY TO survive last week had been to implement a whole new plan.

It was very aptly named: *The Ignore Liv Plan.*

It was comprised of several different components.

*Don't Look at Liv.*
*Don't Talk to Liv.*
*Pretend Liv Doesn't Exist.*

I knew I was pissing her off, and worse, hurting her, but my plan had been working.

Ron stopped watching us. Novek was pulling together with the team and not shooting his mouth off every damn minute. What I'd told Liv was the truth.

I'd had to make the choice – the team or Liv.

I stood by my choice.

The three-legged race, however, rendered the *Ignore Liv Plan* useless.

We were tied together from our hips to our feet. I could feel her breathe. I could feel her breasts against my arm. Her hair against my neck. It was like going from ice cold to on fire.

*Do not get a hard on, do not get a hard on.*

"Hey brother, I'm going to kick your ass!"

I looked over to see Wendy had partnered up with her bartender Dave and was already smack-talking us. Dave was tall and Wendy's speed would be to their advantage, but they didn't know I'd tied myself to a Tasmanian Devil.

"Bring it!" Liv shouted back to her. "No mercy for family."

Then she looked at me a little nervously.

"That's true. Right? No mercy for family?"

"No mercy," I agreed, and then shouted over Liv's head, "I'm going to bury you, sister!"

There were seven other teams on the field which was situated in the center of the town square.

Bobby and Mari, Wendy and Dave. Annie and her new boyfriend Levi.

I didn't know Levi's deal, but Annie had two left feet on her best day.

Jackson had teamed up with Roy since Lola was pregnant, and Vanessa had just had a baby. Those two had me a little worried, but Roy was not a team player in any situation and already looked extremely unhappy being tied together with his brother-in-law.

Vanessa snapped a picture of them and Roy immediately untied himself, grabbed his daughter Nora and walked off.

I looked around for Matt Sullivan. There was a time back in high school, when he and Carrie Piedmont would win this race every year, no questions asked.

Of course, that was back when they'd been in total sync with each other.

I spotted him at the finish line standing next to someone who looked a lot like...

"Holy shit, is that Carrie Piedmont?" Liv asked. "She looks...different."

Different was one way of saying it.

Her famous red hair was chopped into an uneven bob. Was that a Hollywood thing?

"What is she wearing?" Olivia asked.

"Crocs."

"And like a..."

"Grandma's house coat?"

"That can't be her," Liv said, and I would have agreed with her until the red-head caught my eye and waved.

"You'll never beat our record, Heart!" She shouted.

"Why aren't you racing?" I shouted back. Beside her Matt Sullivan went bright red, which was weird. Carrie said something to Matt, who shook his head. Carrie said something else and he shook his head again. Carrie stormed off.

"Giving you a shot!" Matt finally answered, and then walked in the opposite direction as Carrie.

Carrie and Matt only proved my point. Love built on chemistry wasn't something that lasted.

Love was a decision you made when you were ready and committed to starting a partnership together.

A family together.

Love was going to happen for me in my late thirties. When my career was over. When I could dedicate the time to being a lover, partner and friend.

"Hey Sheriff! Just checking, when we whizz by you, you won't give us a speeding ticket, will you?" Liv called out to Bobby.

No. No way was love happening now.

"Hey, wait a minute, Heart, did you bring a ringer?" Mari asked, pulling a pencil out of the bun at the back of her head as well as a plastic pumpkin cake decorator. She looked around for someplace to put them, didn't find one, and so tucked them back in her hair.

"Not a ringer," Liv shouted. "Just someone who plans to run rings around all of you."

"Can you back up all this smack talk?" I asked my partner in crime.

She shrugged. "I can. Can you?"

"Just don't slow me down," I told her, as I wrapped an arm around her waist and felt her do the same.

Mayor Martinez stood on the steps of the gazebo with a bull horn in her hand. She lifted it high in the air.

"On your mark. Get set. Go!"

Like we were shot out of a canon, Liv and I took off. I had to ease up a little to account for the height difference, but she was there, keeping up with me stride for stride. Like we'd been running three-legged races our whole lives.

We crossed the finish line first with stunning ease.

I bent down to untie us while she turned around and continued talking smack to everyone just coming over the finish line.

"Oh, yeah, baby. I can do this all day. You want to go again? How about you Sheriff? You want to go again?"

I had just gotten our ankles untied so that we were free individuals once again, and I dipped my shoulder under her stomach. My plan was to hoist her over my shoulder and do a victory lap, letting her trash talk to her heart's content.

Or possibly to make a breakaway from an angry mob. Bobby was not enjoying the trash talk.

Except the second her feet left the grass she went stiff as a board.

"Putmedown! Putmedown!"

She slapped my back and wiggled like she wanted to throw herself off me. If I wasn't as strong as I was, she might have gotten away with it, but I was able to wrap my arms around her legs and keep her steady as I lowered her feet back onto the grass.

She was shaking like a leaf and I immediately realized her knees weren't going to hold her. So I carefully placed her down on her butt, controlling her descent even as I quickly sat next to her.

I cupped her face in my oversized hand and nudged her to look at me.

"Talk to me, Liv."

"I don't like to be picked up," she said, her face was flushed and her hands were freezing.

Right. Of course not. Stupid of me not to think of that.

"Okay. I'm sorry. I was just having some fun in the moment. I should have asked."

She shook her head and cursed under her breath, but I wouldn't let her look away.

"I'm not mad," she finally said. "At you. I'm mad at myself. I used to be lifted into the air with only one hand. I could fly like that for hours. Now my feet leave the ground or I have a stupid fall and I freak out. It's messed up."

I nodded. It made sense. It also made sense why she'd reacted the way she did the other week when she'd slipped on the ice. The sensation of falling, of being lifted, it was all triggering for her. The fact that she could get back on the ice at all was kind of amazing.

"You're not messed up, you know exactly where the fear comes from, and it's real."

She jutted out her chin and clenched her teeth. "I want it gone."

I laughed at that. Of course someone with her will would hate anything she perceived as a weakness.

"Doesn't work that way, babe."

She grunted and I pushed her hair behind her ear.

"Are you scared of being lifted or are you scared of being dropped?"

"Isn't it the same thing?"

I didn't know the answer to that. Only she did. But what happened to her wasn't just a bad accident. It destroyed the trust she had in her teammate.

Her boyfriend.

How in the world do you trust another person after something like that?

Could she ever trust me? Did I want her to?

The answer to that was absolutely yes.

"Did people see me freak out?"

"It's so cute you think anyone looking our way would be looking at you. I'm the famous one, remember?"

She scowled at me. "I used to be famous too. Little girls in skating costumes would line up for my autograph."

"You want me to get a few kids over here?" I asked her, only half joking because if that's what she wanted, that's what I would do to make her happy.

"Nah," she said. "Let's go win some more shit."

That was my girl. Upset forgotten and on to the next thing.

*Not my girl. Not my girl.*

"I'm hungry. I say we carb up. We can hit up The Lobster Pot for some lobster mac & cheese, Birdie's Falafels are also pretty amazing. Or we can check out Pappa's, but my guess is that will be packed. Or we can sneak into the kitchen at the Gull and I can fry you up some more wings."

"Yes," she said with a definitive nod. "To everything but the diner, I don't want to wait for food."

"I like where your head is Miss Tyler-Branch. We'll start with the falafels, hit the Pot and finish strong with some wings."

I hopped to my feet and held my hand out to her. Something I hadn't done before when she'd fallen on the ice.

For a second she eyed it suspiciously, like she was remembering that moment too, then she took it and I pulled her to her feet.

It was safe to say the *Ignore Liv Plan* was officially dead.

I was going to need a new plan.

## 13

*One-Eyed Gull*
*Dillon*

I t took me a few hours, but I came up with a new plan.

I was calling this one the *Fuck Liv Out of My System Plan.*

Again, not planning on sharing the details with her, but the gist was pretty much in the plan name.

We were sitting in the kitchen of the Gull, which didn't open for another hour. The remains of our takeaway of falafels, lobster mac and cheese and the wings were scattered around the counter.

Liv was licking her fingers and smiling, clearly satisfied with both her victories and our rewards. We'd ended up using her tickets for the falafel.

"Was I right, or was I right?" I asked her.

"You were wrong. The lobster mac and cheese was the clear winner."

I pretended to be outraged.

"Where are the wet wipes?" she asked.

I got up and found the drawer where Wendy kept the store of packets and tossed a few on the counter. I threw away our garbage and checked the clock.

Staff was going to be coming in soon.

So if I was going to ravish her here, I was going to have to be quick.

"That is one thing I don't miss," she said, as she cleaned off her hands. I pointed to something near the corner of my lip to show her where she'd missed a spot.

"What's that?"

"Starving myself," she answered.

I didn't like hearing that.

"Don't give me that look," she said. "I had to be as light as possible while being as strong as possible. Every calorie was counted."

I grunted. "Yeah, that wasn't my problem. I couldn't eat enough food when I started playing. My dad was always forcing cottage cheese down my throat. Cottage cheese and protein powders. There were days I felt like I was a goose he was stuffing for Thanksgiving dinner."

"Did you like it though?" She tilted her head like I was an equation on a white board she was trying to learn. I loved it. "Or were you like, *my dad made me do it and I happened to be good?*"

I shook my head. "You can't get to this level if you don't love it. You just can't. It takes too much of your time, energy, focus, brainpower, willpower. If you don't love every single moment of it, then you burn out before you ever get to the pros. But there was a time...I don't know, maybe sixteen, seventeen, when I wondered who I was doing it for. What about you?"

"My parents would be very happy if I was a high school science teacher." She smiled and shook her head. "But once

I put on skates and found I could go faster across the ice then I could walk... I never wanted to do anything else."

Yeah, I could see that about her. Skating wasn't something she did, it was a joy that lit her up from the inside.

She wiped her hand across the stainless steel counter, and her shoulders, previously relaxed and loose, went up around her ears.

"My parents want me to quit the job and come home and go to college," she said. "They think this whole idea is crazy."

"It's not crazy. You have a serious future in the NHL, Liv. I swear you do. You are miles better than any skating coach I've ever had."

Her eyes opened wide and she blinked like she didn't want to cry.

"Prettier, too."

She stood and tossed all her wet wipes in the trash bin behind her and approached me. I stood up straight, wondering with every fiber of my being what she was about to do.

That was the thing about this woman...she was constantly surprising me.

"You have to choose your team," she said.

"I do."

"And I have to choose myself," she said.

"You do."

"Where does that leave us?"

I grinned at her and she grinned right back. Yeah, we were on the same page.

"Calico Cove," I said.

"You're just a bartender here," she said, looping her arms around my neck. "A beer league player. With some dimples."

I smiled and she dipped her fingertip into the divot near my lips.

"And you're just a gorgeous, smart woman with a competitive streak a mile wide on vacation." I pulled her closer to me. She didn't resist.

"So?" she said, with a gleam in her eye that went right to my dick. "What are you going to do about it?"

"This," I said, and dropped my head the distance I needed to close the gap between us. Her mouth was soft. She gasped slightly when our lips touched, but again she didn't pull away. We both knew what we were doing, where this was going. Like magnets, we were drawn to each other, which is why we both showed up in Calico Cove today.

I cupped the back of her neck, her hair falling over my hands.

Her mouth was everything I'd ever wanted. Like this was how kissing was meant to be. Not just foreplay to get to the main event, but the event itself.

Her hands were on my shoulders and like that first time, it felt like she wanted to climb me like a tree. I cupped her bottom and she hopped, actually hopped up into my arms, her legs secure around my waist.

No fear now.

*Because I wasn't picking her up. She was in control.*

My brain registered the thought, vaguely. Then I was turning her and sitting her ass on the prep counter. I needed room to work, space to explore. I needed her to feel completely secure so I could touch her everywhere my hands wanted to go.

"Dillon," she groaned. "This is bad."

She tilted her head back and I kissed her neck. Softly behind her ear, harder where her neck met her clavicle.

"Honey, this is the opposite of bad."

"They make food here."

My whole body was humming. Like a tuning fork that had hit the right chord. Was I shaking when I slipped my hand up inside the lightweight sweater she was wearing? I touched skin, soft and warm, then met the restriction of a silk bra and wanted to howl with frustration.

Everything. Now.

It's what my brain wanted. It's what my body wanted.

My dick firmly agreed.

Suddenly, a noise registered. A door closing.

"Oh shit. Sorry man."

I came up for air, having buried my nose in the crook of Liv's neck and shoulder and looked around. Dave, the Gull's bartender, was standing in the kitchen, a set of keys in his hand.

It took a few seconds to register his presence.

"I've got to prep the bar, man," he said, as if I needed an explanation. "We open in like an hour."

"Right. The bar."

"Sorry," Liv said, as she hopped down from her seat on the counter. "I told you this was bad," she hissed at me.

I grabbed her hand. "We'll get out of your way, Dave. Uh...maybe you don't have to tell Wendy about this."

"Tell Wendy about what?" Dave asked.

I nodded in appreciation.

Not that I cared if Wendy knew I was sucking face with a woman in the kitchen of her bar, but if she did know there would be a million questions to follow. Good questions about whether it was smart to make out with a member of the coaching staff.

It wasn't smart. But it wasn't going to stop me.

We headed for the back door where Dave had come into

the kitchen and stepped outside into the late afternoon sunshine.

The apple cider sugar smell of the festival filled the air even blocks away. "You want to go back to the festival?" I asked. "There's an apple dunking contest tonight. You could make some kids cry."

She shook her head, her gray eyes gleaming silver in the sunlight.

"I rented that apartment, over the bookstore."

Blood pounded in my dick.

"Perfect. Let's go."

She tucked her bottom lip under her teeth and my tough, strong, hard as nails competitor suddenly looked nervous. Bending down so I was in her face again, close enough to see the ring of black around her gray irises, I gave her the full force of my dimples. There was only one way to put this woman at ease.

"How many times can you come during sex?"

"What?" Yeah, the eyes went wide, the lip came out from under her teeth. There's my girl.

"Come on, give me your stats. Three? Four?"

Laughing, she shook her head, and when I pulled her towards Annie's bookstore and the apartment above it we were going to fucking ruin over the next two days, she didn't hesitate.

"We're not competing over orgasms."

"Fine," I said. "We'll shoot for five and go from there."

THE STAIRWAY to the apartment was behind the bookstore.

Liv unlocked the door, and as I followed her perfect fucking ass up the stairs I got my own weird case of nerves.

When it came to sex, like kissing, I didn't really do a lot of thinking. Get my partner off and then fuck until I come. Rest and repeat.

This was going to be different. I knew it in my toes. I cared less about my own satisfaction and more about blowing her mind, wrecking her world and making this the best sex she'd ever had in her life, so I would be imprinted on her forever.

So she would remember me long after I walked away.

The plan had been to fuck her out of my system, but somehow that had morphed into something else. Something darker.

*Fuck her so she never forgets you.*

I dropped my duffle bag along with a plastic bag, filled with Combos, Doritos, Twizzlers, five different flavors of Gatorade and a box of condoms we'd bought at a convenience store on the way here, at the top of the stairs.

You know how I dealt with nerves? Head on.

"Get naked, babe. Now."

She turned around in the nearly empty living area. There was a couch and a chair. A TV mounted on the wall and not much else.

"Maybe we should talk about this some more," she suggested.

"Sure, you can talk. But my mouth is going to be a little busy," I walked over to her, and pulled the loose sweater she was wearing up and over her head.

God, her skin was perfect. Olive toned and smooth. Her body was lithe, and compact. She was graceful and sturdy all at once.

"Look, you need to know a few things about me first," she said as I unfastened her bra.

"Tits," I grunted, as soon as they were free from the silk prison she kept them in. I cupped them in my palms.

"Seriously, Dillon. I'm not someone who just jumps into bed with guys. I'm more discerning than that."

I bent down and sucked her tight little nipple into my mouth. It was hard and pebbled and no matter how much talking she thought she wanted to do, her body was ready for me.

"For instance, I'm really vocal about what I like and what I don't like. Some guys aren't cool with that. So if you have a problem taking direction..."

*Taking direction. God, she was adorable.*

I released her nipple and found the button and zipper to her jeans. I shoved her pants down her hips and got to my knees in front of her. I lifted one foot and slid off her shoe, then the other. I had fun watching her wiggle out of her panties.

Those I took from her and shoved in my back pocket.

"Did you just steal my panties?"

I lifted her leg over my shoulder so I could have a better angle to work. She was so pretty and pink. Wet already. The hair between her legs was trimmed, not that I cared, and I started licking my lips.

I ran my fingers up the inside of her thigh. Not touching her. Not yet. Just gliding my fingers up and down and around. Teasing the edge of her slit, listening to her breath break. I could smell her, sweet and salty as I leaned closer. Not touching, just breathing her in. I brought my other hand around to slap her now naked ass. Nothing hard, just a tap so I could run my hand over it.

"What the?" she yelped.

Hmmm. So, that was new to her. She squirmed, wetter

than she'd been before. This was going to be fucking amazing.

"Can you come standing up?" I wanted to get my mouth on her.

"No, I can only orgasm in a certain position and only if you let me do it myself."

"Okay," I said, although I wasn't having that. Getting yourself off wasn't nearly as fun as having someone else do it for you. I slipped my fingers across her pussy, slipping through her lips to where she was hot and slick and perfect. Her hips arched. Her breath broke.

"So you can do the...you know... the thing with your mouth down there...but it doesn't really work for me. Just so you know."

I pushed a finger deep inside her. She was hot and tight and her head fell back on her shoulders. I slid my finger as deep as I could and slowly slipped it out.

"No?" I said, fucking her again with my fingers. "You don't like oral?"

"It's...ugh, yes, fuck, that's good. Right there. It's fine...oh, but it doesn't work. Oh."

I parted her pussy lips and ran my tongue from where my finger was working her right up to her clit. I circled her clit then added another finger.

*Doesn't work? Hilarious.*

Her hips started to push toward my face and I fucking loved that. Could feel the precum spurt out of me when she did. I locked my arm around her ass and sucked her clit between my lips.

"Dillon!"

I worked her until I felt it start, that fluttering in her muscles. The tension in her body, and I took my soaking wet finger from her vagina and slid it deep inside her ass.

"What the-"

She shook and came and screamed my name, pushing my face harder where she needed me. I waited for the tremors to settle down before I pulled my hands away and fell back on my haunches.

"Couch is behind you, babe," I told her.

She wobbled backwards and sank into the couch.

"I've never done that," she panted. "No one has ever done that to me."

"Yeah, we're going to have a lot of firsts, I think."

I stood and started stripping out of my clothes. Shirt, pants, briefs, until I was naked and towering over her.

"Oh my gosh," she said, looking at my dick. It was hard and throbbing and leaking pre-cum down my shaft. "Are you kidding me right now? You're that big?"

"Yeah," I said, taking my dick in my hand to give it a squeeze, trying to get it to calm down. I wasn't done playing with her yet. "But you'll get used to it. You need anything before I make you come again? Electrolytes? Protein?"

She rolled her eyes at me, which was adorable. "Dillon," she said, like she was breaking some bad news to me. "I know you're some kind of sex god, but really, I'm not someone who comes multiple times during sex. Most women don't. So if you just want to get to it, that's fine."

She leaned back on the couch and swung her legs up. One long strong leg cocked against the cushions. Like she was going to lie back and figure out the angular velocity of my backward crossovers.

"Are you putting me on right now?" I asked, eyeing her suspiciously. "Is this a challenge?"

"I'm just trying to keep it real. I don't want to disappoint you and I'm not someone who fakes shit."

I walked over, grabbed her ankles and pulled her across

the couch until her hips were on the arm rest. I shoved a pillow under her lower back for comfort.

Didn't want my girl getting a cramp.

I kissed her mouth, then each tit, because I didn't want her to think I was ignoring their perfection.

"You don't fake anything with me. This is real. All of it. Now don't move while I suit up."

I walked back to the kitchen island and opened the box of condoms. I covered myself then turned back to her. She hadn't moved. Her hands were resting above her head, her eyes were closed.

A post-orgasmic blissed out woman.

"You need a little nap?" I joked. She wasn't about to sleep through what I was going to do to her.

"No, I'm awake. You have fun now."

I stepped back between her legs, angled my cock at her slit, then punched my hips deep into her. She was still slick and soft and took me so sweetly.

"Oh!" she cried out, lifting herself up with her stomach muscles. Her eyes were wide open.

"Too much?" I asked. I could feel her body squeezing me from the inside.

"You're huge," she groaned, and her head fell back on the couch.

"Baby, that's not what I asked. Can you take more?"

She did this body adjustment thing, her hips shifting as if trying to accommodate my size inside her. It was that shimmy she did, but better. Because I was inside her.

"I'm good," she muttered. "That feels good."

I took her at her word and didn't ask again, I just fucked her. I lifted one leg so her ankle was on my shoulder and I watched her tits bounce as I pounded into her over the arm of the couch. It was fucking hot as hell.

She was twisting her head from side to side, like she couldn't take it, except she was moaning my name like she didn't want it to end.

"Dillon," she groaned, half surprised, half out of her head. "So good."

"Yeah baby, you like to get fucked real good, don't you? Nice and hard. You need more dick, baby? You want me deeper?"

Her eyes met mine, a flush climbing her chest. She liked a little dirty talk. *Happy to provide.*

I twisted my hips and slammed into her even harder.

"Fuck!" she shouted, and bit down on her fist.

I wanted to fuck her like this for hours, but the come was building up in me. I could feel it in my lower back. I needed to get her there, fast. I pressed my thumb through her pussy lips, seeking her swollen little clit and pressing down on it. I sucked my middle finger on my other hand.

"What...what are you doing?" she whispered.

"You know what I'm doing," I told her. "You fucking love what I'm doing."

"Dillon," she whispered like she was unsure. Shy.

No room for that this weekend.

I slid that finger in her ass. She was overcome with my cock in her pussy, my finger in her ass, my thumb vibrating her clit.

"Dillon!"

There it was. The squeeze of her pussy. The way her leg over my shoulder was shaking uncontrollably. She was coming, so I could too.

I let myself go and felt the orgasm take over my whole being. I needed to come on her, to mark her, but I was so deep inside I didn't ever want to let this feeling go. Of being swallowed by her.

I shot my load into the condom, again and again, and thought how next time I was going to paint her pretty tits with my cum. And maybe watch her run a finger through it to taste.

Yeah, next time, I thought, as I collapsed over her. My open mouth pressed against that magic space between her breasts.

# 14

---

*Later That Night*
*Liv*

I was crunching on some Cool Ranch Doritos when I looked down at my chest and saw the orange crumbs. I had an option, get up, get a towel, clean them up or...
I brushed them off my chest and proceeded to eat.

"We're going to seriously need to wash these sheets before I check out," I told Dillon.

He was lying in the bed next to me, a bed we'd basically destroyed with sex and snacks. With his eyes still closed, he reached over and squeezed my naked thigh.

That's right. I was lying naked in bed, eating Cool Ranch Doritos. There was a bottle of Gatorade on the bedside table and I was perfectly content to listen to Dillon snore as he physically recovered from wreaking havoc on my body for the third time that day.

"Yeah, babe. I got jizz everywhere that last time."

Like everywhere. My stomach, my breasts, the pillow he'd shoved under my butt.

"I was taking about the crumbs, but that too."

I thought I knew sex. I thought, smugly, that I was pretty good at sex.

Brian and I always had a good time when we were together. If you had asked me, I would have said he had a perfectly nice penis.

I clearly didn't know penises. I didn't know how game changing it could be when a man with a very large one knew what he was doing with it. And I certainly didn't know my brain and body would explode every time he came near my asshole.

I'd had control over every orgasm I'd ever had.

Now Dillon was in control of my orgasms, and I wasn't sure what that meant.

*Here it comes. The overthinking.*

It was like feeling a sneeze coming on and knowing you couldn't stop it.

My body was exhausted and happy, so my brain kicked into gear, counting down all the reasons I shouldn't have done this.

*It's a weekend. Calm down. You get back Monday morning and he goes back to being just another player you're trying to make better.*

And he'll treat me like he's never had his mouth between my legs.

Ugh. That thought made me feel like shit.

So what if he was the best sex I'd ever had? Maybe my problem was I just hadn't had enough sex. There was my high school boyfriend, then Brian. But since my accident, my whole life had been about recovery.

I'd only just started going on Hinge dates, which were

not as conducive to having sex as one might think. Strange dudes were weird in person.

This *thing* between us, while enlightening, had to be a one and done deal. Like some wickedly sinful dessert, that you let yourself eat once, then got back on your diet plan the next day.

We would go back to Portland and act like professionals.

Except he was a professional who'd come on my tits and I was a professional who begged him to fuck me harder.

It was starting to feel like we were both self-delusional, believing we could make this be casual when it didn't feel that way.

Maybe what we really needed to do was wait for the logistics of it all to play out.

The reality was, we were just a few more weeks until my contract was officially over. My hope had always been to leverage my time here into a new job with another team.

In another city.

Maybe there I could find someone who could give me out of control orgasms and Dillon and his fabulous penis would be a distant memory.

I glanced over to where he was sprawled out over the bed. His tree-trunk like legs were spread wide, he had one arm over his eyes, his other hand still cupping my thigh. His big penis was flaccid now, but no less intimidating.

I wasn't going to do that thing where I made this more important than it was. I wasn't going to assign some crazy romantic feeling just because we had a lot of fun together and, physically, we were well matched.

Instead, I was just going to lie here next to him, eating all the Doritos I wanted while orange crumbs gathered around me. I wasn't going to do something as stupid as blurting out...

"What's next?"

He groaned. "Babe, I'm going to need a few minutes of recovery here. And probably another Gatorade before I can think about what's next."

"Not sex, you idiot. What happens next with us? Do you go back to ignoring me?"

He turned his head and peeked out from under his arm. "Please tell me we're not having this conversation now. You fucked common sense right out of me, Liv."

I threw my hands up, one hand still clutched around the Doritos bag. "I know! I don't even want to have this conversation. Ever. But I can't turn off my freaking stupid brain. I know this is not serious and just for this weekend. But I want to know if you're going to go back to being an asshole and ignoring me?"

He rolled toward me, throwing his heavy leg over both of mine. I could feel his penis now pressed against my hip.

"Chip me," he demanded, and I gave him a triangle from the bag. He chewed it thoughtfully. "I'm sorry I was an asshole. I'm not going to ignore you. But you know we can't do this back in Portland."

I nodded around the lump in my throat. Of course I knew that. Intellectually.

He rolled away from me onto his back, now both arms up over his head so I could spend some time appreciating his broad chest, the smattering of dark chest hair over his pecs, the contour of his stomach and the way it flattened out.

Dillon was his very own landscape of hills, and mountains of skin and muscle.

I missed his penis touching me already. It was official. I was pathetic.

He sat up, the muscles of his stomach doing all the work,

and sighed. It was a sad sound, so sad that I found myself rubbing his back. I smiled at the trail of orange powder I left across his shoulders.

"It sucks, but guys can be assholes about this shit. I even thought about letting Coach know what's going on. Like keeping things above-board, maybe we sign a consent form or some bullshit. It's not just about you being on the team though, Liv. Having sex with me would make you a woman first, a coach second. Not just in our locker room, but all across the league. In a male driven space, that's not good for you."

"You don't have to explain misogyny to me, Dillon. I've always understood what's at stake. This was fun, now it's over, and we move on."

He looked back at me, his expression somehow managing to be flirty, sad and angry all at the same time.

"That simple for you, huh? A little dick and you're done with me."

"Uh...nothing little about that dick," I said, and he chuckled, breaking some of the tension.

Stop this, I told myself. Stop this now, before you get any deeper. Before it gets any harder. Before you get hurt any more.

"Uh oh. He heard you," Dillon said, and like a sleek predator he climbed over me, and pressed his hips into mine. "I think he likes you."

His penis was rock hard, and ignoring my good sense, I wrapped my arms around him.

"Yeah, well tell him not to get too attached," I muttered and tilted my head back.

"Babe, you're covered in my favorite flavor." He was licking the crumbs from my chest. "This is better than whipped cream."

"I don't know what you're doing," I said primly, even as I was giving him better access to the space under my ear. I really liked it when he kissed me there. "You just said that this thing is over. We should be getting up and finding a laundromat in town so we can clean these sheets."

"No, we have tonight and tomorrow. We don't have to be back in Portland until Monday morning. By my count, I can probably get about six or seven more orgasms out of you before then."

He lifted his head and looked at me. The easy charm was gone. There was only Dillon, with all his intensity, his fierceness. I realized in that moment this wasn't easy for him either. He was in deeper than he wanted to be, too.

It was oddly comforting.

"I don't want you to forget me," he said. "I don't want to be that hockey player you had a hot weekend with that one time. I want you to remember this. Remember me."

I cupped his cheek. "I'm sorry, and you are—?"

"Jerk," he said, then he kissed me, with his whole mouth and tongue and I forgot everything else for now.

*The Calico Cove Laundromat*
*Sunday, Midnight*
*Liv*

"You show me yours," I said.

We were sitting side by side in two chairs, watching the sheets we'd pulled off the bed tumble in the dryer. We still needed to sleep on them tonight when we got back to our place over the bookstore, but at least it wouldn't appear to Annie, the nice bookstore lady who had rented me the cozy apartment, that I'd been having Dorito orgies over the weekend.

"You show me yours first," he countered.

"Why?" I grumbled.

"Same reason you want me to show you my stuff first. Because you think going last means you win. It doesn't."

I hated how well he knew me.

How well I knew him.

Officially, this *thing*, whatever it was, whatever it had been, was over on Monday. We were both cool with that decision.

Except he was going to get his wish.

I wasn't going to forget him.

I could never.

"Fine." I got my phone out and went to YouTube. I shifted a little on the hard seat. My lady parts were feeling every bit of yesterday and today. When we'd finally left the apartment, I was surprised I could still walk.

But no one complained about achy post sex lady parts when the sex was so insane. The cost of doing amazing business with Dillon Le Coeur.

Dillon, sensing my discomfort, pulled me off the hard chair and into his lap. His thighs weren't much softer than the chair, but sitting in his lap, with my legs dangling over his right thigh, I was definitely more comfortable.

Or maybe it was just because I was touching him again. We'd been connected for forty-eight hours. My leg over his. His hand on my shoulder. His arms wrapped around me. Whether he was inside me, or just holding my hand while we ate Chinese takeout, it didn't matter. We were touching.

I didn't consider myself a touchy-feely person. But touching this guy was my jam.

"Okay, you promise not to make fun of Brian's costume?"

Dillon snorted. "No."

I tucked my phone away. "Then I'm not going to show you."

He pulled the phone out of my hand and hit the play button on the screen.

"Hey!" I said and reached for the phone, but he held it above his head and out of my reach. Familiar music began to play.

We were showing each other our best highlights. Mine was obviously the long program when we took the gold medal at Worlds. Our music that year was Tchaikovsky's Romeo and Juliet, and Brian's costume was as dramatic as anything that had ever been imagined by our costume designer. She said she'd wanted his Romeo to be a peacock, and well, he looked like a peacock.

"Is his face green and purple?" Dillon asked, watching the video.

"You're supposed to be watching me skate," I objected.

He continued to watch the video. "Classical music? Isn't that out?"

"I thought you didn't pay attention to figure skating?"

"Whoa, what was that?"

"Side by side triple lutzs"

He grunted. "Nice."

The music started to swell and I knew exactly where we were in our routine. The difficulty level in the second half of our routine was the highest of any teams that year. The following year – the year of my accident – we'd pushed ourselves even further. The lift Dillon was watching was one of my favorites: a triple twist lift.

The muscles in my abdomen and chest remembered their jobs during that lift and I fought to keep myself still.

"Holy shit!" he barked. "How fucking high did he throw you?"

I laughed. "We never officially measured, but it's about six feet."

"And he catches you?"

"Hello, you just watched it," I said, pointing to the screen.

"That's sick as fuck," he muttered.

The music slowed and I did my backwards bend into the Death Spiral. Then eventually we collapsed into each other's arms to end our routine.

I could hear the cheers coming from the phone. Could remember every second of that feeling. The high of performing at that level. Knowing we'd nailed the routine. Realizing we had a shot at winning.

"Look at you, babe," he said, his arms coming around me, pulling the phone closer to his face. "Look how happy you were."

The tears welled up before I could stop them, but I fought them back. No crying over the past. That was my rule. "Yeah. I really loved it."

"Does it bother you to watch these videos?"

"I haven't watched any videos since my accident."

I saw him register what I was saying. That for whatever reason, I was ready to do that now. With him. In a Calico Cove laundromat.

Recovery was weird.

"You're amazing," he said, and kissed me.

Jeez. Why was I so emotional? Too much sex? Was that a thing?

"Okay, now let's do mine," he said.

I rolled my eyes dramatically. "Do I have to?"

"Hey, this is a compilation video set to real music, classic rock, not that old shit."

I drilled my fingers into his ribs and he yelped. "Don't disrespect Tchaikovsky."

"Yes, ma'am," he said and shoved his phone into my hands. "Now watch me kick a little ass."

*Early Monday Morning*

THIS WAS NEW FOR ME. I don't know that I'd ever had sex like this before. It was like riding on top of a tiger. All sleek muscle and bone. So flipping strong.

"That's it, baby. Ride me, work my dick as hard as you like."

I was straddling Dillon and doing exactly that. Filled with his massive cock, I was riding him to a rhythm that suited me. Not him, not his pleasure, not his speed or pace. But mine. I twisted my hips, found another angle and groaned. It all felt so good.

He was playing with my nipples. Pulling and twisting them in a way that at first felt too aggressive in his strong heavy fingers, but now I craved it as hard and as much as the rest of him.

He grabbed my hips and held me still. Our breaths panting together.

"What...what are you doing?" I stammered, trying to grind against him but his hold was too firm. I was powerless.

"Trying...not to come," he said, teeth gritted.

How was a girl supposed to just live her life knowing she could make Dillon Le Coeur struggle not to come? Like, where was my crown? My parade?

I was a sex goddess and I needed him to worship me.

"Some sex toy you are," I said, and squeezed the muscles of my pussy around him.

"Jesus, Liv."

We were on the floor next to the bed. After sleeping on the clean sheets last night, we'd logically agreed on shower sex this morning. But shower sex had turned into me dropping to my knees to give him head. No easy thing considering his girth, but so worth the fun of feeling him lose control. His hands in my hair, my name ripped from his chest like I was killing him.

We'd stumbled out of the shower together. He tripped on his duffle bag and fell by the side of the bed, I grabbed a condom and quickly took advantage of the fact that he was on his back.

One touch of my hand as I slipped the condom over him and he was back in the game. Dillon's recovery time had to be a record.

"You wet enough to take me?" he'd whispered. I nodded.

"Show me," he groaned, and I slid over him, his dick between the lips of my pussy, the head of his cock hitting my clit. I was wet and I was already on edge. This was the very last time we'd touch each other like this.

"You got this wet sucking my cock?" he groaned, and all I could do was whimper. I reached between us, adjusting him so the next time I slid back, he slid home.

This time I was in control. This time I would get myself off instead of letting him take over. Maybe because I needed to prove to myself I could do this again. I could bring myself to orgasm with or without Dillon.

*Why would you ever want to do this without him?*

I squashed that thought as quickly as I had it. This was our last time. The last hour we had together. I would pack up my car and head back to Portland and my apartment. He would head back to his place and we would both arrive at the practice facility a few hours from now as professionals.

This weekend would be over. Like it never happened.

Only it had. It so had. The proof was in me. In my body and my heart. My head.

"Get there, babe. You're killing me," he growled.

I had both palms planted on his chest while I worked my hips on him like he was a stripper pole. I put my hand over his full lips.

"No talking," I demanded of my sex toy.

I was in charge and I needed to concentrate. Focus on just enjoying this ride. The ache of my thighs as they continued to support my weight. The deep satisfying tug in my pussy as my orgasm continued to build.

He grunted and thrust his hips up into me.

I grunted back because if he thought he was going to make me come one second before I wanted to, he was delusional.

Then I felt it. His hands sneaking around my hip, covering my butt cheek.

I slapped his hand away. "No butt stuff. I don't like it."

He chuckled. "Babe, you love it."

Secretly, of course I did, but openly I wasn't admitting to that.

He surged up into a sitting position, and used his mouth on my breasts, sucking my nipples, tugging them between his teeth, something else I loved.

But not the angle of his cock inside of me.

I leaned forward, forcing him to lay back down without pulling away.

"Ahh," I sighed, and for a second stopped riding him just so I could plant both hands on either side of his head, while he feasted on my tits. Everything he did always felt so good. So right, even when I hadn't known it was exactly my kink.

He slapped my butt cheek hard, then harder.

"Get back to work," he growled. "Or I'm taking over."

I looked down into his face. His cheeks were tight, his eyes were ablaze.

"Don't tell me what to do. You're my sex slave this morning."

A wide smile took over his face. His Dimples Grande on prominent display. I wanted to trace the groove of them with the tip of my finger. I always wanted to do that.

"Oh yeah?"

"Yeah," I smiled back. "I'm in charge."

It happened in less than a second, he lifted me up off him and used his strength to wrestle me onto my belly. I was squealing and wiggling underneath him.

"I'm in charge!" I shouted again, which was a hard claim to make when I was on my hands and knees underneath him.

He slapped my ass and laughed. "You were in charge. But I need to come babe, so now you get to play my sex slave. Get that ass high in the air for me."

I pressed my head to the carpet, my weight on my elbows as I waited. Then I screamed when he thrust into me from behind.

"Good?" he wanted to know.

Of course, it was good. It was amazing, but I wasn't going to give him the satisfaction.

I just grunted and rocked back against him until he groaned.

"Make me come," I demanded, like he was still mine to boss around.

I didn't have to say it twice. He thrust hard, shifting my whole body along the carpet in a way I was certain would give me rug burns on my knees, but I didn't care.

I had all of Dillon unleashed. Powerful, overwhelming male behind me taking me like a savage warrior. He shouted and grunted and snapped his hips, sending his cock so deep inside of me I could feel it all the way in my belly. Which I knew was anatomically incorrect, but that didn't matter when your brain was being turned into jelly.

His hand slipped under my body and his middle finger slid over my clit. He pressed it there, not doing anything else but giving me the pressure I needed even as his other hand pressed against my lower back like he was holding me in place in front and back. He slammed against me and it happened. That explosion of pleasure I'd only found with him.

"Yes!" I cried out as my fingers dug into the carpet, drawing out every second of that delicious blast through my body.

"That's it, babe, come on my cock. Fuck, your pussy is so tight. Take it, take my cum. Ahhh fuck."

I collapsed like a pancake underneath him and for a second took all his weight on my back. We breathed hard together. Our chests heaving in unison.

That was really it. That was my last orgasm with him. His last orgasm with me.

We were no longer people who would orgasm together.

He pressed a kiss to the side of my head and slipped out of me, still semi-hard. I hid my wince... *I'll be feeling that one for a week.* I imagined feeling this ache in my pussy on Wednesday while he skated past me not making eye contact, and me wanting to cry.

*Stop it. Stop it right now.*

He choose the team.

I was choosing myself.

We both knew the rules going in, no sense wishing for something different now.

Dillon planted his hand on my butt to push himself to his knees. He stood and I heard him walk back into the bathroom to dispose of the condom.

I was on the pill. Had been since I was eighteen. I could have told him that. Could have let him come inside me without the barrier, but in so many ways it felt necessary to have something between us. Even something as insignificant as a condom.

I was still laid out on the carpet on my belly, caught up in memories of the weekend and trying to reconcile them with the week ahead. He was undoubtedly already thinking of training and team meetings. Preseason games started in two weeks and his head would go right back to work.

"Babe."

I ignored him.

"Liv."

I wasn't listening. He was going to say that we had to get back. He was going to say we had to get dressed and we had to leave. I knew that. It was an hour drive back to Portland. If we left now, I would barely have enough time to shower, change and get to the practice facility on time.

I needed to move. I needed to get up and get on with my life.

This was over.

"Liv," he said again, this time more gently. He ran his

fingertips over my back and I knew I was emotional and not thinking clearly, but that touch felt like pity.

*Hell no.*

I scrambled to my feet and started to walk by him but he wrapped an arm around my waist and pulled me close.

"I need to use the bathroom," I said, even as I smashed my face into his big beautiful bare chest. His penis was touching my hip and I was happy again.

"Yeah. Stay in there until I leave," he said, and pressed a kiss on the top of my head.

"Why?"

"Because I can't leave if I'm looking at you."

I nodded but didn't say anything.

"We good?" he asked,

I still didn't say anything.

"Liv?"

"I need to use the bathroom," I repeated, slipping out of his arms. "See you at practice."

I stepped into the bathroom and shut the door behind me. I didn't really need to use it, so I just sat on the edge of the tub and turned on the water behind me to drown out the sound of him leaving.

# 15

_____

*The Following Week*
*Dillon*

"**S**tep it up, Captain!" Coach McKay barked as I charged down the ice, deeked past Morgan, which wasn't a huge feat. If I was slow, he was slower. It had been a long few days and it felt like I was skating through mud.

Liv had fucked the speed right out of me.

Skalsberg was quicker than Morgan and today he was quicker than me, he checked me against the boards and stripped the puck right off me.

"You better play better than that against Tampa," Coach barked.

Our first preseason home game against the Tampa Whales was slated for the last day in September and the boys were geared up. We were good. We were really fast, thanks to Liv.

*I mean Coach Tyler-Branch.*

Everyone except Novek, whose refusal to listen was beginning to cost him.

O'Rourke was looking more and more like our star winger.

Go fucking figure.

Usually at this point of training I was the biggest, most efficient cog in the Bruiser's well-oiled machine. I loved to skate, I loved to practice, but I really loved to compete. I loved to win.

Look up hockey player in the dictionary and you'll find a picture of me. For ten years this game had given my life focus.

Being a part of a team had given me meaning.

I wasn't going to let my guys down.

I swung around the net at top speed, my crossovers faster than they'd ever been, and sprinted down the ice to where Novek had taken the puck and was trying to score on Smith, who so far was shutting him out.

Today I wasn't a Bruiser, I was Team Orange.

I was playing like shit for Orange. The coach was right to be calling me out for it.

My legs felt weighted down. My chest was tight and I could see Novek lose the puck to O'Rourke who was lightning fast on his way to home ice.

At the boards Liv was yelling at him and I watched in real time as the rookie incorporated her coaching, corrected the alignment between knee, ankle and skate, and left everyone behind.

When he scored, he skated right back to Liv for a high five and a debrief.

She stood there glittering with success. So fucking bright and beautiful it was a wonder we weren't all blinded.

*Don't think about Liv.*

I practically snorted, the idea was so ludicrous. I thought about her every hour on the hour. If not the fucking minute. If she wasn't right in front of me, I wondered what she was doing or thinking or feeling.

Hell, I wondered about all of those things when she was standing in front of me.

She'd destroyed me over the course of the weekend, and as much as I told myself that this infatuation or lust or whatever the fuck it was would pass, I was starting to have doubts.

She was in my head. Seeing her every day at practice was too much.

And not enough.

She had two more weeks on her contract.

I needed her here.

But I needed her gone more.

McKay blew the whistle, signaling my shift change. I skated over to the bench and watched the next line take the ice.

"You're skating like shit, Captain."

Ron, who had been on my shift, slid onto the bench next to me. We were both panting, as we squeezed water into our mouths.

"Fuck you," I said, and spat the water next to his skates.

"Maybe you need to spend some time with your girl-friend. See if she can't teach an old dog some new tricks."

The anger started in the vicinity of my toes. A tingle of impatience and annoyance gathered speed and hit my chest. This fucking guy... this fucking guy had been a problem since the minute he was traded to Portland. I'd done everything I could to incorporate him into the team, but he wanted to sit on the bench and spit venom into every ear he could find.

I wasn't the team fighter. Not even close. That was Skalsberg. We sent our Viking out on the ice to right wrongs and exact retribution. My job was to keep a cool head at all times. It's what the team expected of me. Needed from me.

But I was ready to make an exception for this guy.

"The fuck you say?" I growled at him.

"You heard me," he said, his voice low, his head turned in my direction. "But you better do it fast too. I heard she got a call from Montreal. What do you think they want?"

I whirled on him with fire in my eyes.

"Hey, man," Ron lifted his gloves. "I'm just telling you what I heard."

No one gossiped more than hockey players in a locker room. But I hated that I didn't know that. That I wasn't her very first call. If it was about another job, she must be excited as fuck and I had to find out from Ron?

I hated that as much or more than I hated Ron.

But maybe it wasn't true? Half the shit the guys talked about in the locker room was nonsense.

"I don't know what the fuck happened between you two," Ron said. "But it's damn clear you didn't take my advice. You've been moping around this whole week like a dog who lost his favorite toy and the skater lady wouldn't look at you if you were on fire. Now, on top of being distracted, you're skating like an AHL player at best."

I shook my head to clear away the buzzing. "I'm going to fuck you up, Ron."

"You going to fight the whole team? Because I'm not the only one who's noticed."

Bullshit. No one noticed. We'd been so careful. So careful it was killing me.

I stood up and towered over the old veteran. "Get up."

Ron shook his head. "Punching me is not going to fix your problem."

"Well, we're going to try it and find out."

He sighed like a man who knew he had no choice. No choice but to put up or shut up. I was about to drop my gloves when Coach blew the whistle.

I turned my head then, distracted by Coach, and Ron sucker punched me.

Right under the chin, I went down like a fucking log. Falling back on my ass onto the bench and rolling off.

It was not graceful.

I barely had enough room to scramble to my skates when I felt him behind me getting another shot into my ribs. Right under the pads, the bastard.

"What the fuck?" I heard Coach McKay shout.

In full rage now, I turned on Ron and wrapped my arms around his waist. In one smooth twisting motion, I took him off his skates and sent him crashing down in the space between the bench and the wall, in a takedown move my dad would be proud of. I heard him grunt in pain and barely had a chance to let the satisfaction of that wash through me before hands were grabbing me by the back of my pads and heaving me off of him.

I got in one hard shot to his kidney to pay him back for the sucker punch before I let myself be pulled away.

Coach McKay got in both of our faces. "Knock it off! Le Coeur, you should know better. What kind of fucking example was that for the team? Both of you, hit the showers. Now. And make it cold."

It had been a shit practice and now my chin was throbbing from where he'd clipped me. My side hurt from where he'd connected to my ribs. Worst of all, Ron was right. Hitting him hadn't fixed anything.

We hit the showers as ordered and stayed as far away from each other as we could.

When I was finished dressing, my gear packed up, I finally snapped.

The thing I'd been forcing myself not to do all week was now the only thing I could do.

I made my way from the locker room, down to the hallway where Liv's office was. This was stupid because there was no good reason for me to be down here. If someone saw me I couldn't say, "Oh, just stopping by PT."

Nope. It was just Liv down here.

In my head I did a little recap.

The *Ignore Liv Plan* hadn't worked.

The *Fuck Liv Out of My System Plan* hadn't worked.

I was officially out of plans.

She worked with us after morning warmups, watched the scrimmages and then spent afternoons in her office writing notes and her coach's reports. There had been a couple of times O'Rourke came down here after practice. Even Skalsberg was coming down once in a while to shoot the shit with her. Skalsberg brought Smith one time.

It was a whole fucking party.

Not me, though. I kept my distance.

God, I wanted to see her. I wanted her to kiss my chin better and tell me that Ron was an idiot and I did the right thing getting into a childish fight with him.

Then I wanted to bend her over her desk and fuck her until my head was right.

I stopped in front of her door and looked through the glass.

As I suspected, she was still there. Sitting behind her desk, typing something into her laptop. Her hair was up in one of those messy buns, and I could see her tongue pressed into the corner of her mouth as she concentrated on the screen in front of her.

She wasn't wearing my jersey and I was struck by the reality that she would never wear my jersey. Instead. she was wearing some generic purple and black Bruisers' t-shirt and those ass-hugging leggings she always wore. I wondered if I walked into her office, bent her over the desk, stripped her leggings to her thighs and just sank my cock inside her, if I finally, finally would have some peace.

Not pleasure. Just the secession of pain.

I knocked on the glass and she looked up to see who it was.

I didn't know what to make of her expression. I wasn't that guy who could read all the emotions on someone's face, especially when they were complicated.

Happy. Sad. Pissed. Those were the only ones I could recognize and process.

Her expression didn't say any of those things. Or maybe it said all those things. I couldn't tell.

She waved her hand, inviting me in.

I stepped inside and shut the door behind me. Fought the urge to close the blind on that little window, because that would be extra suspicious. She got up from her desk and met me halfway.

For a moment the expression on her face was easy to read. Worry. She'd seen the fight with Morgan.

"You all right?" She lifted her right hand but didn't touch me. I wanted to grab her hand and put it on my face. Force her to do what we both wanted. Needed. But instead, we stood there like strangers with two feet of distance between us. "That was some fight."

"I'm fine."

"That's going to bruise," she said, like she wanted me to feel worse.

"He looks worse," I said, on edge. Pissed off. Mad that she was just standing there looking at me and I was just standing there looking at her.

"What can I do for you, Captain?" she asked, stepping back like she was going to put the desk between us. Behind her on the wall she had a big calendar and a bulletin board. On the bottom corner she had a picture of her family. I didn't like the way her father was looking at me. Like he knew what I'd done to his daughter and what I was about to do to his daughter.

"I ah…" I cleared my throat. "I don't know about you, but this isn't working for me."

"Fighting? It doesn't work for a lot of people."

I shook my head. "Don't play dumb. You won't even look at me."

"I'm looking at you now."

"Stop. You know what I'm talking about." Morgan was right, and of course I picked up on it. The few times we'd talked, her eyes were locked on the spot right above my left shoulder.

"It makes my stomach hurt when I look at you," she admitted.

Yeah, okay. That was fair. Sometimes my stomach hurt when I looked at her too. Or was it my heart? I wasn't sure.

"I didn't think you'd notice," she said.

Of course I noticed. I noticed everything. She painted her nails two days ago and the red on her thumb was already halfway gone because she chewed on that nail during scrimmages. Her hair slipped out of her ponytail at the end of the day and she would take it out, gather up all that thick honey blonde hair and pile it on her head, securing it there with magic. In the cafeteria she always asked for a grilled cheese sandwich with ham and tomato and she'd only eat half of it.

She stayed late. Came early. Worked so hard.

But I wasn't here to talk about that.

"There's a rumor going around you got a phone call from Montreal. They offer you a job?"

Her cheeks went pink and her eyes went back to that space over my shoulder. "No, they want to meet me though. I was going to wait until my contract was up."

"Don't wait. That's not how it works in this business. Coach Renaud is a good guy," I said. "The team is a bunch of assholes."

Her lips lifted and she ruthlessly flattened them. "You say that about every team."

"You should go," I said. "When they offer a job, you should take it."

She licked her lips and stepped back. Hurt flashing across her face before she could hide it. I didn't want to hurt her, but weren't we already doing that? Wasn't this situation already cutting us to pieces?

"Ready to get rid of me that quickly?" She tried to make a joke, but it fell flat.

Yes.

Never.

"You need to leave," I said, as honest as I could be. It felt like shit. She blinked at me, her eyes wide like I'd just punched her right in the chest.

"This isn't some bullshit plan so you and I can-"

"No," I cut her off. "This isn't about you quitting so we don't have a conflict at work. This is about you messing with my focus, which is messing with my game. I don't do relationships for exactly this reason. I am the team captain and right now I'm useless to them because I can't get you out of my fucking head."

"And that's *my* problem?" she asked.

"No, it's *my* problem," I said, pointing my thumb at my chest. "But you have to help me get over this, Liv. The only way I can think to do that, is for you not to be here. For me not to see you."

"This is my job, Dillon!"

"No, Liv," I said gently. "This is *my* job. And if I'm not here, mentally and physically, we have no shot of making the playoffs. No chance at the Stanley Cup. Everyone in the organization suffers then."

"And that's all that matters to you?" she asked, crossing her arms tight across her chest.

It had to be, right? It was all that had mattered to me for the past ten years. Wins. Playoffs. Championships. MVPs. Records. All of it. All the glory I could suck out of the sport.

I was *The Heart*.

The Captain.

I needed to act like it.

I knew what she was asking. The question behind the question.

*Do you care about me at all?*

"It is," I said. "It is all that matters to me."

My words landed like a ton of bricks in her tiny office. Her father in that picture shot daggers into my face.

"You'll get another job. If not Montreal, then something else. You're good, Liv. You could easily become the best skating coach in the NHL."

"Yet you're asking me to leave? How is that good for the team, Dillon?"

"It's not. It's good for me though. And I'm their captain."

Her eyes were cold hard flint. The color of a sword. She

was right too, she would be an asset to any team she worked with, ours included. But I was a selfish prick with no self-control when it came to her and this was breaking my goddamn heart.

"It's killing me."

All that anger melted from her face and she let out a long hard sigh, her shoulders slumping.

"I know," she whispered. "It's killing me, too."

"Liv," I breathed, and opened my arms to her, praying she'd take me up on the invitation and hug me. Press her body to mine, warm me back up.

There was another knock on the door and we both jumped apart just as Novek walked in.

He had his bag around his chest and he wore a black puffer coat with the word Prada all over it.

"Do all your clothes have designer names on them?" I asked him, irrationally pissed at that coat.

"Do all of your clothes come from Costco?" he shot back, and...well... I liked the Costco brand athletic shorts. Sue me. Sometimes when I went in for steaks and protein powder, I grabbed shorts and a few t-shirts.

Novek grinned at me like he was just taking the piss.

"What are you doing down here with Coach?" he asked. "Trying to get some private training?"

He made it sound filthy without even trying. Or maybe that was me? Inferring filth because I wanted so badly to touch her again. "Nope," I said. "Asking Coach Tyler-Branch about Montreal."

"So that's true?" Novek asked.

"It's just a request for an interview," Liv said, sitting back down behind her desk. "Now, what can I help you two with?"

"Well," Novek grinned. "Cap here needs some help with his left hook."

Yeah, I wasn't standing here for this shit.

"Good night, Coach," I said to Liv and I patted Novek on the back, though I doubt he felt it through his Marshmallow Man jacket. "See you tomorrow, Novek."

I walked down the hallway towards the exit. Ready to head home to my apartment.

So I could count down the hours until tomorrow's practice.

"Cap!" Novek shouted, trotting down the hallway towards me. Gold necklaces bouncing against his chest. He still wore that puffer jacket and shorts.

What a twat.

I kept walking.

"Hey Cap," he said. "Where are you going?"

"Home."

"You want to get a beer?"

I shot him an exasperated look. He did not catch on. "No, Novek. No beers. Thanks."

"I wanted to talk to you."

"About your shit attitude?"

"I've been trying," he said. "To be less shit attitude."

Hmmm. I had to give him that. He was a better teammate than he'd been weeks ago, but he still wasn't giving Liv all the respect she deserved.

"What's on your mind?"

"O'Rourke."

I laughed. "The kid is coming for you Novek. You getting nervous?"

Novek stopped in the hallway surrounded by pictures of past and present teammates and staff. "Yeah," he said honestly. "I am."

The guy wasn't being an asshole show off. He was being human and honest.

"He works hard," I said with a shrug. "Harder maybe than anyone else on the team."

"Yes. I see that. But...I have never not been the best. Wherever I am. At any level. I have never..."

I knew Novek's story. Every pro did. There was always a guy in any locker room who had been touched by God. He never had to work to be the best and so he never did. He just was.

Those guys never made it into the history books.

It was the guys who were touched by God and worked harder than everyone else – the Gretsky's, The Ovechkin's, The Crosby's – they changed the game.

"You could be a legend," I told him. "You honestly could, and I would love you to be a legend on this team. With me."

He preened, chin up like a fucking peacock.

"But if you don't work harder and actually listen to the people trying to make you better at what you do, you'll be left behind."

I continued walking.

He didn't follow and all I could hope was that he'd take what I said to heart and dig in.

And that Liv would take what I said to heart and move on.

## 16

*Liv*

I wanted to bang things. Smash things. Pulverize everything and everyone in sight. I'd had rages like these after my accident. When I was coming to understand that while I'd been so incredibly lucky to retain full brain function, full cognitive ability and make a full physical recovery... I was never going to compete again.

Yeah. I hadn't taken the end of my life as I had known it very well.

Was this as bad as that moment? No. But I was pissed. Righteously pissed.

I knew I could tell Dillon to fuck off. That this was my job, and I would handle it the way I saw fit. We should be able to be adults and work together without letting the weekend we shared interfere with that.

Only I was just as much to blame for not being able to put it behind me. I wasn't lying when I said I didn't like seeing his face. I didn't like hearing his voice. I didn't like being in the same space with him knowing we were nothing more than colleagues to one another.

It didn't feel right. It felt like a lie and I hated lying. It messed with my stomach.

So he was an asshole.

But he was right.

Staying here was bad for both of us.

Sitting back down behind my desk, I opened the bottom drawer and pulled out my contract with the Bruisers.

It was officially up in two weeks. What I hadn't told Dillon was that there was an extension clause included. Obviously it had to be mutual. The team had to want me to stay and I had to want to stay.

I liked working here. I liked the guys and the staff. I'd been holding out hope that I might be offered an extension. Now Dillon was telling me, in no uncertain terms, not to take it even if it was offered.

Montreal? I mean, I guess. It couldn't be any colder than Maine. Also, I loved poutine as much as the next carb and cheese-obsessed girl.

Montreal wasn't here, though. It wasn't the Bruisers. It wasn't watching O'Rourke work so hard and improve so much. It wasn't Skalsberg and Smith calling me Coach and coming down to my office to talk about skating at the end of practice.

It was so far away from Dillon, which was the point, I suppose.

This sucked.

I'd had a Zoom call with the staff in Montreal and they'd asked me to come up to see the facilities and meet the team face to face. I'd been hesitant to interview while still under contract, but what Dillon said about not waiting made sense. A lot of the other assistant coaches had echoed the same thing. When the team called for you, you went. Because you always wanted to keep your opportunities open.

I quickly pulled up the last email from them and confirmed the dates I was available for a visit.

An email came back immediately. Next Wednesday morning, they would send the team jet.

Holy shit. Even with my broken heart I had to smile. That was some baller shit right there. My brother would lose his mind.

I put away the contract and packed up my stuff for the day. My plan was to go home and eat girl dinner until I was sick. Which, knowing the contents of my fridge, meant pickles with mayonnaise on Wheat Thins and a chocolate bar with peanut butter on it. Maybe that and a gallon of wine might make me feel better.

The weather had started to shift and it was getting darker earlier. Tonya was one of the last cars in the parking lot, but there was a figure leaning against it. For a second my heart picked up.

Dillon.

Planning to apologize and say he changed his mind.

No. It was Novek.

My heart sank. This wasn't going to go very well.

"Hey Novek, what's up?"

"Is this really your car?" he asked.

"Yes."

"Does it work?"

Sometimes. Less than it used to. "Of course."

"It is a very ugly car. I think it should be against team rules for an assistant coach to have such an ugly car."

"What do you want, Novek?"

He looked around the entire parking lot as if to assure

himself we were alone. Basic feminine nerves kicked in. Why was it important to this guy, who'd made it clear he didn't like me, that we were alone?

"Is it true about Montreal?" he asked.

"It's just a first interview," I said, as if it wasn't a big deal.

"You can't go." He licked his lips. "I need you."

I picked my jaw up off the floor. "I'm sorry?"

"Yeah. I need you...to make me better."

Oh, I laughed. I laughed so hard I had to put my duffle bag down and wipe my eyes. "You're just figuring this out now?" I asked him.

"I am not...," he stopped like he was searching for a word. "I have never asked for help. My father..." He shook his head and I saw an entire painful relationship in his dark eyes. "Could not abide weakness. Needing help was weak. Not being the best was weak. I am learning his way is not the only way," he said. "You have made that boy O'Rourke into a competitor, so imagine what you could do with me. Huh? Imagine the team we could make."

I could make Novek unstoppable. I could cement my future in the league. Go wherever I wanted.

At what cost? What life would I have seeing Dillon Le Coeur every day? Knowing he wanted me to leave. Maybe growing resentful of me, if I didn't.

"So," he said, like it was decided. "I'll talk to Coach. You will stay."

"No. No, Novek." I stopped him. "Please don't do that."

His eyes narrowed, and listen, I was not in the habit of crediting Novek with an ounce of perception, but even a broken clock was right twice a day.

"Is this about Cap?" he asked. "Is he bothering you? The team sees the way he watches you."

*Oh no. No no no.* "He doesn't..." the words dried up in my mouth.

"It would be a mistake to have a relationship with him. I once fooled around with my former coach's wife and it nearly destroyed the team."

I stared at him blankly. The coach's wife?

"It's true," he nodded. "Hockey and romance are not a mix."

No shit. He was right. I hated that he was right because it made me such a dumbass for messing around with Dillon in the first place.

In fact, I was going to put it up there with the dumbest thing I've ever done. I broke the rules, slept with the big oaf, pretty sure sex will never be the same for me, and got my heart pulverized for my trouble.

"No," I said. "Dillon's not bothering me. But please don't get involved. I'm handling things." This was a lie, but whatever. "In the meantime, let's meet in the morning for some one-on-one."

He smiled like a boy at Christmas. "Six?"

Oh God. That meant getting up at five. But if he was willing to listen, I was willing to coach.

"Let's do it."

Novek high-fived me and walked away to his sleek, completely impractical for Maine, Corvette. I was halfway back to my lonely apartment when what he'd said registered.

*The guys saw the way Dillon looked at me.*

Maybe me leaving wasn't enough. What if we needed better damage control?

The big oaf might ruin my career even while we were doing the right thing. We needed to make sure we fixed this now.

I pulled into the nearest liquor store.

This called for gin.

*Dillon*

My couch was extremely comfortable. And long. Deep, too. Four hockey players could sit on this couch and not touch each other. A guy could stretch out and take a nap on this couch without ever feeling like he was laying on rocks.

I hated this couch.

I kind of hated my apartment right now. It was a beautiful apartment that I'd paid some sophisticated woman a lot of money to decorate. It had high ceilings. An open concept floor plan, so I could see the front door and the kitchen, my massive big screen TV all at once. Behind me there were sliding glass doors that lead to a balcony that was large enough to entertain ten additional people.

But it was cold. Empty.

Did I need a few plants or something? Art on the wall?

I had my framed jerseys from the Olympics and the Stanley Cup win. My peewee jersey from the Calico Cove Renegades.

This is where I lived during the season. At least for home games. The rest of the time it was on the team plane and in hotel rooms. Hotel rooms that all looked alike, smelled alike. Didn't matter how fancy it was, the bath towels were usually scratchy.

Never once, not one time in the ten years I'd been playing professional hockey, did I think I was lonely.

Loneliness had never occurred to me. Growing up, it had

been the four of us in that cramped little house. Mom and Dad. Me and Wendy. When I played club hockey I had teammates. Roommates.

I was surrounded by people all the fucking time.

But now, sitting here on my couch, in my big fancy cold penthouse, I felt it.

Loneliness.

I rubbed a hand over the left side of my chest, like I could soothe away the ache. Only this wasn't a contusion or a torn muscle or a broken bone. It was something that hit me deeper and I didn't know what to do with it.

Beside me, my phone started to vibrate. I picked it up with the desperate hope I would see Liv's name on the screen. But no, she wouldn't call me. I knew better than that.

It was my sister and I jumped on the distraction like an overtime shoot out.

"Hey Wendy, what's up?"

"Whoa! What's the matter with you?"

"What are you talking about? There's nothing wrong."

"Dude, you sound like your dog just died, which is not possible because you don't have a dog."

"Maybe I should get a dog."

Wendy barked out a laugh. "Yeah, how are you going to do that? You travel half the year."

"Did I ever tell you I hate hotel towels?" I closed my eyes and rested my head on the back of my couch. "Like hate them. Hate that they're always white, too small, very scratchy."

"Geezus, are you having some kind of breakdown?"

I stood and walked over to the sliding glass doors where the city of Portland was spread out in front of me. A small, but hockey crazy city, glittering against the jet black ocean. In this town, near the stadium, there was a billboard with me on it. And when I got on the ice, everyone in the arena chanted "Heart, Heart, Heart."

This was my life. My fancy life with the cool shit and all the accolades a guy could want.

And I just crushed a woman at the start of her career.

Such an asshole. I deserved to be lonely. I should feel like shit.

"Why did you call?"

"I wanted to see if I could score some tickets to the opening preseason game. I can use them as a giveaway for the bar."

"Not to come see your big brother play?"

"I've seen you play plenty," Wendy said. Giving me the gears was her love language. "The movie people have left. The tourist season is over. I've got Jackson Dumont's new bar to contend with, and while the locals are being very loyal, I can't just coast on my existing clientele. I need new blood."

"Fine," I said. "I'll hook you up with two."

"Four," she countered.

"Wendy, it's our first game. It doesn't matter that it's preseason. It's gonna be a sellout."

"Fine. Two. Now, are you going to tell me what's happening with you and Liv or what?"

The change of subject gave me whiplash. "What about me and Liv?"

"Uh, the fact that Dave caught you sucking face in the kitchen last week after you kicked our asses in the three-legged race."

*Fucking blabbermouth Dave.*

"You told me things with her were a no go because she worked for the team," Wendy reminded me.

"Yes. Well, things are still a no go. We shouldn't have messed around. It was a mistake."

There was silence on the other line.

"What?" I pressed, familiar with my sister's silences. "Just say it."

"You guys looked good together. That's all. Even when she was smack talking her ass off at me I thought...yeah, that's who he needs."

"I don't need anybody," I said, fully embracing my shit mood. "I can't need anyone. I need to be focused on my game."

"Right," Wendy agreed. "Everything for the sport, for the win. For the high of being on top."

"You know what Dad taught us," I reminded her.

"Oh, I do." She dropped her voice so she sounded like a talking bear. "No marriage, no relationships, no happiness until I'm done playing."

"Is that supposed to be me?" I asked, confused by the impression.

"Dillon, I adore Dad, but did you ever consider it wasn't us that ruined his wrestling career? That maybe Mon Ami was just a freaking dumb character. And maybe, all that traveling he did to try and make it big, wasn't the thing that ruined his and Mom's marriage. Maybe they got divorced because they weren't right for one another. So you can wait. Until the sport and wins abandon you. And the guy you walked away from asks you if it was all worth it, and you're like, how can I possibly know, and he keeps texting you even though he's told you he's moved on with this life."

I frowned. "Are we talking about my life or your life right now? I'm confused."

"All I'm saying is that we tend to be very focused people, which is great, but lonely."

"You should get a dog," I told her gruffly. "I would feel better knowing you had someone to walk you home every night after the bar closes."

"You know I love it when you go all big brother on me. I'll think about it, okay?"

"Okay."

"And I'll just say this. When I saw you with Liv, in the short amount of time I saw you together...it looked real. Like real, real. Don't discount that."

I wasn't discounting it. I was simply choosing to walk away from it. For the sport.

The sport first. Always.

"See you, Wend. I'll email the tickets."

"Thanks, Dillon. Love you."

"Ditto."

I disconnected the call and shoved my phone in my back pocket, still staring out over this city where I was a hero.

Liv was going to leave and I was going to skate out onto the ice against Tampa. The fans would do the chant and we would win, or we wouldn't. No matter what, I was pretty sure I would still be hung up on Liv.

I had no clue how long it was going to take to put Liv firmly in the rearview mirror, but I knew it wasn't going to be measured in days or weeks.

There was a knock on my door and it startled me

*Bang. Bang. Bang.*

This was Portland, Maine. Not New York City. We didn't have staffed doormen in the lobby, but we did have a locked building door that required people to be buzzed in. It hadn't happened too often, but there had been a fan or two who had tried to follow me home after a game. The residents of the building were cool and they knew not to let just anyone inside.

Maybe a neighbor needed something?

I stalked to the door and opened it. When I saw Liv standing on the other side of the door with a bottle of gin tucked under her arm, I felt all the jagged edges of bones and joints and muscles in my chest resettle into a puzzle where all the pieces fit.

*She's here.*

*Thank God.*

"Your neighbor on three recognized me," she said. "She thinks we're doing an Ice Capades charity event together and I'm here to help you pick a costume. Let me in, Dillon. Let's say goodbye the right way."

## 17

---

*Liv*

I set the bottle down on the island in his big ass kitchen.

"Tell me you have tonic," I demanded.

"And limes," he said, walking over to his fridge. He pulled out two small bottles of tonic and a lime. He wore a pair of gray sweatpants that sat low on his hips and hugged his ass. Those sweatpants should be outlawed in all fifty states.

I found the cabinet where he stored his glasses. Of course, his fancy refrigerator made ice. so I filled both glasses to the top and set them on the counter. I hit each glass with some gin and Dillon came around me with tonic, a squeeze of lime, then he popped a lime wedge into each glass.

"Cheers to never seeing me again," I said, raising my glass.

He said nothing. Just looked down at his glass.

"For the record, you fucked this up, not me."

He nodded. I liked that he looked unsure. A little shattered.

"Novek told me the guys have noticed how you watch me. So it's not just Morgan who is on to you. On to us, I guess. But now I'm leaving before your behavior costs me the rest of my career."

"Fuck. Liv-"

"Cheers," I said, cutting him off, and tapped my glass against his. "To me."

I sucked back half my drink while he just stood there.

"Drink up, buddy. I'm going to Montreal for that interview. On the team jet, no less. If you can stomach the sight of me for two more weeks, I should be out of your hair permanently."

He lifted his glass but set it down again.

"Novek said what?"

"Everyone sees the way you look at me. Which I'm going to assume is like a goddess you'd like to worship."

"When did he say this?"

"He was waiting at my car when I left. He's asked for some one-on-one time."

His eyebrows lifted like he was impressed.

"Yeah," I said, on a roll. "So when your hot shot forward gets better, you can thank me while I'm in Montreal making sure everyone else on that team is faster than you."

God, I loved trash talk. It was like armor when you were in pain.

Dillon turned his glass on the counter. Very precise quarter turns. "I'm sorry."

I shrugged. "Don't be sorry. You were my mistake and I own it."

His face flushed and those ice blue eyes of his went glacial. Okay. Maybe too far.

"You done getting all your shots in?" he asked.

"My parents and brother are coming out for the first preseason game. They wanted to see...well, I guess what I was doing. Just stay away from them. From all of us, okay?"

He knew what I was asking. I didn't want them to know anything about him, and in turn, us. If they saw us together, they'd be able to see what he meant to me all over my face.

Maybe over his face, too. Since he was so shitty at hiding it, apparently. Which I also secretly loved. I mean *loved*. He should be hurting. He should understand I could have been the best thing to happen to him.

*C'est la vie, Le Coeur.*

"Sure," he said. He took another sip and I finished off my drink. I drank it too fast and on a stomach full of anger and pent up longing, so the gin went right to my head. I had to get out of there before I made another stupid mistake.

"That's it. That's all I came to say. I'll leave."

He pushed off the island towards me. "You don't have to."

"I told you I'm a one and done girl. I need to drive."

"Then have a second drink and stay the night." Dillon said. "With me."

He didn't corral me, but his presence was so all consuming. Like he took up all the space and oxygen in this big empty apartment.

"I didn't come here for that," I said, but I didn't make a move to leave either.

"I know. But stay for that anyway."

I sucked in a breath, the air between us sizzling and hot.

"We already did the crappy goodbye thing back in Calico Cove. Do you really want to go through all that again?"

He stepped around the corner of the granite countertop

and took my hand. I didn't jerk it away, which was probably a mistake.

"If it means another night with you? Yes."

My knees were going weak. All of me was going weak. Had I been planning this when I drove over here? Maybe. Probably. But I wasn't going down without a fight.

"Your face is all messed up," I said, pointing out the bruise on his chin. "I can barely even look at you."

"Okay," he pulled me closer, until I felt the warmth of his chest. I could smell the lime on his breath. "Close your eyes."

"I don't think I like you anymore either. I don't sleep with guys I don't like." I said this even as he wrapped his arms around me and I planted my face against his chest. This was so stupid. But he smelled really good, and I could feel his erection against my stomach.

*Hey buddy. I missed you, too.*

I wanted all my clothes gone. All of his clothes gone. I wanted his rough hands on my breasts. His mouth against mine. I wanted to curl my nails against the muscles of his chest until he begged for mercy.

I wanted him inside of me.

I wanted to be whole.

One last time, I thought. What would it matter? Would it break my heart any more than it was already broken?

Nope. Not possible.

"Then how about this?" he said, his hands rubbing big circles from my neck to the top of my ass. "How about we pretend you're not a former figure skater and I'm not a hockey player who told you to leave? I'm just a guy who works at a bar and you're in town looking for a vacation fling."

I didn't lift my head.

"Hmmm. What do those people do?"

He paused like he wasn't sure either. We'd never had a chance to be so normal. "Well, I think they... chill and watch Netflix. They order up some pizza and drink G&Ts. And... they talk all night."

"Talk? All night?" I said, looking up at him to see if he was really serious.

"Yeah. The girl on vacation can tell the bartender about her parents, and the bartender can tell vacation girl about his sister. She can tell him about her first kiss and her favorite teacher growing up and the worst hangover she ever had."

"He can tell her about growing up in Calico Cove and how his father maybe passed some of his own dreams onto his son, and it's hard, but it's also part of what made him what he is today."

"That sounds boring," he joked, his hand sliding down to squeeze my ass. "You know what else bartender boy does?"

"What?"

"He goes down on vacation girl until she can't form complete sentences. He licks and tongue fucks her sweet pussy until she screams."

"I like this bartender boy, do you have his number?"

He grabbed me around my waist, not lifting me up over his shoulder because he knew that was a trigger for me, but lifting me up enough that he could carry me to his king-size bed. He laid me down and I pulled him over me.

"This is another big mistake, isn't it?" I asked him.

"A'yup."

*Dillon*

I DON'T EVER REMEMBER sex like this. In high school it was all about the thrill of doing it for the first time. Fucking and blow jobs and what worked and what didn't to get me off. To get the girl off.

When I was climbing the leagues, sex felt like an extension of hockey. A sport. A competition. Trying to keep up with every puck bunny who wanted to take a ride on my dick.

It got old. Fast.

But this? This?

I'd never expected anything like this.

Like Liv.

I knew the clock on us was ticking, but nothing about her felt short term.

She was comfortable and familiar despite this only being our second time in bed together.

Her calf muscles had this curve that fit directly in the small of my back. Our tongues, when we kissed, knew how to play together. From the first kiss I was ready, dying to be inside of her. She was arching against me like she wanted it too. Like it had been too long and she needed me as much as I needed her.

But I wasn't ready to start fucking her yet.

Because I didn't want this part to be over. The kissing part. The naked bodies pressed together part. Her legs wrapped around me. My arms wrapped around her.

"Dillon," she breathed, as I bent my head to that spot on her neck she liked to have sucked.

I'd already given her an orgasm. Reveled in the sound she'd made when I'd thrust my tongue deep inside her hot wet pussy. She writhed when my thumb pressed down on her clit.

My girl didn't need a lot to get off. Just exactly the right pressure at exactly the right moment.

She was her own math equation.

I wanted to give her a G-spot orgasm. One that started deep inside her body and would blow her mind. I'd found that little shelf, now I just needed to hit it exactly right with my dick.

She thought it was impossible.

That only made me more obsessed.

I paid absolutely no attention to my own pleasure. It felt secondary to hers. Sure, I was going to get off. Eventually, I was going to put on a condom and have at her when she was so wet and swollen and limp from all the orgasms I gave her, but my side of things seemed so anti-climactic.

Huh. How was that for irony?

"Dillon, are you going to fuck me, or what?" she asked, squeezing the back of my neck in a way that sent electricity down my spine. Who knew I was sensitive there?

I pulled away from her neck so I could look down at her face. Her hair was spread out on my pillow. Her cheeks were bright red. From her arousal or my beard stubble, I wasn't totally positive.

I'd left every light in the bedroom on, because her body was something out of my dreams. Her tits when they bounced in time with my thrusts were next level hot.

"You don't like foreplay?"

"We've been doing this for hours," she whined.

I looked over at the clock. "We've been doing this for twenty minutes and you've already come once."

"I know, but I want to get to the good part," she said with a pout.

"What part is that?"

Her cheeks flushed even hotter and I couldn't stop the chuckle that rumbled through me. Another first. Had I ever laughed during sex?

"Your big swinging dick. Is that what you want me to say? I need you to dick me. Hard. With your big massive cock, you jerk hole."

"My dick does not understand sarcasm."

She slipped her hands down over her breasts in a way that made my jaw loose.

"I'll do it myself," she said, her hand sliding down her taut belly.

I knew when I was beat. As much as I'd love watching her get herself off, I needed to be inside of her.

"Okay, honey, let me get a condom and I'll take you for a ride." I climbed off the bed to get the condoms I'd left in my kit bag from our weekend together. "Roll over on to your belly, babe. I want to take you that way, fill you up nice and tight, yeah?"

"Dillon?"

I stopped halfway to the bathroom door and turned back.

"I'm on the pill," she said quietly. "If you're clean..."

I was clean. The entire team was tested at the beginning of every season, with a firm reminder from the team doctor to wrap it up if we were going to get some strange on the road.

"Yeah?"

"Only if you want to. I'm clean, too. There hasn't been anyone since-"

"Don't fucking say his name," I said a little too harshly, because she flinched. "Not when you're naked in my bed.

He's gone. He never existed. You're mine while you're in that bed."

She snorted and rolled her eyes. "Okay, Hulk."

I was tempted to lift her up off that mattress. Throw her over my shoulder and slap her ass, showing her how much of a Hulk I could be. Except picking her up would freak her out because that dickhead dropped her.

It wouldn't matter how many times she told me it wasn't his fault. In my head, it was always going to be his fault. She put herself in his hands and he hadn't done enough to protect her.

But enough about him.

I stalked back to the side of the bed. "Roll over."

She turned like a cat in the sun, all lazy stretching. Her back arched, her arms under the pillow, her head turned to the side, to watch me. My cock was hard as fuck, but still I took it in my hand to stroke it, like I needed to communicate to it, its responsibility. This woman was going to let us come inside, no barrier. No protection. Because she trusted me. It was heady stuff, and again, unlike any sex I'd ever had.

I'd never not used a condom. But goddamn, I didn't want to use one now. I wanted to push inside her and know what it felt like to feel her on the skin of my dick. I wanted to pump inside her wet heat and feel every twitch of muscle inside of her.

But mostly I wanted to come deep inside her. Fill her up with my cum so I would always be planted there. Deep.

I wanted to get her pregnant.

The thought shook me. It also made me squirt precum over my knuckles. I had to squeeze my dick hard enough to stop myself from coming, which wasn't easy when Liv reached out and swiped her thumb over the head of my cock. Taking that drop of cum and sucking it into her mouth.

I climbed on the bed, knelt between her thighs.

"Spread them," I said. When she didn't immediately comply, I smacked her ass. "More."

I braced my hand by her waist and cocked my hips to the right angle. I thumped my dick against her ass and thought maybe someday she'd let me take her there, too. It would take a lot of time to get her ready, but fuck, that would be hot.

*There won't be time. She's leaving soon.*

I shoved that thought away and I lifted her hips with my big hands and slid home hard, deep inside of her.

Hot. Wet. Perfect. When I died, heaven was going to be my naked dick in Liv's pussy.

She screamed, the sound muffled by the pillow. I pulled the pillow out from under her head and stuffed it under her pussy. "No, Liv, I want to hear it. Every sound. You tell me when I've got the pillow right on your clit."

I shifted the pillow underneath her, felt her wiggling beneath me, getting the pillow right where she needed it.

Fuck me, I wasn't going to last. I was raw and balls deep inside her. It felt like my head was going to explode.

"Ooh, there, there," she crooned.

I was not some purist who believed I had to get a woman off every time with my fingers, my tongue or my cock. Any tool was up for grabs.

*I should get her one of those rocket vibrators. Make her come until her voice was hoarse from it.*

Except there wasn't going to be time for that either.

This was it. The last night.

I braced my hands on either side of her shoulders and

slammed inside her. As if I could root myself there indefinitely.

"Yes! Again!"

This time there was no pillow to muffle her screams and I was helpless to do anything but comply with her wishes.

Again and again I fucked her into the bed, into that pillow that was rubbing against her clit. I slid out of her just enough to fuck her at a different angle, and the sound she made wasn't human.

I'd never felt more alive. Never felt more connected. The slick heat of her, the sounds, the way she was pushing that ass back up against me even as she chased her own pleasure on the pillow that was smashed up against her pussy.

It was the end of me.

She was the end of me.

"Babe, I'm going to come." It was the last coherent thought I had before I pressed my hips against her ass and gave up control in a way that felt profound. Vulnerable.

This was sex without a condom, sure.

But we were naked in so many other ways.

When it was over I crashed onto her back. I knew I had a solid minute of recovery time before it would be uncomfortable for her, and I took every second to just breathe her in.

"Liv," I muttered into her ear.

Nothing.

"Liv," I said a little louder.

She grunted so I knew she was alive.

"Did I get you there?"

She turned her head to the side. "Well, technically, I think the pillow got me there."

I laughed with her, the sensation a pulsating massage over my semi-erection.

"Whatever works," I said, and kissed the cheek that was turned to me.

"Get off, you're heavy."

"Nah, I gotta wait and let my cum get up inside you."

"What are you talking about? I told you I'm on the pill."

"Babe, ten thousand years of evolution is telling me to stay deep inside you. I can't fight that."

"Yeah, well, two hundred plus pounds of caveman laid out on top of me is telling me I can't breathe. Move, you oaf."

I rolled off her on to my back, never happier with my king-sized bed then I was now. There was all the room in the world for us together on this bed.

*Not for long.*

"I should go," she said on her belly, face pressed against the mattress.

"What are you talking about? You're staying."

"I have to get up early," she moaned.

"So get up early. But you do it from here. I'll put the TV on. We can fall asleep to Netflix." I planted my palm over her ass just to drive the point home. She wasn't going anywhere. Certainly not in the middle of the night.

That was some big-time bad idea caveman shit that she would never agree to, but I could win her over.

Winning was kind of my thing.

## 18

*Liv*

"**S**hit. Shit, shit, shit."

I turned the key in the ignition again only to listen to it attempt to turn over and fail. *Not today. Any day but today.*

"Tonya," I said, as sweet as I could muster. "Honey. I know you're cold. I know you don't like it, but I have to get to work."

I gave her to the count of ten and turned the key again.

Tonya was not starting.

*Shit.* Did I say that already?

I was supposed to meet Novek at the rink at six which was fifteen minutes from now, only I was twenty minutes away with a car that I hadn't been able to start for the last ten minutes.

I was stuck in the parking lot of Dillon's fancy condo

building with limited options. There was no way I could go back upstairs and ask him for a ride. Forget the fact that he was fast asleep and snoring like a bear in hibernation. Rough night for the guy who'd dedicated himself to balling me stupid.

I could feel myself smiling and told myself not to look in the rear view mirror to check out the expression of smug satisfaction on my face.

But I was not showing up to the training center in Dillon's car. We did not need to add any fuel to the rumors.

An Uber was going to be expensive as fuck at this hour and would leave me without a car at work. But desperate times...

I pulled out my phone, ordered the Uber and let Novek know I was going to be late. After which there was nothing left to do but check my Gram, watch some TikTok videos... or replay over and over what Dillon and I did in his bed last night and try not to beat myself up about it.

Was it smart? No.

Was it the best sex I ever had? Absolutely yes.

Could I do it again? Absolutely not.

It was too easy to hang with him, too easy to sleep with him. Just sleep. He was a warm solid weight in bed and he kept everything super cozy even though he slept with the air conditioning on full blast.

So no repeats. We both knew the deal. This was temporary. We were temporary.

There was no other option.

"THERE YOU ARE!" Novek shouted from the ice. With his accent it was hard to tell if he was accusing me of something or worried about me. Previous to the conversation in the parking lot, I would have said he was accusing me of something. Now I wasn't sure. He skated over to the boards, sweat already streaming down his face.

"I had car trouble," I shouted. It was close to seven, but it had been out of my control.

"That's why I have two cars," he said without irony. "You okay?"

I narrowed my eyes, wondering what his angle was. Could it be he had no angle? He was just a clueless, incredibly gifted, supremely self-absorbed athlete? "I'm fine," I said.

"You could have called me," he said, skating backwards.

"I'm not showing up to work in your car, Novek."

"You could have called Cap."

My eyebrows lifted. Was he fishing for drama? If so, he wasn't getting it from me. "I can get myself to work."

"I'm just saying, Cap is one of those white knight guys, you know? Howdy ma'am and all that."

"Is that why you give him so much trouble?" I asked him. Novek skated around me and slid to a stop. "You think he's too nice?"

"Where I'm from," he said, his face soft without his sneer. God, he was young and extremely handsome. "You eat or get eaten. Teams only wanted one thing from me, score goals. Fill seats. I don't understand all the things the captain wants from me."

"Well, if you want to be on the team, you have to try."

He held out his arms, his white teeth blinding. "How does that woman singer say? This is me trying."

My jaw dropped open. "Are you quoting Taylor Swift to me, Novek? Did that just happen?"

"She has the voice of an angel and the legs of a super model. Undeniable."

Fucking right undeniable. I didn't see this coming, but I found myself rooting for Novek.

"Let's go, buddy. Center ice. We're fixing that momentum problem in your c-cut."

∽

*Dillon*

> Dillon: LIV, WHERE THE FUCK ARE YOU?

> Liv: Calm down. I'm at the practice facility. I told you I needed to be here early.

> Dillon: Why is your car still in the parking lot?

> Liv: The battery died. I had to take an Uber.

> Dillon: Why didn't you just wake my ass up so I could drive you?

> Liv: GIF: DUCK SNORING.

I CHUCKLED as I looked down at the image of the duck blowing through his beak like he was about to blow the roof off the house.

> Liv: Also, I'm not showing up at work in your car. Exactly what we're trying to avoid.

I stood outside my building, my near freakout when I saw her car in the parking lot without a trace of her around, slowly subsiding.

She was fine. She took an Uber instead of waking me up.

This was going to work in my favor, because she was going to need a ride home tonight. I would be there like a knight in shining armor with some takeout and a dirty mind. In the meantime, we needed to get her car to a garage and have them do a diagnostic on everything.

Tonya needed a new battery. An oil change. A tune up definitely.

Especially if she was considering driving that old thing to Montreal.

*No disrespect, Tonya.*

I fucking hated the idea of her driving away all by herself to start a new life someplace else.

Without me.

Montreal was six and a half hours away. Once the season was over maybe we could meet in Calico Cove. Better yet...

Holy shit. A lightning bolt of an idea came to me.

I opened up Google to check the Bruisers' schedule this season.

Bingo. Early November. Away game in Montreal.

Maybe we could do this long-distance. She would have her life and her career and I could have mine. When our schedules worked out we could see each other. No pressure. No compromises. No commitment.

Not that I was asking her to be my long-distance, low-commitment casual girlfriend or anything. Dudes had to be careful about that shit now.

No, this was just an opportunity to see her again. Maybe. If she got the job. Who was I kidding? She would get the job. I opened my phone to text Coach Renaud, who I once played for in the minors, to give her a glowing recommendation.

But I didn't.

She'd hate it if I meddled.

I put my phone in my pocket with a smile on my face.

I didn't have to choose the team over her. I didn't have to choose anything, I could just let it all happen.

## 19

---

*Later That Afternoon*
*Liv*

"You ready to leave?"

"Oh my god, Dillon, you startled me." I looked up from my computer, surprised to see it was after five in the afternoon. It had been a long day and tomorrow would be another one.

I was meeting Novek again, hopefully at six am, this time. If I was being honest with myself, I was excited. Away from all the other guys, he dropped his guard and actually wasn't an asshole. He was also an exceptional student. He'd made big improvements with just a few corrections.

"Hey, how was Novek today?" I asked.

Dillon's eyebrows went up. "Weird, actually."

"What do you mean?"

"Smith told a dumb sexist joke in the locker room and

Novek called him out on it. And he actually wanted to work on passing drills."

"I think he's trying to be a team player," I said.

"I'm not holding my breath," Dillon said. "But it would be amazing if he was. Now, you ready to go?"

"Go where?"

He looked around the hallway before stepping into the office and closing the door.

"Back to my place. You left a car there, if I remember correctly."

Right. The car. I'd planned to take an Uber back to his place. I wasn't going to be so stubborn that I didn't text him and ask him for a jump – battery jump only. But I hadn't thought about driving back there with him.

"You didn't have to wait around for me," I said.

He just gave me that look that said I was being stupid.

Spending money on an Uber when I was probably going to have to dump a whole bunch back into Tonya wasn't the smartest decision.

Please, let it just be a battery.

I packed up my stuff and followed him through the complex out to the parking lot.

"Coach tell you we start practicing at the arena next week?"

"Yes," I said, following closely behind him. "Although that would have been a next level prank. Moving the team and leaving me behind."

"Baby, I would have sent you GPS coordinates."

I snorted. "You're all heart, Heart."

We drove back in a relatively companionable silence to his building. For my part, I was putting the script together in my head.

*Sure, you can jump the battery.*

*No, you can't jump me.*

*No, I'm taking the car to the mechanic myself because I'm a big girl.*

*Okay, fine. If you want to come along just to make sure I'm not getting dicked over by a mechanic because I know nothing about cars – you can. But we're not getting something to eat after, so don't even suggest it.*

Be firm. Stick to my guns.

~

*Liv*

"CAN I get you guys any dessert?" our waiter, a nice young man named Jeremy, asked us. Of course he wasn't looking at us. He was looking at me. The woman.

Who more than likely wanted dessert. Because hello, it was dessert.

"Yes," I said. Because I did want dessert. "But no." I also said. Because I had restraint, and of course knew that dessert was a total luxury and not something I needed after demolishing a Nashville Hot Chicken sandwich with fries.

"So that's a no?" Jeremy asked, looking for clarification.

"Yes. I mean no. I mean, yes, I would like a dessert, of course, because it's delicious. But no, I won't be ordering it, because it's not necessary."

A lot of the night had been unnecessary. The mechanic had swapped out the battery but then Dillon insisted on a full diagnostic check and an oil change, which meant the mechanic was going to keep my car until tomorrow.

When Dillon suggested dinner, it wasn't like I had options because he was driving.

*Weak, Liv. Really super weak.*

So, I still didn't have my car, but the chicken sandwich had been delicious.

"This is clearly a process," Dillon said, sitting in the booth across from me. His big fat knees were touching mine, the booth was so small. "I'm so glad this isn't a date. Like if this was a date, I would think you're a little flaky right now."

I kicked his shin under the table.

"Ow!"

"I'm sorry, Jeremy. I admit, I tend to be a little indecisive when it comes to dessert, but no, I'm totally firm now. I do not want dessert. Thank you."

"Cool," he nodded.

"I'll have a piece of chocolate cake," Dillon announced.

My jaw dropped. "What are you doing?"

"Ordering dessert. I don't have a problem with indecisiveness."

"You can't order, if I'm not ordering," I insisted.

"Why not?"

"Because what am I supposed to do, just watch you eat cake right in front of me? How unfair is that?"

"Then I'll share," he said to me. To Jeremy, he tilted his head. "Dude, I'm sorry about this. My not-date is going through some things."

"I don't want to share your stupid chocolate cake," I muttered, crossing my arms over my chest.

Annoyed. Dessert-less.

"Then what would you share?" he asked me, nudging my calf with his stupid foot. "Liv?"

"The bread pudding with vanilla ice cream," I said quietly.

"We'll take the bread pudding with vanilla ice cream.

And two spoons," Dillon said, a smile spread across his face, making his Dimples Grande stand out.

I wanted to punch him in that smiling face.

Unfortunately, I also wanted to make out with him.

*Dillon*

"DILLON! YOU PROMISED."

"It's not even ten and you said you wanted to watch the end of it," I told her as I parked in front of my building. "What's the big deal?"

"The big deal is that we agreed. Food and that was it."

"Hey, I'm not the one who got all moony eyes over some Belgian guy on a Tour de France documentary. I'm also not the one who doesn't have a Netflix subscription. And before you ask, no, I'm not giving you my password because Netflix is cracking down on that shit and I already gave it to Wendy."

"First of all, do not disrespect the Green Jersey," she shot back. "Also, I can't believe you dismissed the entire sport like that. What those guys do is incredible."

"Do you want to come upstairs and watch the last two episodes, or not?"

We'd hung out in bed with our postcoital glow on, watching the Netflix documentary. It had been nice. So nice I wanted that again.

I held my breath while she bit down on her bottom lip. Poor Liv, she'd been fighting a losing battle all night. The countdown was on in our relationship and I was going to spend as much time with her as I could. So I wasn't making any of this easy for her.

"I guess I would like to see how it ends," she said. "But right after, you have to drive me back to my apartment"

"Absolutely. Two episodes and then I'm driving you back to your apartment."

"You know, we could just log into your account from my apartment."

"And sit on that instrument of torture you call a couch? No thank you, I don't want to start the season with an injury."

"You're a baby, you know that?"

"A baby with a Netflix subscription and a giant, very comfortable couch."

She blew out a long breath. "It is a really comfortable couch."

I did a quick, two fisted, Olivia Tylor-Branch style fist pump and she laughed.

"You're stealing my moves," she said as we got out of the Bronco and made our way back up to the penthouse.

The documentary was about last year's race, so all she had to do was Google the name of the winner if that's all she wanted to know.

However, if she wasn't going to say anything, neither was I.

*Liv*

"Don't let me fall asleep," I said. He had one of those L shaped couches. He was stretched out and I was laying down horizontal to his vertical. On his thigh. We'd finished the documentary on the Tour de France and we were now watching one about a new space telescope that came up as a recommendation. My excuse was, I was willing to watch all the free Netflix he would let me.

"'Kay."

"Seriously, once this is over you have to drive me back to my apartment."

"'Kay."

"Because I had that bread pudding so I'm really stuffed and when I'm full like this, I tend to get sleepy."

"Don't forget the vanilla ice cream," he said.

I would have pinched his jean covered thigh, but it was too muscle dense and I couldn't get a grip.

"Your thigh is too hard," I grumbled, and settled my body even deeper into the couch while I rolled my head on his thigh to find the perfect spot. "Also, you need throw blankets and pillows."

"I'm a man. Men don't need throw blankets."

"Men are weird," I sighed. "Throw blankets are delightful."

"Babe, watch the show," he said, then settled his palm softly on the top of my head.

"'Kay," I said, and my eyes drifted shut.

*Dillon*

I OPENED my eyes and squinted against the light. Shit. What time was it? The TV screen was off. Which meant Netflix had asked me if I was still watching, decided I wasn't, and turned itself off.

I picked up my phone that I had set on the couch arm.

2:40 am.

Shit. We'd both fallen asleep.

The question was now, what did we do?

If I woke her up, was she really going to make me drive her back to her apartment? She wouldn't, right? No one wanted to go to Siberia at three in the morning.

But I didn't want to spend the rest of the night on the couch. It wasn't good for my neck or back.

I glanced down at Liv and heard the soft sounds of sleep coming from her mouth. Not a snore. Nothing so inelegant. Just the steady sound of her breathing, and if I wasn't mistaken, a little wet patch had formed on my jeans where she'd drooled on me.

I smiled. That was another piece of her I had now. Something she would probably deny, but Liv drooled in her sleep. It shouldn't have made my heart ache, but it did.

Okay, we could do this. I was going to shift out from under her and gently lower her head to the couch. If she woke up, we would just go to bed, and forget any stupid protest she made about needing to get home. It was too late for that.

If she didn't wake up, I would just snag a pillow from the guest bedroom, and the duvet, and throw it on top of her. She could sleep out there and I would go back to bed.

The first part of the mission was easy.

I was off the couch and she was still sound asleep. She definitely needed a pillow and a blanket since she wouldn't have my body heat to keep her warm.

Or, if she was this passed out, I could just pick her up

and carry her to bed with me. She'd ultimately be warmer and more comfortable with me.

Except she didn't like to be picked up without her consent. It was a trigger for her. If she woke up, while I was carrying her, she might freak out. What if I dropped her? Hurt her?

No, the smartest thing to do was get her a pillow and a blanket and call it a night. I turned to go grab them from my guest room when she stirred.

"Whereareyougoing?" she said, all in one sleepy mumble.

"Bed," I whispered, tucking her hair behind her ear.

She lifted her arm, her eyes shut. Was this...? Was she asking me to carry her?

Gently, reverently, I bent down and got my hands under her. Given the amount of weight I lifted in the gym, she was nothing to pick up.

Despite the bread pudding.

The second I had her in my arms and I was standing straight, she curled into me. Buried her face into my chest and let out a soft sigh as she fell back asleep.

"I would never drop you. Ever."

Her faith...her trust...it was humbling. Intimate. More important than anything we'd done together. More important than half the shit I thought was important before this moment.

And that was terrifying AF.

## 20
———

*The Next Morning*
*Liv*

Ugh. The alarm on my phone was going off in the other room. I must have left it...

My eyes snapped open. I wasn't in my room. Or my apartment.

Milky gray sunlight crept through the curtains in Dillon's bedroom.

So much for all my tough talk yesterday. I'd been about as firm as Jello every time Dillon suggested anything else that would allow us to spend more time with each other.

Shit. I still didn't have my car.

Dillon rolled over and threw his arm over my hips, hauling me into the nest of his body. Like I was his very own snuggle pillow.

He was in his underwear, but I was fully dressed.

Huh.

A night together without having sex. Why did that feel like a weird milestone? Like we were a couple. Like we were friends.

I slipped out from his arms and made my way to the bathroom. He'd given me a spare toothbrush the other night, so I used that again and when I was done I dropped it in the cup where he put his own brush.

Something about that sight. About the toothbrushes in the same cup made my stomach do weird things. Weird things I didn't have time to think about. I washed my face, put my hair up into a ponytail, gave my armpits a good sniff and decided they'd be fine until I took a shower after the workout with Novek.

Out in his living room, I put on my shoes and grabbed my phone.

It was 5:30am. I was going to be late again and I was going to need to get an Uber. Again.

I still didn't have my car because Dillon couldn't leave well enough alone with just a new battery.

*Stupid, Liv! Weak, weak, weak.*

"Hey, come back to bed."

I jumped and almost dropped my phone. There was Dillon, in all his naked glory, completely unashamed of his body and his very evident morning wood.

"Can't. I have to get to the facility early."

I tried not to stare but failed.

Was my mouth watering? If you had asked me what attracted me to a man, I would have said personality. Humor. Overall energy and spirit. Certainly nothing as shallow as his looks. Or his body.

But looking at the cut of his shoulders, the way his waist tapered down into a V. Every muscle of his body defined. With his big proud dick on full display?

I had to amend my answer. Apparently, I was about as deep as a puddle.

Dillon was the walking definition of everything attractive in a man.

Did I have enough time to stuff as much of that cock into my mouth as I could, to tease him into coming? Groaning and shouting my name while he did? I'd have to brush my teeth again, so I didn't have cum breath when I met Novek for practice.

So, the answer was no. I didn't have time.

But I did have Novek's cell so I could tell him I was going to be late. Again.

*So weak, Liv.*

"Novek is making you show up this early again?" he was running his hand over the stubble of his jaw.

He was letting his beard grow out temporarily. It was a tradition to stop shaving once the team made the playoffs. But Dillon did it in the preseason too. Coming in with scruff on his face out of the gate was Dillon's way of announcing to the league what to expect from him by the end of the season.

Guys were so weird.

"Don't worry about it. Go back to bed. I'll Uber to work."

I was pulling the app up on my phone, when he walked over and took the phone from my hand.

"Hey, give that back."

"I'll drive you."

"You can't-"

"Liv," he said cutting me off. "You having car trouble and calling the team captain to pick you up is not a scandal. It's almost what any other coach on the team might do. They know this is my thing."

I bit my lip. He wasn't wrong. Novek had basically implied the same thing.

"Text Novek, tell him your car is still in the shop and you called me to pick you up. It will make sense. We'll get there when we get there."

"Fine," I said, reaching for my phone. I did what he said and tossed it on the couch.

"Now say good morning to me properly," he said, pulling me into his arms for a hug.

Great. Now I was swallowed by warm, naked muscle man and his penis was pressed against my stomach.

His penis seriously wanted me to be late.

"Good morning," I said, my voice muffled against his big chest. "Dillon…" I sighed.

"Don't say it." He must have interpreted my sigh. "I know."

"Yeah," I acknowledged, even as I held tight. Now he was rocking me side to side. "It's not good for either of us."

"Nope."

My hands cupped his butt, squeezed. He groaned into my ear.

Yeah. Fuck this. We had enough time.

I slowly sank to my knees in front of him and did exactly what I imagined earlier with this cock.

"Babe," he sighed, his head falling back on his shoulders as I worked the head of his dick with my mouth. One hand I used at the base of his cock to give him short tight pulses, while my other hand gently cupped his balls.

He made whimpering sounds in the back of his throat that made me believe he was wholly and totally a captive of the pleasure I gave him.

He was perfect. Everything about this moment was perfect. The quiet morning. The way he felt in my mouth.

Hard and hot. So full. He cupped the back of my head, not to force anything, it wasn't that kind of blow job.

He just wanted to touch me.

"Fuck, you're killing me, baby. Suck me like that. Just like that. Yes! Liv, fucking take off your shirt. Now."

I pulled my mouth away from his dick and let him go just so I could pull my t-shirt over my head and quickly toss my bra aside because I knew what he wanted.

I was going to be so late...

But he liked to see his cum on me.

And I felt like giving that to him.

He planted himself in front of me, bending down enough so that he could play with my hard nipples. Teasing them, tugging on them, until I could feel my own orgasm building.

"Your mouth," he muttered. "One more time."

I opened my mouth wide and slid him inside with my hand controlling him. Using my tongue, I played with that spot that drove him nuts, just under the head of his dick. I could taste the salt of his cum.

"Yes! Fuck, that's good!"

He jerked backed and braced a hand on my shoulder. His other hand reaching for his cock, which was in full explosion mode. Stripes of cum splattered my breasts and belly, and I reached inside my jeans with my hand to stroke my own clit.

I was so freaking close.

"No, let me." Dillon sank to his knees beside me and pulled my hand out of my pants.

"Ugh, I'm so close."

"Then let me do it with my tongue. Please, baby." He pushed me on my back and jerked at my jeans, until he could pull them down to my thighs. I felt the scruff of his growing beard on the top of my thighs, and then his tongue fluttered over my super sensitive clit. The orgasm hit me like a rocket.

It went straight through me and back again, but he didn't stop. He slid his finger deep inside me, and the way my jeans pinned my legs, the sensation was so filling. He wiggled that finger deep inside as his tongue worked my clit and then it happened.

Again.

It wasn't possible. Not this close. One on top of the other. But I was shaking and he was the only real and solid thing in a world dissolving into sparks.

"Dillon!"

He eased off and put one giant warm hand on the center of my chest as if to steady me. Or to feel my heartbeat to verify I'd survived. The other he pulled from between my legs. As I watched, he sucked on the finger that had been inside me like it was his favorite dessert.

"Better than bread pudding and ice cream, babe."

I snort-laughed and rolled towards him. "I'm going to be so late."

"We'll shower together," he said, helping me to my feet, his eyes pinned to my boobs.

"My eyes are up here, jerk," I said, although there wasn't much sting to it.

"Your eyes are up there, but your pretty titties are right here and I'm looking at them for as long as I can," he said, smiling at me. "Now, here is the plan. Quick shower, then we stop for coffee, then I'll take you to practice."

I nodded, following behind him to the bathroom.

"Hey," I looked back to the living room as something occurred to me. "I fell asleep on the couch last night. How did I get into the bedroom?"

Dillon turned. "You don't remember?"

"I remember a little bit of the space documentary and then I was waking up in your bed."

"You got up to pee, and you were half out of it. I just nudged you toward the bedroom and you crashed."

That made sense. Half the time I never remembered getting up to pee in the middle of the night, although I knew I did it.

"I didn't do or say anything embarrassing, did I?"

"Does drooling all over my leg count?"

"You know a gentleman would never tell a lady that she drooled."

"Oh babe. We both know I'm no gentleman."

I put my hand over his cheek, the Dimples Grande vanishing as the laughter faded from my face.

"Didn't we agree not to say it?" he said.

"I feel like we have to. Or we'll keep slipping. We can't do this anymore."

"I was thinking, if you take the job in Montreal we could still see each other sometimes. When our schedules worked out."

It shouldn't have hurt. I mean, of course he'd think that. I could take the job in Montreal and we could start some kind of casual long distance thing. Something that would fade into the background whenever he needed it to.

I would fade into the background while he did things that mattered more to him.

I shook my head. "Dillon, I can't be casual," I said. "Not with this. Not with you."

"Yeah, sure. I get it," he said. "We'll just see how things go."

Only I didn't think he did get it.

When I left. I was gone.

## 21

---

*The Following Week*
*Liv*

The contract from Montreal was burning a figurative hole in my figurative pocket. I couldn't think about anything else.

Three years. More money than I'd ever made in my life. My meeting with them this morning had been the kind of meeting a person dreams of. Red carpet. Donuts. I met the staff. I met the team.

Everyone from the maintenance guys to their star center forward had been excited to meet me.

Did I mention the money?

On the private jet back from Montreal I'd forwarded the contract they emailed to my dad.

He'd gotten back to me pretty fast with a, *looks good to me,* and, *is that salary a misprint?*

So why didn't I sign right there?

Instead I came right here to the facility from the airport so I could see the tail end of practice.

Which was bullshit. I came down to see Dillon. I needed to be honest with myself. Brutally honest.

I wanted to talk to him about that interview. About the city. About that salary. The office with the window and the chair with wheels that didn't squeak. I wanted to know what he thought and if he still thought me leaving was the best idea.

THE TEAM WAS WORKING a battle drill and everyone looked tough. Especially Smith, who wasn't letting in a single shot. Novek went up against O'Rourke and they went tooth and nail at that puck, but Novek squeaked it out in the end and the two of them bumped fists (that was new) and got back in line. Dillon won easily against Ron.

Coach blew the whistle and the guys headed my way to get water.

I took the opportunity to trash talk them all. With love, of course.

"O'Rourke, that looked like you were pulling a carriage behind you. Novek, those crossovers were so flat I'm surprised you didn't trip."

The guys all smiled at me and it felt like I was finally being embraced by some of them. Like a big pack of older brothers. Some infuriated me, some baffled me, but they were mine.

That's why I hadn't signed the contract.

*You'd feel that way about the guys in Montreal too. It would just take time.*

But what if none of them were as smart and coachable

as O'Rourke? Or as hard working as Skalsberg? Or as funny as Smith?

Or as captivating as Dillon?

"Where have you been?" Novek asked, and then squeezed water in his mouth. The guys were all catching a breath, leaning on their sticks. "Why are you dressed like that? Were you at a funeral? You look like you were at a funeral. Or court. It is very ugly."

I was wearing my navy-blue pant suit, the only thing I owned that wasn't athletic gear.

"Thanks, Novek. I ah...had an interview. In Montreal."

"For what?" Skalsberg asked. He took off his helmet to squirt water over his head and then shook like a dog, spraying everyone around him.

"A job." The guys didn't seem to be catching on. "Skating coach."

"For Montreal!" Smith said, like I'd said I was taking a job for Satan. "Those guys are assholes."

"Are you taking it?" O'Rourke asked, and the guys all echoed the question.

"Please say yes," Ron muttered under his breath as he skated past me.

Except, of course I heard him, which naturally only made me get my back up.

"I'm considering it," I said, making sure I did not look at Dillon, even though all I was aware of was Dillon scowling at me.

"Why are you leaving?" Novek asked. "Is it him?" Novek pointed at Dillon, whose eyes went wide.

"The fuck?" Dillon said.

"No," I said curtly. "My contract with the Bruisers was always going to be temporary. But enough about me. You guys get back to work."

I stepped back and the coaching staff split the team to do more specialized drills.

Dillon skated over, making a show of putting the water bottle on the bench.

"It went well?" he asked, and I nodded.

"Is it a lot of money?" I nodded again, unable to stop my smile.

"Let me take you out to celebrate."

After my sleepover last week he'd respected my space, but I kept thinking about those toothbrushes in the cup. I was a fool for wanting what was never going to happen.

But before I could say anything, Coach McKay was walking over to me.

"Coach Branch, a minute?"

Dillon skated away.

"Yes, Coach?" I asked.

McKay had started coming to the skating practices a few weeks back. He asked smart questions, made even smarter suggestions. I felt like we had a real partnership, so I'd told him about the Montreal interview a few days ago. I hadn't wanted to blindside him.

In some ways, it had felt like I was telling my father I wanted to move out. But he was cool and echoed what the assistant coaches had told me. This was just how it was done in professional sports. Nothing was ever permanent.

As far as bosses went, he was the opposite of a micro-manager and he led by example. He trusted his staff and let us do our thing. I didn't love the offensive assistant coach, Gary, more because he was an ass-kisser and less because I could tell he didn't respect me. I preferred straight shooters.

McKay was about as straight a shooter as they come.

"Can you stop in my office in an hour?"

That didn't sound good. "Sure. No problem. Is this about Montreal? Because I cleared the morning with Joyce."

"No," he said. "Well, yes, but we can discuss it further later today."

Shit. Had I screwed this all up? Was there some sort of unwritten rule, that sure you could interview with another team while under contract, but the second you did, you would be fired. McKay was probably going to just tell me to go ahead, clear out my locker and leave.

I could kiss that extension clause goodbye. But I'd already done that, really. Because Dillon didn't want me here and I couldn't be where I wasn't wanted.

Still, a sudden rush of panic filled my chest. This was happening. I was leaving Dillon. I wouldn't see him or talk to him or...

*Breathe. Breathe.*

Focus on the future. Things were going well.

The first preseason game was this Friday. My parents and brother were flying in tomorrow. I wondered if my dad had told my mom about that contract or if he was waiting so I could make a big announcement. They would be so proud. So proud.

Maybe they would apologize for not believing in me. Mom might cry. Dad would absolutely cry.

Everyone would be happy.

Only not really.

Because I could never tell them about this guy I liked. Who I was crazy about. I could never tell them how he made me think I could trust someone again. Be vulnerable with someone. I couldn't tell them how my heart was getting crushed.

Not from disappointment, or failure, but from straight up...

*Don't say it. Don't say it. If you don't say it, it's probably not true.*

He asked me to leave. He chose hockey over me. The team over me.

Dillon Le Coeur would *always* choose the team.

Which meant I had to choose myself. My life. My future career in skating. All of that was in Montreal.

Back in my office, I kicked off my very uncomfortable heels and put on my flip flops. Pulling open the laptop, I started to go through my emails. Despite the beautiful food that the team had put out for me, my stomach had been so nervous I hadn't eaten all day.

I opened the big drawer in the desk where I had learned to keep some snacks, and blindly reached inside for my family-size bag of peanut butter M&Ms. What I got instead was a handful of condoms.

My drawer was stuffed to overflowing with condoms. Individually wrapped, ribbed and mega-sized.

As pranks went, it was fairly generic. Swap out M&Ms for condoms. But I wasn't crazy about the sexual component of it. Was this Novek? It didn't feel like Novek. After these past few days of one-on-one practice, I thought we had some mutual respect. Even casual friendship. The guy had the ego of someone five times his size, but he was kind of funny.

These condoms did not feel like mutual respect.

Something chilling rolled down my spine.

Tentatively, I opened the other drawer on my left. Hoping for something innocent like a bunch of fake snakes. Instead, inside the drawer was a massive pink dildo. A typed note on top.

USE THIS INSTEAD

This wasn't a prank. This was a message. Every ounce of

outrage came to life. I wanted to take the stupid dildo, toss it on the ice, and ask which one of them thought this was funny.

Show some damn courage instead of an anonymous note.

Shit like this didn't work with me. Shit like this only made me want to stay and fight.

But there was no way to fight. My contract was up and Dillon told me I wasn't good for him.

So what was there to fight for? I'd thought today, watching them on the ice, that we were coming to feel like family.

Boy, was I wrong.

One asshole really didn't want me to be a part of the team.

One asshole and Dillon.

I slammed both drawers shut, careful to school my expression so that if I passed any of the guys on the way to the coach's office they wouldn't know how pissed I was.

By the time I reached Coach McKay's office, I was calmer. At least more in control of my emotions. I'd felt so good today. I'd felt important and successful and... special. Like all my hard work had earned me some VIP treatment.

Now I just felt like I'd been put back in my place. In a box.

I knocked on the door.

"Come in."

Just as I reached for the door handle, the door opened. Novek was on the other side.

"Hey Coach," he said with his chin nod.

"Did you put that shit in my desk?" I asked him in a low tone. I wasn't here to rat him out, but I needed to know if it was him.

He looked startled, but then he nodded. "Yes. The gloves? That was me."

"No. The shit that's in there now?"

He blinked at me, his dark, perfectly groomed eyebrows lowering like a storm cloud. "What's in there now?"

Novek was a lot of things, but an excellent actor he was not. He had no idea what was in my desk.

"Nothing. Forget it."

"Are you okay?" he asked, and for a second I thought about hugging Novek. Not as a guy or a member of the team, but as a human. Because I could really use a hug.

Then I thought of the asshole putting the condoms in my desk and I held myself firm. I wasn't giving the gossips anything else to work with.

"Great. Talk to you later," I said with a big smile, and stepped aside so he could walk by. I put my chin up and strode into McKay's office like it was center ice and I had a gold medal to earn.

"Have a seat, Olivia," he said, glancing up at me and then finishing what he was typing on his laptop.

I sat and crossed my legs, only to reveal my flip flops and my gnarly feet. Whatever. He could deal with it. His office was nice. Huge. He had a big couch along the wall that faced the floor to ceiling windows that looked out over the rink. The Zamboni was doing it's snail-like laps, leaving slick ice in it's slow wake.

Behind him, there were pictures on a shelf. He had three daughters and a round faced wife with a huge smile.

McKay pushed away his laptop and smiled, which was a little bit like seeing a bear smile. It kind of put a person on edge.

"So...Montreal?"

"Yes. Montreal," I repeated. "Thank you for letting me take the morning to interview."

He waved his hand. "You have every right to be looking out for your future and I knew about their interest before you did. The GM called me weeks ago and I gave you a glowing recommendation. He knew a coach you worked with on the Junior's team."

"Thank you," I said, feeling myself blush.

"But," he said. "I hope you will give us a shot to make our offer before you make your decision."

"I'm sorry...what now?"

"I know you had a rocky start with Novek and some of the guys didn't make it easy on you. More women in the NHL is good for everyone, but there are going to be some Neanderthals on every team."

The dildo and condoms were on the tip of my tongue.

"But you held your own, Coach Branch. Admirably. You made incredible progress with many of the players and have been a big part in turning our star forward into a team player."

"It's been a pleasure," I said. "Especially, if I may say, O'Rourke. He's the most coachable kid I've ever worked with."

"Yeah, you've lit a fire under him too, and made my job a whole lot harder, because now I might have another mega star ego on the team."

I shrugged like *whoops,* which made him laugh.

"I've gotten the okay from management to extend your contract through the regular season."

It took several seconds to process what Coach McKay said. "Wait. What?"

"Whatever Montreal has offered you in salary, we will

match, and knowing their cheapskate GM, they low balled you, so we'll add ten percent."

Oh. My. God.

"They...it was a three-year contract."

"Then so is ours," he said, and took a pen to a piece of paper in front of him. "I've also included a housing stipend so you can move to a place in town of your choosing."

"Three year contract, same money and you'll pay for my apartment?" I asked.

"Okay, twist my arm, I've seen your terrible car. I wouldn't let my daughter drive that rust bucket in a Maine winter, we'll throw in a stipend for new transportation."

"My dad hates my car," I said, numb with surprise.

"Good man. Now, I know you'll need some time to think. To look over the new contract. I'll have the changes made to this one and email it to you as soon as possible."

Two contracts in one day? Five months ago I didn't have a job, and now I had two?

"Does the team know you're offering me this job?"

"No, Coach. I didn't want to get their hopes up."

That was the nicest thing he'd ever said to me. That anyone had ever said to me.

I couldn't feel my legs when I stood and made my way out of his office. Like a zombie, I closed the door behind me and made my way back to my office. I didn't want to think about cleaning the drawers out. I didn't really want to think about anything negative at all.

So, I took myself down to the cafeteria for a celebratory grilled cheese.

That contract...more money? They would pay for my apartment and my car? How could I say no to that?

This was everything I could have wished for.

There was just one big problem.

A six-foot two man with Dimples Grande who wanted me gone.

Was I really going to give up something so good for me, for him? What a terrible compromise – I gave up a great job and got my heart broken and he...what?

What exactly were the consequences for Dillon? He got to go back to playing in top form because I wasn't around to distract him?

My phone binged and I saw I had an email from McKay. The new contract.

Well, I thought, the first thing I had to do was see if this deal was as good as it seemed. I forwarded the email to my father.

*Check this one out for me too, please? Let me know if it's as good as it seems? Or if there's something I'm not seeing.*

What was I going to do? More importantly, what did I really want?

I was going to need more than a grilled cheese.

This kind of decision making required chocolate cake.

## 22

---

*Bank Trust Arena*
*Thursday*
*Liv*

I watched the team take the ice at the arena. The echoes in the place enormous compared to the much smaller practice facility. I tried to imagine what it would sound like filled with fans chanting Dillon's name. How he might pull their energy into himself.

It's what I used to do when I skated. Just reach out and take the crowds thrilling excitement and let it fuel me.

God, it had been such a high to perform. To skate in front of a cheering arena.

That life was over for me, but Dillon still had it. Still craved it.

It was for all of this, that he was willing to turn his back on us.

I needed to talk to him. I still hadn't made a decision.

Dad got back to me about the Bruisers' contract with

one word: *WOW*. He went on to say it was a better offer on every level.

But he said if I really wanted to go to Montreal I could use the Bruisers' offer to nudge the Voyageurs' higher. That seemed like a level of negotiation I was not comfortable with. But how could I take a lesser deal just to give Dillon what he wanted?

I couldn't.

I needed to tell him.

I hadn't been sleeping well. Eating wasn't much fun. I almost caved and paid for Netflix just so I could rewatch the documentary we'd watched together, but then realized how pathetic that sounded. Like watching a documentary might bring him back.

The worst part of all of it was, he seemed totally fine. Just skating away, laughing with Skalsberg like he didn't have a care in the world.

Didn't he miss me?

We'd only been together a handful of days total, was it stupid to think I'd made any kind of permanent impact on him?

I needed to let his indifference fuel my ability to get over him. Put him behind me and move on. Except taking this job meant staying put.

*You have to tell him.*

I was going to. Every day after practice, I planned it, but then I turned chicken and ran.

"Intimidated by the big stage?" Ron came up behind me from the stands as I stared out over the ice, lost in my thoughts.

I jumped, because I hadn't heard him come up. And because it wasn't common for us to talk. He'd made it clear over these last several weeks he was not a fan.

I didn't really know how to respond.

"It's just ice, like any other ice. Come get your feet cold," he said, with a smile. Then he took off his blade guards and headed out onto the ice.

Had the coach told him to be civil to me in an effort to get me to sign the contract? That seemed the most likely answer. I didn't believe Ron suddenly had a change of heart about me all on his own.

Whatever. I removed my own blade guards and stepped onto the ice.

It was a casual practice today. There was also a group of kids from a local school sitting in the stands, excited to see their heroes goofing around. Today the players were just getting used to the sounds and size of the arena.

Sweet O'Rourke looked just as wide-eyed as the kids.

The first preseason game was tomorrow night at seven.

I took to the ice and dug my blades in, feeling them catch and bite and propel me forward. This feeling never got old. Pure freedom. Like if I could just go fast enough, my blades would leave the ice and I would be flying.

Soaring.

The guys circled the ice. Everyone looked easy and loose ahead of the first game. They were waving up at the kids who were losing their minds. I thought about sharing the ice with these monsters of men, proud of how I'd been able to improve almost all of them. At this level of athleticism, the only improvements that could be made were going to be incremental. But everything counted.

"Hey, Coach," Cody skated by me with a wave.

I gave him a chin nod, then I caught Dillon out of the corner of my eyes. The big oaf took to the ice like he'd been born to skate.

Maybe Dillon wouldn't care anymore if I took the Bruisers' job. Maybe these days apart had shown him he wasn't as into me as he'd thought. And if he didn't care about me, then I couldn't be a distraction for him.

Great, that only made me feel shittier.

It felt like there was no good answer in this for me.

Our eyes locked across the ice, the way they did when we met in Calico Cove. Everyone on the ice disappeared and it was just him standing there. So big and solid and real.

His dimple flashed when he gave me a tiny half smile, but then he turned and skated away like I wasn't there.

My chest hurt. No. It was my heart.

How long until I wasn't turned inside out by every half smile, every passing glance? How long before he was just one of the guys?

Would he ever be? Could all the money in the world make it easier to get over him?

Music suddenly filled the arena. One of those loud hard rock themes that played at every sporting event. A song that was meant to motivate the crowd to cheer louder and harder. It was blaring and distracting, but that was the point. The players needed to not be distracted by it. They needed to be focused on the opponent and the puck.

A few of the guys had come to a stop on the edge of center ice. They were looking up at the Jumbotron screen above the rink. Two big screens facing either end of the arena. Something up there got their attention.

All of them winced and then pointed up. They were probably showing highlights of some past game. Maybe Skalsberg smashing someone against the boards.

Their groans got louder. While I had no interest in whatever gross display of violence they were watching, if hockey was about players getting smashed up and I was going to be part of a hockey team, then this was stuff I needed to get used to. Even revel in when we came out on the winning end.

Except when I skated to a position where I could see the screen, I realized it wasn't a hockey game. There were only two people on the ice. In costumes.

It was a pairs figure skating routine.

It was strange too, because I recognized Brian before I did myself.

Like for a second I thought I was watching him with a new partner. Was this some kind of a prank? Showing my old partner with this new partner on the ice? Was I supposed to be jealous?

Except the skaters blew by the camera at a dizzying speed and I saw me. Arms stretched, my joy in competing absolutely beaming out of my face. My entire body. I was vibrating with happiness. Focus. Drive.

Only the routine didn't look familiar to me.

What the hell was I watching...

I felt it in my stomach first. That moment when Brian lifted me up in the air with his right hand. The heel of his palm digging into my pelvis. We'd practiced that lift every day for weeks, months. Over and over again. He spun around one, twice, his other hand lifting as he prepared to drop me in a controlled, dramatic descent so he could launch me into a spinning throw across the ice.

"Shut that off! Now!"

Through the buzz in my head I recognized Dillon's voice. He was angry.

I couldn't close my eyes. They were locked, instead, on Brian. Watching as my descent started. There was no control. The drama was raw and unplanned and horrific

I'd never seen this footage. Not once. There had been no point. Brian and our coach told me my blade had gotten caught in the lapel of Brian's costume, which threw off his balance and... it had been an accident.

All of it an accident. No one to blame.

Only there it was on the giant screen in the middle of the rink. Like it was moving in slow motion when in reality it only took seconds. There it was, my skate just a shade out of position. He lost control and then it was my head crashing into the ice, my skull cracking, the blood...

The buzzing got louder, my vision filled with black dots.

I didn't feel a thing as I dropped to the ice.

*Dillon*

"Liv!"

She dropped like a stone. Like she had no bones left in her body to hold her up. Her head hit the ice and I felt a spike of fear that felt like someone had shot me with an arrow.

"What happened?" Coach McKay was in sneakers making his way to the ice.

I looked around, but the team seemed to be in shock. Like they had no idea that watching the video of Liv nearly dying would be so traumatic to her she'd pass the fuck out.

Falling onto my knees next to her, I gently turned her, so she was flat on her back. Her eyes were closed, and her breathing was shallow.

"Liv, baby, come back to me," I said gently slapping her cheek gently, all while the rage roared inside me.

"Dillon, back off," Coach tried to tell me. "We should get a doctor."

"Don't you fucking touch her! Nobody fucking touches her. Do you understand me? Who did this?" I shouted at those who had dared to skate closer. "Who put that video on the fucking Jumbotron?"

Liv's eyes were still closed but she was coughing and trying to breath at the same time. The fall probably knocked the wind out of her. I gathered her in my arms. There was no blood. Arms and legs didn't look out of position. Her right cheek was red under her eye. She'd fallen on that side of her face, but it didn't look broken or too swollen.

She'd fainted and it had knocked the wind out of her. That was all.

"Liv," I whispered to her. "Baby, open your eyes."

She shook her head in a jerk. "Can't watch," she croaked.

"I know, I know. I'm going to get you out of here."

She was poised to have a meltdown and I knew the last place she would want to do that would be in front of the team and the coaching staff.

"Listen to me," I said, bending down to her ear. "I have to pick you up."

"No," she said, pushing her hand weakly against my chest. "No!"

"I'm going to pick you up and take you off this ice. Liv, you can't skate on your own."

She curled up into herself. Right there on the ice in front of me. Tight in the fetal position. I had no idea what was going through her head right now, but it wasn't good.

"Come on, baby. You know I'm stubborn. We're going to get you off this ice."

"You'll drop me," she whispered.

I bent down over her, as close to her ear as I could. "I swear on my life I will not drop you, Liv. You trust me. I know you do. Please, Liv. I. Will. Not. Drop. You."

I must have gotten through, because she didn't fight me when I slid my arms under her body. Instead she curled into my chest, her arms circling my neck. Just like she'd done that night she'd fallen asleep on the couch.

More careful than I'd ever been in my life, I got up onto my skates and slowly, like my life depended on it, took her off the ice.

Gary had a medical kit in his hand on the home side bench. I waved him off. We were going directly to a hospital to see if she had a concussion.

"Dillon, talk to me. What the hell happened?" Coach McKay was following us to the locker room.

I didn't bother with an answer. I needed to change into sneakers and get her stuff too. She wasn't talking now, just had her face pressed into my neck. Her body felt like dead weight and it made me murderous.

I turned before I reached my locker and looked at the coach, who seemed perplexed by the whole thing, rather than angry.

"You find out who did that," I told him coldly. "Find out whose idea it was to play that video-"

"Dillon, be serious. They only thought it was a joke," Coach said, cutting me off. "They couldn't have known how she would have reacted."

"How did all those kids in the stands like it?"

I saw Coach realize the PR nightmare this little joke had brought his way.

"You find out who did that," I repeated, as serious as I had ever been in my life. "Or I don't play tomorrow."

Coach opened his mouth only to shut it when he saw my expression.

"Now leave us alone. She doesn't want anyone to see her like this."

"We're not done talking," he said, and left the locker room.

Gently, I sat Liv down on the bench, but I wouldn't let her go. Not until I could see her gather herself. I looked into her eyes. They didn't appear dilated, which was a good sign. I'd seen enough concussions in my day to recognize the look of a badly rung bell. I didn't think she was concussed, but I knew something else had broken deep inside her.

"I'm changing, we're getting your shit, then I'm taking you to a hospital to get checked out."

She didn't say anything, just reached up and placed her hand against my face. Her eyes said everything I needed to hear.

"No, babe," I said. "I didn't drop you."

## 23

*Dillon*

She refused to go to a hospital.

I insisted she see a doctor. So, we settled on an urgent care not far from her apartment. The doctor checked her out and said she didn't see any signs of a concussion. There didn't even appear to be a lump on her head. According to the doctor, Liv's cheek had taken the brunt of the fall. She had a bruise forming under her eye that was going to be painful.

Liv answered all the questions like she was completely checked out and I knew she just wanted to lie down and pull the covers over her head.

I wanted to take her back to my place, but she insisted we go back to her apartment because that's where her stuff was.

She didn't tell me to leave when she unlocked the door to her place, but she didn't exactly invite me inside, either. I just followed her through the small living room to the bedroom and waited.

She was in her head. *So* in her head right now. Replaying the accident, reliving the pain and suffering that came after it. I didn't know where she was, I only knew she wasn't here with me and I hated it.

It felt like I couldn't touch her. It felt like she was far away. It felt like...

Like I'd lost her.

Ironic, considering I'd pushed her away.

She took off the Bruisers t-shirt and stared down at it. All she'd wanted to do was help those guys and one of them had done that to her as a thank you. I was going to kill whoever was responsible. And it wouldn't be enough. It would never be enough for having done this to her. Having put her in this state.

"I liked being a part of a team," she whispered. "It's why I skated pairs. And the guys..." she took a deep shuddery breath. "I thought we were a team."

She balled the shirt up and threw it in the corner.

She peeled off her leggings like she didn't care that I was standing in the doorway. Wearing only a sports bra and a pair of black cotton panties, she retrieved a pair of sweats and a sweatshirt from a dresser drawer and pulled them on. Comfort clothes. That's what she'd wanted.

She crawled into bed and rolled to her side, facing the wall.

I should leave. She didn't want me here. She was about to have some major crying jag and it was going to make me as uncomfortable as hell. I hated it when the women in my life cried. Wendy, or worse, my mom. It made me feel useless because I couldn't *do* anything. Couldn't fix it. I could only sit there and feel it all with them.

Maybe that was the point.

Liv lifted her arm and waved me over. Like she wanted me inside the room. Maybe even in the bed with her.

"Get naked please. I want your penis, but not like that. Okay?" she said quietly.

I shouldn't have understood what she meant. But, I knew exactly what she wanted. My body heat. Physical connection. Comfort.

In seconds I stripped off everything, dropping my jeans near the bed, and slid in behind her on the far too small mattress. I pressed my dick into the small of her back, so she could feel me there. I wrapped my arms around her chest and pulled her back against me, my knees against the backs of hers. I tucked my nose in behind her ear and just breathed her in.

Fuck. I'd missed her.

I'd been short tempered and angry all week. I didn't want to sleep in a bed that she wasn't in. I didn't want to eat a meal where I wasn't sitting across from her. I'd done a pretty good job of not showing her how I felt, but inside I was a raw mangled mess of emotions.

This, here, now, with her in my arms, was the first peace I'd felt in days.

From the moment we met, she had filled up this space inside me I hadn't known even existed. And this whole week, that space had throbbed with emptiness. A fucking echo chamber in my chest that just kept asking, *where is she? Where is she?*

She was here. Now. Safe in my arms.

"It's okay to let go," I said softly. "I've got you."

Her shoulders, her chest, her whole body started to shake. The sobs when they came were so mournful, so painful, I clenched my teeth hard, feeling her heartbreak inside me.

"Why did they do that?" she cried.

"I don't know, baby."

"That was the end for me. That was it. Everything I loved. Everything I was."

It was hard to make out the words. She was crying and hiccupping through it, but I understood.

"No, Liv. That wasn't everything. That was just a part of you. You're so much more."

"I lost everything!"

This, I thought. This was how it was going to feel when hockey was over for me too. In a way like…dying. But Liv was wrong. Not everything was gone the day she fell.

She hadn't even met me yet.

I wanted to tell her that. I wanted to tell her that this moment, the two of us here in her bed, mattered. That this was important. And the team…the guys who listened to her and the work she did so they could improve.

So important, and it all came after the fall. But how could I say any of that when I knew she was leaving? When I was the one who told her she had to go.

Through her tears I could hear the sound of a doorbell ringing. Then a knock on her apartment door. She sucked in a breath and pulled the blankets over her head.

"No!" she cried. "I don't want anyone to see me like this."

I couldn't imagine who it was. Maybe the neighbor downstairs who heard her crying and wanted to check in on her. Maybe Coach McKay had a name for me and wanted to deliver it in person. That was enough to motivate me away from her body and out of her bed.

I pulled on my jeans and my t-shirt. Whoever it was, wasn't staying long.

If this was the fucking UPS guy looking for a signature, he picked the wrong damn time.

"This better be-" I pulled open the door only to find a couple on the other side of the door. A dark-haired man with glasses and a silvery-blonde woman with gray eyes. The smiles on their faces froze when they saw me, then slowly melted away.

An oversized teenager stood behind them.

"Holy shit, you're The Heart," the kid said, all smiles.

Oh *shit*.

"You're Liv's family?"

Her mother eyed me up and down, taking in my rumpled hair and bare feet. I might as well have been naked under her steely gaze.

HER FATHER CLEARED HIS THROAT. "I'm Miguel and this is my wife Caroline and our son Billy."

"Dad."

"Sorry, Bill. We're here to see our daughter, Mr. Heart. So if you wouldn't mind."

"Dad, no. It's Dillon Le Coeur. He's team captain."

Her mom had enough of this and called out over my shoulder. "Olivia! Honey! We're here."

"Mommy?"

The sound of her daughter crying was like a siren. She pushed past me and ran across the living room, through the kitchen and down the tiny hallway to her daughter.

"Why is my sister crying?"

I'd clearly gone from hero to zero in the kid's eyes. He also pushed past me, but made sure to bump his shoulder against mine on his way past.

Protective brother.

Her father pushed his glasses up his nose and also assessed me.

"If you're the reason my daughter is crying like that, I would suggest we go someplace and have a conversation," he said.

This small man, in his mid-fifties, with a dad-bod paunch was calling me out. Completely not afraid.

But like her protective brother, it only made me like him more.

"I can explain," I said lamely.

"Yes, then you should do that," her dad said.

CAROLINE AND BILL stayed behind with Liv, who was in no hurry to leave her bedroom. Miguel and I walked down the street to the Starbucks on the corner. It felt like a job interview and an interrogation rolled into one very strange experience.

We sat at a little round table in the corner and I didn't know what to do with my knees or elbows, but Miguel sat there, patiently.

"Dillon," he said. "Tell me what this team has done to my daughter."

I told him about the pranks. The gloves left in her office, the puck fired at her ass.

"Yes, she told us about that," he said with a dark frown.

But when it came time to explain the video on the Jumbotron, I felt my throat closing up.

Miguel clapped a hand on my shoulder like he understood what I was going through. When I was done, Miguel leaned forward, his dark eyes behind his glasses damp with emotion. I liked this guy. I liked that Liv had a dad like this.

"She's never seen it," Miguel said. "We made sure in the beginning while she was recovering. Brian insisted that we show her. He said it would bring her closure. I called bull-shit on that. I think he needed to prove to her it wasn't his fault."

"The fucker dropped her," I said. "It *was* his fault."

Miguel lifted a hand like it was ancient history. "We refused. And when she was fully recovered, she had no interest in seeing it."

"Why would she? Who wants to relive that?"

"Indeed. To be forced to relive it, in front of colleagues, and," he tipped his head towards me. "Friends. Well, it's especially cruel, isn't it?"

"I'm going to find out who did it."

"I appreciate that it matters to you. But all I care about is my daughter, and that working environment isn't good for her."

I couldn't disagree. How could I? The Bruisers had put her through the fucking wringer, and she deserved so much more. So much better.

Miguel let out a long breath and looked out the window. "I remember it all too well. Imagine being in the stands. Imagine watching it happen in real time. I thought she was dead when I saw the blood. There I was. Her father. Sitting a hundred feet away and there was nothing I could do to stop it. I just watched it happen and I thought... my baby is dead."

My throat closed up again and my eyes burned. I could not imagine the pain her family went through watching that live. The video was bad enough.

"But my Livvy, she's a fighter. Always has been. She gets that from her mother. When they told her she was never going to skate competitively again though..." He stopped and took off his glasses, used his napkin to wipe his eyes. Watching this father pull himself together was humbling. "Well, for a while, Caroline and I thought she would never pull out of it. We encouraged therapy. Even medication for depression, but Livvy would have none of that. She told us she was grieving and to let her do it in peace. So we gave her that. Then she started working with Billy's hockey coach to improve the teams' skating. All the tips and tricks and bio mechanics her coach had drilled into her for years, and suddenly she was reborn. One thing led to another and she got the job out here. We thought she was taking too big of a leap, moving too fast. But we were wrong. The job offers prove she's doing exactly what she needs to do."

At this point I had to interject. "Offers? I know about Montreal, but..."

Her father looked confused. "The Bruisers offered her an incredible package."

"What? When?"

"Same day as the Montreal offer."

I leaned back in my chair. It was like a blow to the chest. A part of her life she hadn't shared with me. "She didn't tell me."

Her father lifted a shoulder, and his expression slid right between my ribs like a blade.

*Why doesn't she trust you?*

Because I told her she had to leave. I felt sick to my stomach.

"I can't tell if you're upset or relieved," he told me.

I couldn't tell either.

My phone buzzed and I took it out of my back pocket. Coach McKay, but I wasn't ready to pick up yet. I'd texted him from the urgent care that Liv was okay. So this call was about me refusing to play. I was probably in violation of my own contract. No doubt my agent would be hounding me next.

I declined the call and put the phone back in my pocket.

"None of this was supposed to happen," I muttered.

"I assume you're talking about getting involved with my daughter. Olivia hasn't told us anything about you, but it's obvious you have some kind of relationship."

My laughter had no humor behind it. "We knew it was a bad idea. But it was like...it was like we didn't have a choice."

From the second I saw her on the ice, we had seemed inevitable. Undeniable.

"Hmm. That's the crazy thing about love. You can't plan for it, it happens on its own schedule."

"This isn't love," I said, shaking my head.

Miguel didn't flinch. Just pushed his glasses up his nose and sipped on his coffee.

"No?"

"No, sir. I'm sorry. Your daughter doesn't love me, she deserves someone who puts her first and that's not me. Not right now. A man can only have one love at a time, and for me that's hockey. I only have so many years left and I'm giving it everything I have for as long as I can. Relationships are a distraction. Liv and I have proven that. I can't think straight when she's not around. I can't think straight when she is. I can't focus like I need to."

"Oh, I see. Well, then *clearly* it's not love."

"We were a mistake. From the very beginning. It would have been better if we'd never met."

Behind me, I heard a gasp. Miguel lifted his eyebrows, his expression clear: *You've stepped in it now, son.*

Slowly, I turned to face Caroline, Bill and Liv.

"Liv-"

She held her hand up to stop me.

"I heard you," she said. "Loud and clear." Her eyes were swollen, her throat sounded raw. Her cheek was starting to bruise. She looked beaten down. It broke my fucking heart. "I just came for a Frappuccino. Mom, can you get that for me and bring it back to the apartment?"

"Yes, honey. Of course."

She left the store, striding past the window with her chin up and her back straight. A fighter, every step of the way.

I stood up to follow her, but her brother stepped in front of me.

"No, man. I don't care who the fuck you are. You don't disrespect my sister like that."

"I'm not... I didn't mean it like it sounded. I have to talk to her."

Caroline patted my arm. "I think what she needs is space right now. You understand that, right? Mr. Heart."

"I'm not...my name isn't-"

"Oh honey, you just broke my daughter's heart," she said calmly, her expression equal parts fury and pity. "I don't really care what your name is. Now, if you'll excuse me, I need to get a Frappuccino. You have much success with your hockey career."

Without another word towards me, Miguel stood and joined his family at the counter.

And just like that I was dismissed by the entire Tyler-Branch family.

Friday morning, an email was distributed team-wide that Olivia Tyler-Branch was no longer with the team. That she would be starting with the Montreal Voyageurs in two week's time and the Bruisers' organization wished her the best of luck with her new team.

# 24

*Montreal*
*Liv*

The calls and texts started to come as soon as I got to Montreal. I should have blocked his number, but I didn't. Couldn't. However, I was strong enough not to pick up his calls.

Just too weak not to read his texts.

Dillon: Liv, please pick up the phone. It can't end this way between us. I won't let that be the last thing you hear me say, because it isn't true.

Dillon: I found the condoms and the dildo in your office. Fuck. Olivia, that isn't a harmless prank. I took it to the General Manager and HR. We had a team meeting, so far no one is fessing up. But I'm going to find out who did this. I'm so sorry that happened to you. I'm so sorry you didn't think you could tell me. You're the strongest person I know.

Dillon: Did you see they are making another Tour de France documentary?

Dillon: O'Rourke says hi. He's sitting out the next game with me. Sometimes I forget he's only 24. Did you know he was married?

Dillon: You're not texting me. Clearly. You're stubborn as fuck. You know that about yourself, right?

Dillon: I miss you. It's the thing I'm absolutely not allowed to say, right? I mean, all of this is my fault. I invited you back to Calico Cove. I made you stay with me at my place. I made all of that shit happen. It was just… I liked you, Liv. I liked spending time with you so much even though I knew it was a mistake. I still like you. I needed to say it. Maybe you'll read this, maybe you won't, but I needed to say it. I like you more than anyone.

Dillon: My agent called and the team is making noise about me not playing. I have to play. I'm sorry I didn't make the person pay for what he did. I'm sorry for everything, Liv.

Dillon: We open at Cleveland. I'm going to score and when I do, I'll find the camera. When you see me looking into it, I'm looking at you. So watch. Okay. You hear me, Liv?

"Oh no," Billy said, even as I plopped down on the couch next to him. "You are not watching this game."

I kicked my feet up on the brand new ottoman in front of the brand new – and very comfortable - couch, and grabbed a handful of the popcorn from the brand new popcorn bowl in my brother's lap.

"I can watch a stupid hockey game, Billy."

"How many times do I have to tell you to call me Bill?" He pulled the popcorn bowl out of reach.

"A million and it won't be enough," I said.

"Mom, she's doing it again!" Billy shouted over his shoulder towards the kitchen, where my mother was filling my freezer with food. She'd been a casserole queen while Dad, Billy and I bought and put together an entire furniture store in my brand new Montreal apartment. "She's being morbid as fuck and now she wants to watch him play hockey."

Mom popped into the living room, a dish rag in her hands and a frown on her face. "Billy, language please. Olivia, do you really think this is a good idea?"

My mother only ever called me Olivia when she thought I was being stubborn or stupid. I'd been getting a whole lot of Olivia the last few weeks. They didn't love me going to Montreal. They were scared that the team would treat me like the Bruisers had. They were worried I didn't speak French and there was that hassle with the visa.

It was endless and I loved my family very much, but it was time for them to go. Really.

Dad, without me knowing, had negotiated a few of the Bruisers' offerings into my contract with Montreal and they signed it without a fuss. So, I had a new car. A sleek hybrid SUV that looked nothing like Tonya. In honor of my new Canadian home, I was naming her after legendary speed skater and cyclist, Clara Hughes.

"It's just a game, Mom. It's not going to kill me. I mean, I was an assistant coach for the team. I had a hand in improving the play for some of those players."

"What's not going to kill you?" my dad asked, stepping into the living room from the guest bedroom where Mom and Dad had been sleeping. Billy slept on the couch. Did I mention I was ready for them to leave?

"Liv wants to brood over her ex-boyfriend," Billy said to my dad.

"I'm not brooding. I'm just watching. He's not my ex-boyfriend. He's not my ex-anything."

*Then why does it hurt so much?*

"Hmm," Dad said, joining us on the giant couch. There was still room for mom if she ever stopped cooking. "Then you'll be okay with us changing the channel."

"Change it and die, Old Man." I gave him my scary scowl and my father laughed.

Dad reached for the popcorn and I was sandwiched between them. It felt good. It felt safe. But it didn't feel as right as it did when Dillon was holding me. Or when he tucked my thigh over his so we would fit better together.

I hated that. I hated that he'd ruined me like that.

"Fine, we'll just sit here and watch a hockey game. What's the harm in that?"

"Exactly," I muttered.

The commercial break was over and the teams were stepping onto the ice. My heart froze at the sight of those guys; O'Rourke and Novek. Skalsberg, looking terrifying. Smith in his custom stars and stripes goalie mask.

"Hmm. Oh, look. There he is. Your Mr. Heart."

"Dad!" Both Billy and I groaned at the same time. I knew he was putting me on with the whole heart thing, but still it was annoying.

"I feel sorry for him," my dad said as the camera switched to the commentators.

"Because he blew it with me? I don't think he cares, Dad. He's doing what he loves, remember?"

"No, I feel sorry for him because he doesn't understand

how life works yet. He reminds me of you actually. Back when you were competing. Only winning mattered. You didn't have the whole picture back then."

I didn't know what to say to that because he was right. My focus was so narrow that skating was my whole life. And honestly, there was a certain easiness to it back then. Only one thing mattered and so I didn't have to let in anything else.

But that all changed when I fell.

I thought my world was ending, but it was only changing.

"Life should be bigger than just a sport," Dad said.

"This is why they're making me go to college," Billy muttered, rolling his eyes.

"And you'll thank us for that," Dad said.

With some distance and perspective, I could see how my family had sacrificed so much for me. Everything was always about me back then. Now they had this whole other world.

Billy's hockey. My dad was in a chess club. And my mom was on the board of an organization dedicated to saving the historic landmarks of Seattle. Things they never had a chance to do when we were all focused on my skating career and goals.

"Did I ever thank you guys for putting up with me? When I always made everything about skating? I owe you so much and I don't think I ever said thank you."

"Oh, here we go," Billy groaned. Just like an eighteen-year-old would when feelings were complicated. "She's going to get all mushy on us because we built her furniture."

"I'm not mushy. I'm just...seeing things a little more clearly."

My dad patted my knee. "That's good, honey. That means you're growing up."

We watched the referee drop the puck on the ice. Dillon's instincts in a face-off were unmatched in the league. He immediately took control of the puck and passed it back. Cody was actually on Dillon's line with Novek. Not only had he made the team, he was starting and I could take some pride in that.

Game play happened so fast. A pass, then another pass, then Dillon was in front of the net and he hit the perfect shot in the goalie's five hole.

The red siren behind the net lit up and started blaring. The TV commentators were talking about how Dillon hadn't lost any of his form from last season.

The cameras followed him as he glided past the home beck, taking fist bumps. Then he turned towards the camera directly. He smiled and there they were. His Dimples Grande.

*"For you,"* he mouthed.

I didn't want to watch anymore. It hurt too much.

"I'm going to go to my room," I announced.

They both looked at me like I was a time bomb about to go off, but I just wanted to be sad all alone.

Three hours later my phone dinged.

Dillon: Did you watch?

I told myself, don't do it. Under no circumstances was I allowed to respond to his texts. It was just prolonging things between us and neither one of us needed that.

But in the end, I was weak.

Liv: Yes.

> Dillon: I'm going to be in Montreal the
> beginning of November. Will you be there?

That one was easy. Watching him from a distance on TV was one thing. Being in the same space with him, breathing the same air, that was something else entirely.

> Liv: No.

∾

*Dillon*

> Liv: No.

OF COURSE, I didn't blame her. I mean, I thought as an assistant coach she would *have* to be there. But maybe there were exceptions for having to be in the arena with a team that had treated you like shit.

But I was a selfish bastard and I really wanted to see her.

I climbed on the team bus ready to head to our hotel for the night. Some of the guys were talking about celebrating, and as much as I wanted to lift a glass to how well O'Rourke and Novek performed in their first NHL game, not knowing who pulled those shit pranks on Olivia put a bad taste in my mouth about this team.

We'd won tonight but it hadn't been pretty. The team was splintered and I didn't care.

Which wasn't cool. That wasn't leadership. It was part of my job to bring us together.

I just didn't know how to change it. I looked at some of

these guys and all I saw was Liv curled up in the fetal position on the ice.

"What the fuck was that tonight?"

I looked up at Ron who was standing in the bus aisle looming over me. I didn't need any clarification. I knew exactly what he was talking about.

"We won, didn't we?" I asked him. Wasn't that all that mattered?

"No thanks to you. Outside of that first goal, you played like shit."

"Bad night. Players have them."

"You don't. Shit. This is still about her, isn't it?" Ron said, shaking his head. "I've never seen anyone so fucking pussy-whipped in my life."

I didn't think. I didn't pause or consider my actions or the ramifications on the team. I leapt from my bus seat and tackled him into the aisle. I landed three solid punches to his face before the guys pulled me off him.

"It was you, wasn't it? The shit in her office drawer, the video. You did it to push her out."

Morgan wiped his nose and smiled. "I'm only sorry I didn't do it sooner."

I lunged towards him again, and it was only O'Rourke's strength keeping me back.

Coach McKay raised his hands. "For fucks sake. I need this like I need a hole in the head. Do you know what kind of exposure you opened us up to with that little stunt?"

"It was a prank. Like all the other pranks," Ron said. "Ask Novek."

Novek, who had been holding Morgan back, scowled. "Nah, man. The gloves in her office was a prank. The video. That shit was messed up. She was helping us."

"Were you fucking her too, Novek?" Morgan asked. "Le Coeur one night, and you the-"

Novek spun him and punched him in the face and then shoved him down in a seat. "Don't move," he said, and followed it up with a string of low muttered threats.

"What is he talking about?" Coach asked me. "Tell me you did *not* have a relationship with her, Dillon."

I nodded.

"Goddamn it! Are you asking for a lawsuit? Is that what all of you want? Enough of this. Olivia is gone. If she chooses to sue, then I'll testify on her behalf as to what a bunch of assholes you all are. Other than that, I don't want to hear her name mentioned again. We're moving forward. As a team. Without her."

"As long as that piece of shit is on the team," I pointed at Morgan. "Then I am not on this team."

"Dillon," Coach said, carefully like I was a bomb about to go off.

"Him or me, Coach," I said.

"You know that's not how it works. There are contracts-"

I shook my head. "Don't give a shit. I'm not taking the ice with him again."

"You're a team captain," McKay said tightly. "Get your head straight. We all liked Olivia, but you need to let her go and focus on what's important."

It was almost funny. Almost. It took losing her to figure out what mattered most. She couldn't see me doing this, and would probably never know, but someone needed to fight for her. Choose her.

"This team never deserved her," I said.

And neither did I.

## 25

*Liv*

After the Bruisers' season opener, I went to work the next day only to be greeted breathlessly by Veronica and Marci. Veronica was a physical therapist for the team and Marci was the equipment manager.

They'd welcomed me the first week with brunch in Old Montreal. I'd asked them about the men connected with the team I needed to look out for, and they told me Coach Renaud was working hard to eradicate that kind of shit.

But Mike in marketing gave them the creeps.

We'd been fast friends ever since.

"Did you hear?" Veronica asked, the edges of her box braids practically trembling.

"You had to have heard," Marci said.

"My parents just left this morning and all I have heard for days is my mom in my ear telling me I needed warmer clothes. What's going on?"

"Dillon Le Coeur quit hockey."

It was like the building fell down. "That...can't be true."

"Marci is being dramatic. He's threatening to quit the Bruisers," Veronica said.

"Why?"

"No one knows," Marci said.

I hadn't told them about me and Dillon, we weren't that kind of friends. Yet. But I'd told them about the bullshit pranks and the video when they asked why I left the team.

"You've got connections with the team. Go find out," Veronica said.

"And then tell us," Marci said. "Hockey drama is the best!"

They made plans to meet for lunch in the cafeteria and I agreed without thinking. I couldn't think. My brain was static noise and nothing else. There was no way I was reaching out to the team to find out what was happening.

Could I text Cody?

No, instead it was best to just not pay attention.

Except as the days went by, the rumors continued to spread as Dillon didn't play against Nashville.

*Chaos in the Bruisers' locker room. McKay has lost control of his players.*

Was Dillon being benched? Traded? By Friday, headlines screamed that Dillon and McKay were in a standoff for control.

Of what?

I broke. I mean, anyone would break, right?

I texted him.

Liv: What is happening over there?

Dillon: Hey babe, how is Montreal?

Liv: Are you joking? Everyone is saying
you're quitting hockey?

> Dillon: I'm not sure if you know this, but
> there are more important things than
> hockey.

Liv: Is this Dillon Le Coeur?

HE SENT A SELFIE. Dimples Grande on full display. I could
have wept, he was so handsome. So familiar and dear.

> Dillon: How is Montreal? Have you tried the
> bagels? You gotta go to Schwartz's for the
> smoked meat.

Liv: TELL ME WHAT IS HAPPENING!

> Dillon: Ron Morgan pulled all that shit with
> you and I have made it clear to McKay that
> he can have that POS on this team, or he
> can have me. He can't have both.

Liv: You would quit the Bruisers?

I paused, breathless and unsure.

Liv: Over me?

> Dillon: I know I'm too late with this. But I am
> doing what I should have done the second I
> saw you in Calico Cove. I'm choosing you.

Liv: …

Liv: …

In the end, I didn't know what to say, so I said nothing.
Maybe that was cowardly. Or maybe it was just self-preser-
vation. I didn't know anymore.

Dillon: I got this, babe. Well, the lawyers do.
You just focus on killing it in Montreal.

The news broke the next morning that Ron Morgan was retiring from hockey and taking some time to be with his family.

Dillon gave a press conference with Novek and O'Rourke beside him. O'Rourke had a Believe Women t-shirt on. Novek wore head to toe Gucci and kept winking at the camera like he was on The Bachelor.

"That Novek is hot," Marci said. The three of us were standing in the PT room, watching one of the zillion screens in the facility. Everyone connected to professional hockey was watching this press conference.

"You've got to be kidding me?" Veronica asked.

"He looks like a bad boy who is also sweet."

Dillon read a statement regarding The Bruisers' commitment to providing a safe and inclusive environment for everyone on staff. He didn't mention any names, so the world may not know exactly what happened, but everyone knew he was talking about Ron Morgan.

"We can't change the past," Dillon said, looking right at the camera, looking right into my soul. "But we can learn from our mistakes. Hold ourselves accountable. Make better choices. I am dedicated to doing that."

He flashed those dimples one last time and stood up.

Novek leaned forward and said "We miss you, Coach."

Then he stood up and walked out behind his captain. O'Rourke stood, let the photographers get a bunch of pictures of his shirt, and then he left too.

Without a word to my friends, I went to my office, locked the door and cried.

*Red Center Arena*
*Montreal*
*November*

"I CAN'T BELIEVE you came back for this," I told my dad. I pulled the visor of my ball cap down low as if Dillon might see me up here in the cheap seats and come running through the arena for me.

"I wasn't going to let you watch this man play all by yourself."

We could have sat in the team suite with some of the other assistants and the wives and families of the players, but I didn't want to have to make small talk while my heart was going through a grinder.

Every night since that press conference I got a text from Dillon wishing me good night. Sometimes he told me what he ate for dinner. Once I got a picture of the bread pudding from that restaurant we went to.

*Dillon: I can't eat all this without you.*

He never pressured me for a response. He didn't call me stubborn anymore. He didn't beg me to talk to him. I had the impression that he could do this every night for the rest of his life. Like he was just stacking up blocks to tip the scales back in his favor.

And I was...frozen.

Part of it was work. Time flew by. I was learning and implementing new systems every day. Getting to know the team, figuring out strengths and weaknesses. Although now,

I was doing it with way more confidence. Not feeling like I constantly had to prove myself.

I went to work energized and came home exhausted.

But the truth of everything I wanted to say to Dillon was too big for a text. We needed to be face to face. I needed to see his eyes to know if I could believe him.

I was skulking in the cheap seats so I could watch him play without anyone seeing my reaction to him. Then my plan was to find him after the game. What happened then? No clue.

Dad and I found our two seats in the last row and sat down. Dad had popcorn, a hot dog and a beer. I was too nervous to eat or drink anything.

"Honestly," Dad grumbled. "I really think I am going to get a nosebleed."

"Is this foolish?" I asked him.

"Sitting up here when you could be in a booth? Yes."

"No," I laughed, because he was right. "Believing he really means it. That he can change from a guy who only cares about hockey...to someone else."

"Oh honey," Dad said, pushing his glasses up his nose. "People change all the time. They learn and they grow and believing in that is a gift. It's hopeful. Never foolish."

"Do you think he's changed?"

My dad thoughtfully chewed some popcorn, taking his time to answer. "I know certain things are facts. The sky is blue. The sun is going to rise in the east, your mother is the smartest person in the world, and that man down there on the ice is in love with you. He was in love with you in the coffee shop, too. He just didn't have enough faith in himself to see it for the blessing it is."

For a lawyer, my dad could be pretty poetic.

"You wearing that jersey is a pretty bold statement, Olivia," he said.

"I know." Another thing that had felt like a risk given my current employment, but I thought about how he might react when he saw it. How it would be able to tell him what I was struggling to find the words to say.

A cheap trick maybe, but I knew it would make him smile.

"If you saw his face, when he declared he was *not* in love with you, you might be a little more confident. After all, they call him The Heart."

Maybe it was silly to put all this faith in my dad's impression of Dillon, but I wanted to think it was true. I wanted to believe that Dillon had changed. That he missed me as much as I missed him. That I mattered most in his life, and not a sport.

That love was possible.

"Damn, they're fast," my dad muttered beside me, watching the men as they warmed up on the ice. He had mustard on the side of his mouth.

"Billy's that fast," I said. My brother might be going to college, but he could have gone pro if he'd wanted. For now he needed to bulk up and hone his skills on a feeder team, but some day he'd be playing for glory and a whole lot of money.

My dad looked at me, his expression serious.

"Don't look so upset. Most parents are thrilled when they realize they have a child who is professional athlete caliber."

My dad just shook his head. "It just makes it harder to teach them about life. Not everything has to be a competition. There is beauty in losing, in not having to be the best."

I'd been forced into that position. My competitive

dreams taken away from me and I could see the value in what dad said. My life was richer now than it had ever been while competing.

I tried to forget I was here to see Dillon. To watch him play. To exist in the same space that he did. When he wasn't on the ice, that was easy. But now that he was out there, all my attention was on him. He was a magnet and I was nothing but metal shavings.

The game started and control shifted back and forth across the ice.

Every time he took the ice I was blind to everything but him. His size, his agility.

A brief flash of what all that size and agility had felt like in bed crossed my mind and I squirmed in my seat. I shouldn't be having carnal thoughts sitting next to my dad, but when I was thinking about Dillon, remembering Dillon, it was hard not to have those thoughts.

One of the Voyageurs' checked Dillon into the boards. The crowd, of course, loved it, but I groaned at the thought of him taking the pain. They scrambled for the puck between his skates and then suddenly Dillon was flat on his back on the ice.

The play moved forward, but Dillon wasn't getting up and going after the puck.

He rolled to his side, clutching his right leg.

I got to my feet. Dad grabbed my hand.

"What happened?" he asked.

"I can't...I don't know."

Play was stopped and trainers ran onto the ice, blocking my view. I looked up at the Jumbotron screens, but the view wasn't a whole lot clearer. Dillon was yelling something, but the trainer shook his head.

They got him to his feet. His right leg bent, so his skate

didn't touch the ice. Their arms around him, supporting his weight, two trainers helped him off the ice.

The crowd clapped. The guys pounded their sticks against the boards. Dillon lifted his hand in farewell to the crowd and then he was gone.

I took off for the visitors' dressing room.

THE RUMOR WAS a ruptured Achilles tendon.

"It's just a rumor," Dad said, as I paced the hallway outside the visitors' training room. They'd cleared this area, but my staff badge gave us access. Above us we could still hear the muffled roar of the crowd as the teams kept playing.

There was no reason for me to be here. I wasn't family. I wasn't even his ex-girlfriend, technically. I was just a person who he texted every night and who might be in love with him.

No big deal.

My dad knew that going home without seeing him was not an option for me.

The door at the opposite end of the hallway burst open and two security guards were trying to stop Wendy.

"Miss, you can't..."

"That's my brother, jack off, and I will break every bone in your hand if you try and stop me from seeing him."

"Hey!" I stepped up, lifting my badge. "She's with me."

"Are you sure?" The security guard asked. "Because I think she's with the devil."

"I'm sure," I said, biting my lip. Dillon was going to love that one.

"Where is he?" Wendy asked, once the security guard made the sign of the cross and left.

"They're still looking at him." I said, and she pulled me into her arms.

I gasped as she held me tight. Wendy was a powerful hugger. I patted her back awkwardly. I wouldn't have thought we were at the hugging stage having only met a few times, one of those times trash talking her during a three-legged race competition, but I wasn't going to say that.

It was nice being hugged by Dillon's sister. It made me feel closer to him.

She pulled back and shook her head, laughing softly. "Sorry. It's just that he's been talking about you so much, I feel like I already know you. I flew up here to be moral support for him tonight if you didn't show, and now this."

"He thought I wouldn't be here? I work for the team."

Wendy shrugged. "Oh, you have turned that man inside out. He doesn't know what to think. I was supposed to be his drinking buddy, if he was right."

"I'm here. And I was planning on talking to him. I just...I don't know what to say."

"Well, you could start with calling him a big dumb idiot. Then you could call him a buffoon."

"I like oaf."

"Good choice." She smiled, but her eyes were filling with tears. "Do you know anything?" she asked, her thumb jerking back towards the closed door. I shook my head and hugged her again. I wasn't going to get her worried by rumors.

"Oh, hey," I said, stepping back so I could introduce my Dad. "Dad, this is Wendy, Dillon's sister. Wendy, this is my dad, Miguel Branch."

"Nice to meet you," she said, offering her hand.

My dad shook it and winced. "Uh, strong grip."

"Shoot," Wendy said. "Sorry. I'm nervous. When I'm nervous, I forget myself."

The training room door opened, and, Juan Carlos, the Bruisers' head physical trainer, stepped out.

"Wendy?" he said, and Wendy stepped forward. "He thought you might have broken a few jaws to get down here. He wants to talk to you."

"Okay," Wendy said, and vanished into the room. I could hear her start to yell at Dillon, but I couldn't see them.

"Juan?" I asked. "How bad is it?"

"Ruptured achilles," he said, his face grim. "We have to get him back to Boston for surgery."

He went back into the room, shutting the door behind him and I collapsed against the wall.

Without the grace of God and an excellent surgeon, a ruptured Achilles tendon could be a career ending injury. Even if he did fully recover, there was a good chance he wouldn't be the same.

"Honey," Dad said, wrapping me in his arms. "Don't start borrowing trouble."

There was yelling inside the room. Something hit a wall.

"He will need you to be calm. Steady."

The way my father had been calm and steady for me when my career ended.

If I never considered how deeply my love ran for my father, I knew it in that minute. He'd gotten me through the hardest thing in my life and now he was standing next to me during what could be the second hardest. Because now it was my turn to be there for Dillon.

"What are you going to say to him?" Dad asked me.

"He might not want to see me."

"He's been saying good night to you every night for four weeks. He wants to see you. But what will you say?"

"No clue," I admitted.

"Strong plan. Is there any place I could get us some coffee?" I gave him my badge and pointed him in the direction of the staff coffee room.

Alone, I tried to focus. What was I going to say to him? Had he really thought I wasn't going to come tonight?

One thing was for certain, neither one of us was moving on with our lives. Whatever happened to us back in Maine, it still had control over both of us.

Maybe that was all that needed to be said.

We weren't quite done with one another.

Dillon's season was over. Recovery time for a surgery like this was twelve weeks in a cast, followed by several months of intense physical therapy to get the leg and ankle back to full mobility. I knew that just from my experience with other skaters' histories with the injury.

What if he never fully recovered? What if he never got back to the level he was performing at now?

Dillon was thirty-two, which wasn't ancient in hockey, but a year of recovery meant he wouldn't be back with his team until he was thirty-three. Was that too old for a comeback?

No, I told myself, firmly. Dillon was a man of tremendous dedication and focus. He hadn't gotten to where he was without those traits. He would come back from this, it was just going to take time.

The question was, would he let me support him, or would I continue to be his greatest distraction?

The door opened and Wendy stood there, smiling. Not a joyful smile. More like a baring of the teeth. It was a very stressed out and worried smile.

"I told him you were here and he wants to see you," she said.

As I walked past her in the doorway, Wendy grabbed my hand and sighed. "He's going to be a complete jerk. He's my brother and I love him, but he's hurting. He knows his season is done and he's going to be an asshole to everyone around him because that's just how this goes."

"Right," I said. "I imagine he's going to be grumpy."

"Grumpy is an understatement, but you have to know it's not personal, Liv. No matter what he says, I know what he's been going through these last few weeks and that guy cares about you. Deeply."

"We weren't even together, Wendy. Not really."

"If you really believe that," she said, her blue eyes ice cold. "You better take off that jersey before you go in there."

I shook my head. I wasn't going to take off the jersey and I could take whatever he needed to dish out. I'd been where he was right now, I knew exactly what he was going through.

"He's safe with me," I said.

I pulled my hand away from hers and went to face Dillon.

The training room was a mess. His gear was everywhere and there were ice packs and tons of bandages.

He was sitting up on a table, cushions behind him. His leg held stationary and elevated by a lift. He wore his compression shirt and shorts, but that was it. He looked like a grumpy god. Honed from stone and steel and hard work.

Quite frankly, he took my breath away. All I wanted to do was crawl onto that treatment table with him.

I cleared my throat and he looked up from his phone. I watched a million emotions cross his face as he eyed me up and down. I waited for a scowl. I waited for him to turn away. To tell me he had to focus everything he had on his recovery.

That he'd been wrong to try and start something with me.

Again.

Instead, it was a full-frontal assault of the Dimples Grande.

"Hey, babe," he said, like he wasn't laid up with a potentially career ending injury.

"Hey," I said, not at all hiding my confusion.

"Look at you, you're wearing a Bruisers' jersey," he said. He lifted his hand and twirled his finger, asking me to turn around.

Slowly, I turned to show him whose jersey I'd chosen.

Le Coeur was in big white letters across my shoulder blades.

"Now that is a beautiful sight," he said. "So? How have you been?"

"Are you kidding me right now?" I asked. "I think you have more important things on your mind-"

He grabbed my hand. "Not more important. Nothing is more important than you. I hate that I ever convinced you otherwise."

I blinked at him. "Is this a prank?"

That made the smile drop from his face. "No, no more pranks."

"Your leg! Dillon! What about your leg?"

"It's busted up," he said with a shrug. "They're getting the jet ready to take me to Boston for surgery and then I don't know."

"Am I upside down right now?" I asked. "Why are you being so casual about this? Why aren't you angry?"

"What's the point of being angry? Shit like this happens. You said it-"

"Don't say it," I growled.

"Puck happens," he smiled.

"Your career..."

"Might be over."

He shrugged. He actually shrugged, like the cafeteria was out of the protein powder he liked.

"Is he on drugs?" I asked Juan.

"He wouldn't take any until he talked to you," Juan said.

"I wanted to be clear-headed," Dillon said.

Suddenly the whole world went red. I stepped up to his side and wrapped my hands in his compression shirt.

"You are Dillon Fucking Le Coeur," I said, right in his face. "Dillon Le Coeur's career doesn't end like this. You are going to have surgery and then you are going to fight as hard as you've ever fought, and it's going to be awful and painful but you are not going to give up. Not until you are right back on the ice, better than you've ever been."

"Babe," he whispered.

"What?" I snapped.

"You are really giving me a hard on right now."

"Oh my god, Dillon!" I cried, and let go of his shirt, but he grabbed my hand.

"All that...everything you just said? It sounds like a good time." He smiled and I laughed because I knew he wasn't joking. The man loved hard work and impossible odds. "I'll do it. I'll do all of it."

"Good."

"On one condition," he said. "With you by my side."

It was a dream. The dream. My dream. Respect and love and teamwork all rolled into us.

I didn't hesitate. There was no point. I loved the stupid oaf.

"Fine. I agree to those terms," I said.

"Liv, don't agree so fast. This might be the end of my career and you're going to have to decide if you really want a future with a washed out hockey player."

I leaned in close, planted a hard kiss on his mouth and looked him straight in the eye. "Your dick still works, doesn't it?"

## 26

*Three Weeks Later*
*Dillon*

"Are you sure this is smart?" Wendy asked, as she threw open the passenger side door. I tossed my crutches in the back seat of her Jeep and hauled my ass inside.

"Doc says I can put weight on it," I said.

What I couldn't do was drive. Which was why my sister was here pulling chauffeur duty. She came for all my doctor's appointments, and all she asked for in payment was for me to get the entire team to celebrate in her bar if we ever won the Stanley Cup.

"That is a ridiculous thing to ask for," I'd told her when she asked.

"It's epic," she'd said. "It will be a party that will go down in the history books of Calico Cove and I want it at the Gull."

"It might not happen," I'd told her.

"Oh ye of little faith."

So, yeah, somehow the women in my life had all the faith in the world when it came to me. And I did hate disappointing the women in my life.

"That doesn't mean this is smart," she said, climbing in the driver's seat. She turned the ignition and we both shivered until the car's heat kicked in. My phone binged.

> Liv: You need to eat prunes. I read that a lot of people recovering from surgery don't move enough so they tend to get constipated. Prunes will help.

"You know every time she texts, you get this shit eating grin on your face," Wendy said like it bothered her. And maybe it did. But I couldn't stop.

"She's worried I'm constipated."

"You guys are gross."

Wendy put the Jeep in gear and drove away from the doctor's office. After the surgery, she'd wanted me to come to Calico Cove to recuperate so she could take care of me, but that house was nothing but stairs.

Liv wanted to take a leave of absence from her job so she could come down and take care of me. But there was no way I was asking her to give up her amazing job with people who valued and respected her, just to help me get back and forth to the bathroom.

No way.

Besides, I wasn't a good patient, I knew that. I was scared shitless that this was the end of my career and I didn't want to be an asshole to the two most important people in my life.

So instead, I let Novek come over and stay with me at my penthouse to help me to the bathroom when I needed it. I bitched at him that my cast itched and he called me names in his native language and I wondered how this guy ended up being the one I could count on.

Liv drove down to Maine whenever she could take the time. Mostly when the Voyageurs played out of town and on weekends. We watched TV and talked hockey. She made buckets of soup that she said I could freeze and I tried my level best to get her naked.

Except she told me it was against doctor's orders. The sex part, not her getting naked, but she didn't want to be a tease.

But the doctor gave me the all-clear this morning to put some weight on my leg and I felt the bone deep longing for my girl. *My girl.*

"Where am I taking you, Dillon?" Wendy asked me, stirring me out of my thoughts.

"Oh, sis. I think you know." I'd asked her to bring her passport, after all.

"Montreal? Really? It's going to cost you."

"Whatever the price, I'll pay it."

"You have to dress up like Dad behind the bar this summer. The locals will love it."

"No. No way. You're insane."

"If I am driving you five hours to Canada to get laid… you're wearing the beret."

"Fine," I said. I'd wear a thousand berets to get inside Liv. "But I'm not wearing the shorts."

IT WAS in fact a five hour drive west from Portland to Montreal and my sister drove like a bat out of hell. We got to Liv's apartment at dinner time.

Her townhouse was a million times better than the shitty apartment the Bruisers put her in. Every time I thought of the way she'd been treated by my team, it made me mad all over again. But Coach was putting his money where his mouth was and the whole organization had been revamped. More women were being hired in high level roles and all of us were attending workshops on harassment in the work place.

Novek felt so much guilt about the hockey puck incident, he donated time and money to a Portland women's shelter.

Liv had no idea the changes she'd left behind on that organization. I knew McKay wanted her back. The skating coach he'd hired to replace her had none of Liv's innovation and team-building skills.

I pulled the crutches out of Wendy's Jeep, got them under each arm and took a few tentative steps forward.

"So? What?" Wendy asked. "I just sit here while you go get your rocks off?"

"Don't be crass, sis," I said, and pulled my wallet out of the pocket of my gray sweatpants. "Take yourself to dinner and book a suite at the Four Seasons."

I tossed the wallet over my shoulder, knowing she'd catch it.

"Don't forget all the exercises you need to do every day and don't get crazy with the wild monkey sex. The doctor said you could put some weight on it. Not swing from the ceiling."

She gave me a jaunty salute, popped back into her Jeep and was gone. Probably already booking an appointment at the spa.

Before I got all the way to Liv's townhouse, the door opened.

And there she was. Hair pulled back in a pony tail, no makeup. Wearing black leggings and a familiar Bruisers' jersey that I knew if she turned around, would have my name on it.

"Did my sister tell you we were coming?" I asked.

"She texted me at the border. What are you thinking coming up stairs..."

She stopped. Her eyes went wide.

"Weight-bearing activity, baby."

She threw her front door wide. "Get that dick in here."

"I love you," I said abruptly.

We hadn't said it and I'd thought, maybe stupidly, that we didn't need to. Because we *knew* it. That was enough.

Her eyes went wide and filled with tears.

Yeah, that's why I needed to say it. Because it filled her with light inside.

"I love you more than hockey. I love you more than anything else in my life. I want to get you pregnant. Like a bunch of times. I want to listen to you trash talk anyone who thinks they have a shot at beating you in a three-legged race. I want to listen to you trash talk our children."

"Dillon," she laughed through her tears.

"You're all I want. More than hockey, more than my leg to get better, more than my team. Definitely more than some damn trophy. I want to be distracted by you every day of my life and I'll be grateful for it. I promise."

"Wow," she finally said. "That was really good."

"I know. I think I surprised myself. Turn around and let me see whose jersey you're wearing," I said, feeling my heart thudding in my chest. This was happening. It was as real as the cast on my leg.

Liv loved me.

Injured me. Bartender me. All of me.

She did a slow twirl with her thumbs pointed to the name on the back. I realized this jersey was different than the one she'd worn to the game in Montreal. A different jersey that she must have had custom made.

Because it didn't say Le Coeur on the back. It said The Heart.

"Yeah," I muttered. "That looks right."

"Come inside before you slip and do even more damage."

"You're a brat," I said, limping through the doorway. "You know that?"

She danced back inside her townhouse. "What are you going to do about it?"

"Take me to your bedroom, woman, and get naked." Then I had a second thought. "No, wait. Leave the jersey on."

## 27

*Liv*

Yes! Finally! Wild Monkey Sex. It had been months. *Months*. And it wasn't going to be all that wild, thanks to that cast, but it was going to feel wild because it was going to be us. Together after all this time apart.

There had been nights on that couch at his place when I thought I'd lose my mind if he didn't touch me. But I was strict about following the doctor's orders and the first thing Dillon asked after surgery was when he could have sex again.

The answer: when you are cleared for weight-bearing activity.

My body was practically purring.

Naked, he stretched out on my bed, his leg propped up on a bunch of pillows, his arms folded behind his head, showing off his massive biceps, that wide chest and his stomach with all the ripples. He was nothing but muscle and he was nothing but mine.

"Slowly, babe," he said, while I stripped out of my leggings.

"Much slower," he said, cupping his dick while I pulled down my panties.

I girl tricked my bra off without removing the jersey.

Naked except for his colors. His name.

"Baby, I think I need you to come sit on my face right now."

"You sure you can perform injured?" I asked him, a small smile playing on my lips.

He jacked his cock. A drop of cum pooling at the tip. So. Hot.

"My dick is confident in its abilities. Now, Liv."

I didn't want to try and coordinate his mouth on my pussy and my mouth on his cock. All while trying to keep the weight away from his leg. That we could save for later. Now, I just wanted him inside me. Deep. Hard. All the way.

I got on the bed and carefully straddled his hips. I pulled his hand away from his dick and locked my fingers together with his. I slipped my wet pussy against his heavy erection, until he pushed through my lips to hit my clit.

I tipped my head back and sighed.

"Give me your mouth, Liv. I want to taste you. I want to swallow you whole. And when I tell you, you're going to take me inside you and ride me hard."

I shook my head, some of my hair coming loose around my shoulders. I rocked against his cock, feeling like I could come from this alone.

"We have to be gentle," I groaned.

"Fuck gentle." He kissed me, just like he said he would. Hard and wet and like he could swallow me whole.

His hands were underneath the jersey, cupping my

breasts. He found my nipples and did all those things I loved to them.

Yeah, this would work. This was going to work just fine. Him sucking on my tongue, playing with my nipples while his cock head pressed against my clit.

"Dillon," I sighed. "Make me come."

He grabbed my hips and pulled me harder against him, rocking me back and forth until it felt like the world was coming apart.

"Fuck. Liv. I have to..." he pushed me up so he could press his cock up inside me.

He was heavy and full and I forgot how he stretched me. How connected he made me feel to him. I rocked my hips and he gripped my butt cheeks to control my pace.

"I want to come now," I groaned. My hands pressed against his thick heavy pecs, relishing the feel of his tight little nipples against my palms. I wanted to claw him, tease him, settle into his body like it was mine.

I kissed his chin. His cheek. Each closed eyelid.

"I love you," I said.

His eyes flew open. It was the most intimate moment of my life. I could not imagine being more vulnerable and in love with someone as I was with this man, right now. It was us and nothing else.

I didn't have a speech like Dillon's beautiful one earlier. It was just my body and my heart reaching for him.

"Again," he grunted.

"I love you. All of you. Make me come, Dillon," I whispered, trying to speed up my thrusts against him, only for him to take firm control of my hips.

"No, I'm not ready. I want this to last. For fucking ever."

"I can't," I whined, wiggling against him.

"Let's make it a contest?"

"A contest?" I asked, my curiosity piqued.

"Who can last the longest," he muttered.

His cheeks were flushed, his eyes wide. He looked so fucking smug. So certain that he would win. And to be fair, this wasn't going to be the hardest game to lose. Because the loser got to come.

Still, he said the word contest.

I sat up, changing the angle so he was completely inside of me. I squeezed my inner muscles around him.

"Oh fuck," he groaned.

Then I fired off the big guns and pulled his jersey off my body so he was face to face with my breasts that he loved so much.

"God, you're so fucking beautiful."

I cupped my own breasts, teased my own nipples, which was a double-edged sword of pleasure. In the end it was very close, but technically he started coming before I did. I could feel it happen inside me, right before I fell over the cliff.

"Tie," he gasped, when he could breathe again.

"Bullshit," I said, crumpled against his chest because all my bones had dissolved with pleasure. "I'm the undisputed champ."

"Yeah," he said, kissing the top of my head. "You are."

I WAS CURLED up against his left side, listening to the sound of his breathing, feeling everything settle around me. This was right where I was supposed to be. I knew it in my bones. Now that he could handle stairs, it was time for him to move up to Montreal, so he could continue his recovery with me.

I assumed he was asleep, but then I heard him take a weighty breath and I knew instinctively what was coming.

"Liv, I might not be able to make it back," he said. "You get that?"

I nodded against his chest without saying anything.

"So I'll be one of those really annoying boyfriends who wants to go to the super market with you, and sit with you while you get your hair done and shit like that."

"We'll get side by side pedicures. You'll love it," I said, squeezing him in a hug to offer all my support in the only way I could.

"Are you really okay?" I asked, lifting my head to look down at him. "All that stuff you said in Montreal, about if this is how it ends?"

"I always knew that someday there would be an end, but I didn't spend any time imagining what that would look like. I thought the rest of my life would just fall into place and now I can see how naïve that was."

"My father would say that means you're maturing. He was rooting for you, by the way. He thought you loved me."

"He was right. I need to go back to Seattle. To apologize properly for the way I acted."

"Let's worry about that later. We don't need to worry about anything except you getting better. That's it."

"I'm never going to ask you to give up your job, you know that, right?"

"I know. We can make this work."

I stroked his face and sighed. Sleep was creeping up on me. I'd been running ragged driving back and forth to Portland and still keeping up the schedule at work.

But even with the stress and the schedule and my worry for him, I'd never been so happy.

"Dillon, are you happy?" I was pretty sure he was asleep and I fully expected a snore instead of a response.

But he surprised me and replied. "Liv, I can honestly say, here, now, I'm happier than I've ever been."

"Me too."

"Good. Now rest up so we can go again. I want that pussy all over my face."

I smiled. "It's how romantic you are that really gets to me."

# EPILOGUE

*Eighteen Months Later*
*Bank Trust Arena*
*Game 7 of the Stanley Cup Finals*
*Liv*

"L*et's face it, if the Bruisers win this game tonight, this might mark one of the greatest comebacks we've seen in a long time."*

*"That's right, Frank. When Dillon Le Coeur came back, those first few months were tough to watch. A lot of us wondered whether he was ever going to play at his previous level."*

*"Well, I'll go so far as to say, not only has The Heart returned to his former self, I think he's improved. Is it my imagination, or is he skating faster than O'Rourke?"*

"THAT'S RIGHT, GENTLEMEN," I said, with a proud smile on my face. "He's skating faster than he ever has. You're welcome."

"Smug much?" My brother nudged me with his elbow.

I looked at him like maybe he'd mistaken me for someone else. "Uh, yes. Have you met me? I'm taking basically ninety-nine percent of the credit for Dillon's full recovery and speed improvement."

"So Dillon did nothing?" Wendy asked, chuckling. She had a plate full of food that I did not understand how she could eat. I was a nervous wreck. This wasn't just a game. The tension was so much more elevated being in the finals.

"Dillon did...this much." I turned away from the ice to look at Wendy and pinched my finger and thumb together.

Everyone in the team suite knew I was full of shit. Dillon had killed himself getting back into hockey shape once his tendon had fully recovered. He'd become my best student, improving on every metric. Speed, agility and power.

Dillon was a freight train on that ice and no one could touch him.

By the second half of the season he was stronger, faster and playing at his personal best. Which was a big part of how the team got to the playoffs, then the championship series, and now... Game Seven.

Tied up at three games apiece with the Seattle Sea Titans.

"I don't think I can take it anymore," I said. We were surrounded by family in the suite. My family, Dillon's and the extended Bruisers' family. Skalsberg's sister was here from Sweden with a stunning friend who watched Skalsberg on the ice with rage in her eyes. I would have tried to find out more about that, but I really was sick to my stomach.

We were only up by one with the third period to go. My nerves were shot. My hands were clammy. My stomach was in knots.

Game after game, I lived every breath through Dillon's play. Reveling in every win and despairing every loss. Dillon was surprisingly sanguine about the losses. Especially in a seven game series. He was only ever irritated if he thought he'd missed an opportunity, but otherwise he would shrug when I met him outside the locker room and say that we'd get them next time.

Always *we*.

Like we played these games together. His team, but also our team. I broke my contract with Montreal and came back to Portland once he rejoined the team. We'd decided the long distance thing was not for us.

The sports world was calling Dillon and me: An NHL Love Story.

We'd said no to all the media that wanted to interview us, but if The Bruisers won the Stanley Cup, we'd have to say yes to something. I was thinking People Magazine. Dillon would grumble, but it would be nice to get a good picture of us. Something to put up on his wall with his jerseys. Honestly, the peewee jersey had to go.

This, I realized, was love. I felt his ups and his downs because they were mine too. It was the same for him. My victories were his and so were my disappointments. Though professionally, these days there weren't many disappointments. Skalsberg was asking for private coaching this summer and I told him I'd only consider it if he came to Calico Cove, where Dillon and I were planning on spending the whole off season.

To my surprise, he agreed.

Calico Cove might never be the same.

My dad came over to stand next to me. "It's always harder to watch from the stands."

"Tell me about it. The result of this game is out of my control and it's absolutely maddening," I said.

"You're with him though. Down there on the ice. Tucked inside his chest because he knows, win or lose, you're still going to love him."

I hugged my dad because he was the bomb and love made him a poet. "You are so right. But winning is better."

He laughed and we all stood and crowded the front of the suite as the team took the ice.

The guys, I thought, all looked a little ridiculous in their full beards. Poor Cody had tufts of hair coming out in patches on his face and looked like a troll. His wife hated it.

The core of the team was still together. Tighter and better than they'd ever been. We vacationed in the off season with O'Rourke and his wife. Skalsberg and Novek came over for barbecues in the summer. Their favorite thing was to heckle Dillon when he worked behind the bar. Of course, they all got selfies with his dad's picture in the background.

This team was a family. And they took Dillon's lead whenever he was on the ice. A lot of the time off the ice, too. O'Rourke, especially, seemed to look up to Dillon like an older brother.

The best part, they all seemed to sense when Dillon was about to get hot.

Like now.

He hit the ice like he hadn't been playing two periods of fast, brutal hockey. So fresh. So ready. He wanted to take advantage of a defense that was getting tired keeping up with them. Novek came out, hockey hair flowing behind him. You could see his mouth moving as he skated past the Sea Titans.

Novek was a golden-tongued trash talker. Even I had to tip my hat to him.

"That's right, baby. You got this," I muttered to myself. My palms flat against the glass as if I could mind meld with him. "You own them. Now make them pay for all that hard work you did. You show them what your wife taught you."

The game started.

Uncharacteristically, Dillon lost the face off, but Skalsberg stripped it right off the Titans. Dillon came back on the ice, accelerated through the line with the puck, passed it to Cody on his right, Cody passed it back out to Novek on the left.

And...I could see it happen. Like a puzzle falling into place. Dillon picked his spot, skated circles around every defender. He found an opening, Novek met him with the puck...

Slapshot and score!

*Dillon*

"WHERE'S MY WOMAN?!" I shouted, looking around the throng of family members and friends just outside the locker room, waiting to celebrate with the team.

I didn't have to wait long before Liv was jumping into my arms.

"I'm not a woman, I'm your wife!" she shouted, as she showered my bearded face with kisses. It was an old joke between us, a line from a movie she got wrong, but refused to admit. "You were badass tonight, babe. A game seven hat trick? Eat that, Gretsky."

"That third one was for you," I said, burying my face in her sweet-smelling neck. I'd joined a very small, very elite group tonight and it was some heady shit. I felt like I was floating. "Did you see my sign?"

Liv unwrapped her legs from around my waist and hopped off me. She moved her index finger in a circle, making the turnaround sign. The same sign I made every time I scored for her. I didn't dedicate every goal to her, otherwise it wouldn't matter as much. But the special ones... they were all for Liv.

"Show me, babe," I said.

She turned around, her back to me. The Heart in big white letters on the back of her jersey.

It's where mine lived these days. Not in my chest, not for the game, my heart belonged to Liv.

The crazy part about the whole thing was that as much as I thought love might be a distraction, it turned out to be the opposite. Liv didn't take away anything from my game, she only elevated it. Not just with her coaching techniques, which had clearly helped, but her presence in my life.

I was a better man because of her. Which made me a better leader. A better teammate. A better brother. A better friend.

More importantly, I'd just won the Stanley Cup, the greatest achievement I could accomplish in this game that I loved. But sharing it with Liv? Getting to go home with her to celebrate? That was the victory.

Someone should have told me how much fun having a wife was going to be. Guys never talked about that part.

But maybe it was because my wife was so much fucking fun.

"Let's go home and celebrate," I said.

"Yes!"

"I'll let you shave my beard," I told her.

"Ah," she said, rubbing my fuzzy face. "I was sort of getting used to you this way."

"Babe, you just like it when I go down on you with all my scruff," I whispered into her ear. "I'll do that before I let you shave it."

"Awesome idea, Cap," she said "But you know we're not doing any of that. We're headed back to the Gull for a huge party. Wendy has already left to get ready. Half the team, all of our families and most of Calico Cove is planning on being there."

"Ugh," I groaned. "It's going to be like the wedding all over again. You need to tell Billy he can't spend the whole time gaping at Carrie. Or he's bound to get his ass kicked."

"On it."

"And no karaoke this time. That town gets a little out of control the second a karaoke machine shows up."

"On it," Liv said.

"My dick?"

"On it," she said, and tipped back her head to laugh. It shouldn't have been so funny, but I was a man on top of the world and deeply in love with his wife. I laughed until I had to wipe my eyes.

We made our way outside the arena where fans were still celebrating in the streets. Novek and O'Rourke were already there, talking to fans. Someone handed Novek a beer and he chugged it. He lifted his arms, foam dripping off his face and the crowd went wild.

"I hope you're not driving," I said to Novek.

"He's coming with us," O'Rourke said, his arm around his tiny red-headed wife. She was cute and kept her husband on a tight leash. "We will see you at Calico Cove."

I couldn't believe these guys were driving an hour and a half to celebrate at my sister's bar in my hometown with a bunch of fisherman and locals they didn't know.

"See you there!" I shouted.

"Your sister?" Novek said.

"What about her?"

"I will be trying to get her to sleep with me. You are fine with this."

"Oh," I laughed. "Good luck to you Novek. My sister is going to chew you up and spit you out."

"Yes, this is what I am hoping for."

Liv was going to love that.

I signed as many jerseys and pucks as I could. Took a few selfies, fist bumped every kid that came up to me and then looked around for Liv.

She was behind me, on her phone, no doubt coordinating the guys and my sister and her family and where everyone was going to stay tonight.

The high of winning was something else. Especially when we were celebrating it with so many diehard fans. Still, it was nothing like celebrating with my number one fan.

The urge to knock her up was undeniable.

"Heart," a reporter called out from the crowd. I could see the credentials around his neck. "Want to tell us what inspired your hat trick tonight?"

I wrapped my arm around Liv's waist and brought her against my side. She leaned in to kiss my bearded cheek.

There was a shower of flashes. "You're looking at her. My wife is my inspiration. For everything. Forever."

"Ahh," she said and kissed my cheek again. "You *are* a romantic."

"Just a guy in love," I whispered into her ear. For her and her alone.

"Someone is getting lucky tonight," she smiled.

"Yeah," I barked out a laugh. "And it isn't Novek."

"I love you," she said, and every time she said it, it filled me to the brim.

"I love you more," I told her.

"Wait? Is this a contest?"

She did that head tilt thing, and I laughed again, picking her up into my arms, because she totally trusted me to do that these days, and letting her wrap her legs around my waist.

"Let's go, babe. We're off to Calico Cove to party!"

*Did you love Liv and Dillon as much as I did? (Don't tell the other couples - but these guys were my favorite.) Want a bonus epilogue set three years into the future where we find out if Liv is going to run in the 3 Legged Race - while pregnant?*

Check it out:

Bonus Epilogue

# ACKNOWLEDGMENTS

Because it takes a village we just wanted to give a shout out to our amazing cover artist Ecila Media. The fastest copy editor in all the land, Andrea Stocks. And our assistant, proof reader and all round go to person, Becca Habina, who finds all the wrong *it's!*

Thank you for making Hailey Shore 2023 work!

# ALSO BY HAILEY SHORE

Happily Ever Maybe?

(Beauty and The Beast retelling/Grumpy Sunshine/Age Gap)

Not My Prince Charming

(Cinderella retelling, childhood friends to enemies to lovers)

The Grump, The Bride & The Baby

(Marriage of convenience, single dad, grumpy/sunshine)

Fake Date For Christmas

(Friends to lovers, fake dating)

Can't Take The Heat?

(Enemies to lovers, found family)

Flirting with Disaster

(Opposites attract, fake dating)